The PepperAsh Redoubt

Franky Sayer

Published by Sirob Press

British Library Cataloguing in Publication Data.

A CIP catalogue record for this book is available from the British Library.

ISBN: 978-1-9997108-1-1

Prologue

Sunday, 29th July 1990

Rosalie and Henry Stickleback had argued bitterly the morning after their wedding night, which they spent at the exclusive Thrimbale Hotel in Cliffend. The dispute ended their honeymoon. Rosalie travelled alone in a taxi back to her home at the Old Police House in Pepper Hill. She wore only a flimsy negligee and nothing on her feet.

In her arms she clutched the large, ugly brown teddy bear with a gold locket on a chain around its neck that Henry had presented to her earlier. The driver noticed that she worried at the rings on her finger, as if they were alien to her.

When Rosalie arrived, she was agitated to find her brother, George, was not at home. She had promised the taxi driver he would pay her fare. Not having the house keys with her, she was relieved to find the spare to the front door still on a hook hidden behind a hanging basket. During the summer months when her parents had been alive to tend them, these held bright pink and purple fuchsias.

The taxi driver was very understanding and waited while she went inside. When she brought the money out, he noticed she had wrapped a coat around herself, although she was still bare-footed.

George Tillinger, two years younger than his sister despite looking much older than sixteen, returned home at lunchtime to find Rosalie locked in her bedroom. In a desperate telephone call, Henry told George that she'd left him at the hotel, apparently without explanation.

George knocked on her door and called, 'Rosie?' He was the only person who dared to shorten her name: everyone else called her Rosalie. She gave no reply. He tried the handle but she had locked herself in.

'Why are you back here?' he asked. She remained silent. 'What has happened? Why aren't you two on your way up to Inverness for your honeymoon?'

He repeated these questions many times over the next half an hour. He finished with, 'I'm going to put the kettle on. D'you want a cuppa?' Rosalie still did not answer. He pressed his ear to the door but could hear no sounds.

George walked quietly away along the landing and down the stairs. In the hall he stopped near the front door, turned and looked back up towards his sister's room. He waited for several minutes, just in case Rosie came out when she thought he'd gone. But the door remained firmly shut.

Inside her room, Rosalie sat on her bed still in her overcoat with her negligee underneath. She was clinging to the teddy bear. Tears streamed down her cheeks. Her face was creased as she clenched her teeth and held her breath against the pain. She was too miserable to cry properly and too desolate to call out. In her hand she clutched the gold locket, pressing it into her flesh so hard that raw imprints were made.

Chapter 1

Ten weeks had passed since Rosalie and Henry married and subsequently separated.

Rosalie stood by the side of her bed staring at her profile in the full-length mirror. There was a slight swelling to her lower stomach; she was waiting for the results of a home-pregnancy test. These devices were still relatively new. Rosalie felt guilty purchasing one at the chemist in Cliffend earlier. Not only did she think the cost was exorbitant, but she didn't want anyone she knew to see her, especially not Henry, nor anybody who was likely to tell him.

The white stick now rested on a tissue on the floor. She had two minutes before the results showed. She tiptoed barefoot out of her bedroom and crept down the stairs.

Rosalie had only spoken to Henry on two occasions since their wedding day. The first was a telephone conversation.

'Hello Rosalie, it's Henry,' he had said quickly into the receiver as soon as she answered. An angry silence followed. 'Are you there?' he asked.

'Of course I'm here,' she retorted. 'What d'you want?'

'I just wanted to see if you're okay.'

'No, I'm not okay.' She spoke slowly and with deliberate harshness. 'My *husband* stole the memorial I'd left for my parents. He then desecrated their pictures and stuck his mother's stupid diamond in the locket instead. How d'you expect me to feel?'

'I'm sorry, Rosalie. I really am. But I was only trying …'

'Why did you dig up the locket?' she snapped, interrupting his explanation. The tears started to drown her eyes, block her nose and choke her throat. Not waiting for his reply, she clicked the phone off, sat down, held her face in her hands and sobbed.

The second time Henry contacted his new wife was for a more practical purpose, and he allowed no time for her recriminations. He banged hard on the front door of the Old Police House and demanded that Rosalie answer.

'Are you going to return the wedding presents, or shall I?' he asked without preamble.

'You do it! They're all at the pub anyway. It'll be something to keep you busy!' Then she had slammed the door shut.

In the end it was Nora, Henry's mother, who found herself unwrapping the gifts and listing them. She marked which were to be returned and to whom, and those to be retained. Acknowledgements and explanations were due to everyone who attended the wedding, along with a note to those who had not been there.

As she worked, Nora adjusted her reading glasses and quietly coughed. She had suffered a bad cold not long after she was widowed. Although it was not actually diagnosed as influenza, it had drained all her energy. That was two years ago, but she still felt as though she had not fully recovered. In the short term, she had concentrated on looking after George, Rosalie and Henry rather than focusing on her own health - plus she'd also been engrossed in organising the latter two's wedding.

Nora had been looking forward to a quieter time after the young couple left for their honeymoon - if that was at all possible for the landlady of a busy and popular country pub like The Fighting Cock. Henry's unexpected return home the morning after his and Rosalie's first night as a married couple robbed Nora of her self-promised rest. Now she felt more like a woman in her early seventies than someone who was only fifty-two.

'You should be doing this, you know, Henry,' she told her son as she gathered together the batch of Thank You cards she'd bought in Cliffend.

'I know, but I just can't face it. I don't want to talk to anyone. The first question people will ask is why aren't Rosalie and me together anymore. And I can't explain,' Henry said quietly. He didn't usually talk much and this was the longest speech Nora had heard him make since the wedding day.

Nora sighed. Her own wedding gift to the newly-weds was Tidal Reach, a cottage and small holding just across the road from the pub. The dwelling needed redecorating throughout; it was a project she hoped Henry and Rosalie would enjoy doing together. That was obviously not to be now. Nora advertised for a tenant rather than leaving it empty indefinitely. She found a young couple who, at a considerably reduced rent, agreed to take it on as it stood.

Two months had passed between Nora dispatching the last of the gifts and cards and Rosalie taking the pregnancy test. To fill in the time now, as Rosalie waited for the result, she rang Henry.

Nora answered the phone but quickly handed over the receiver, not quite trusting herself to speak civilly to the person who was breaking her only son's heart.

'What did you do with the two pictures that were inside the locket? You haven't messed them up, have you?' Rosalie asked. Her voice was quiet but harsh.

'No, I took them out very carefully. There's a slot in the lining of the jeweller's box, the opening is just above their name. I tucked them in there.' Henry was pleased she had contacted him, even if she did not appear to want to chat.

'I won't be able to put them back in the locket, will I? The diamond won't come out!'

'I didn't mean to upset you, Rosalie.' He could hear the pleading in his own voice. He hoped she would not think he was weak.

'Well you did. You should never have interfered with it.'

'I just wanted you to have something from your parents, and from mine. Dad gave Mum the engagement ring that the diamond comes from, and your Mum and Dad gave you the locket. I just put them together.'

But Rosalie was gone. Henry did not know if she had listened to any of his explanation.

Rosalie was too upset to talk. She slowly returned upstairs to her room and picked up the stick, telling herself not to be either glad or disappointed whatever was shown: she knew the results were not fully guaranteed, and if it was positive she would have to see her doctor for confirmation anyway.

She finally dared to glance at the tiny window. There was a blue line across it. A flash of yearning, fear and excitement rippled through her.

She breathed in deeply as she placed her free hand on her stomach. And she knew. Yes, after just one night as Mrs Henry Stickleback, she was pregnant.

Chapter 2

Postman Jim's last call on Tuesday morning, 9th October, 1990 was The Fighting Cock public house in Ashfield, the eastern community which, together with Pepper Hill in the west, formed the village of PepperAsh. Nora Stickleback retrieved two envelopes from the entrance mat in the lounge-bar. She noted that neither were cards for her birthday tomorrow.

The first was a brown, business-looking missive, addressed impersonally to The Landlady.

She turned quickly to the second. The paper was sky blue in colour and light in weight, with a red and darker blue squared border. Next to the stamps - Italian - was the oblong Air Mail sticker. She flicked it over, saw the sender's address and smiled: it was from Miss A. Childs, aboard the RMS Vaguaries.

Alice used to work as a supply teacher at Cliffend High School. She and one of Nora's regular customers, Max Podgrew, a farm labourer from Ashfield, were at one time *an item*. And the youngsters - her own son, Henry, daughter-in-law, Rosalie, together with Rosalie's brother, George - would forever associate Miss Alice Childs with an unfortunate incident involving Year Ten students.

Two years ago, in the name of sex (the *safe* variety) education, Alice was supposed to teach George's class how to put condoms on carrots as part of their Personal Development course. Alice had been a somewhat shy and seemingly innocent spinster, who had enlisted Max's help in procuring the condoms. He had obliged by emptying the contents of the vending machine in the pub's Gent's toilets.

Alice herself had incurred the wrath of Poskett, Pepper Hill's shopkeeper, when she purchased the carrots - all carefully picked for size and suitability. But the night before the new school year was due to commence, Alice experienced some kind of nervous breakdown. This was witnessed by Max, but he never spoke to anyone about it, which was unusual because he normally liked to gossip. Alice's refusal to carry out the head teacher's instructions led to her ultimate resignation.

Safely unemployed and far more financially secure than she could ever have believed possible, thanks to a lump sum severance pay out from the local authority, Alice booked a holiday on a cruise ship and found her niche in life at the roulette wheel in the on-board casino. Alice and Max originally met in a bookmaker's shop in Cliffend, and for many years Alice suppressed her urge to gamble, although she did allow herself the occasional flutter.

Max brought the last postcard he received from Alice into the pub one evening a while ago. Reading about all the ports and fascinating places the ship had docked and the sights the retired teacher wrote of, Nora yearned for an opportunity to free herself of her responsibilities at The Fighting Cock and explore the world.

However, Henry, at twenty was not yet old enough to hold the licence for the pub, although he had helped out ever since he could remember. He had fetched and carried until he was eighteen when he could serve behind the bar. He then also become involved in the everyday management, including the accounts. Young George Tillinger had simplified Nora's own rather complicated system during his and Rosalie's sojourn after their parents' deaths. The Stickleback family was financially secure thanks to a legacy from Nora's mother and a matured life assurance policy. But luck in money did not guarantee happiness or prosperity.

The past two years or so had been particularly unkind to both the Stickleback and Tillinger families. Rosalie and George lost their parents on the same night Nora's husband, Woody, who was an alcoholic, died.

Annie and Derek Tillinger lived in Pepper Hill, a mile or so along the road from Ashfield, in a former police house, unimaginatively now called the Old Police House. Derek was due some holiday from his work at Tasker's Engineering. This coincided with the pub where Annie helped as a cleaner, closing for refurbishment. They hired a river cruiser - the *Peach Dream*, Nora wistfully remembered it being called - from the leisure company Perrona Dawn's marina in Cliffend.

Their two youngsters, Rosalie aged sixteen at the time and George fourteen, had been left in Nora's care. They were deemed old enough to look after themselves during the daytime and Nora had arranged to stay at the Old Police House overnight with them. Henry was eighteen and infatuated with Rosalie; Annie privately confirmed to Nora that this was mutual.

It was decided that Henry would stay at the pub with his father, but not because the adults feared any shenanigans would take place between him and Rosalie. They were all aware that, if a teenage couple wanted to misbehave, they would find a time and place to do so regardless of how careful their parents thought they were being. The pub's stock was deliberately run low in order not to have too much in store while the business was temporarily closed. The remaining alcohol was securely locked away. But Woody, despite his infirmity, somehow stole the keys and helped himself. He subsequently died of alcohol poisoning and cirrhosis of the liver.

At the same time Annie and Derek Tillinger, on the first night of their holiday, moored the boat at Ashfield Staithe. It was a remote site but still just within view across the fields and marshes from Nora's bedroom window. The couple chose the spot because there wasn't a telephone kiosk nearby. Although mobile phone ownership was spreading, neither possessed one. They felt they needed to be out of contact so that Annie would not ring Nora, or Rosalie and George, to check on them. They wanted the youngsters to feel they were being independent, but Rosalie was due to start her GCSE examinations shortly after the holiday and was a little anxious.

This was Annie and Derek's first experience on board a river boat. As evening drew in, it was surmised that they had felt chilly and switched on the gas heater without checking the flue was open properly. The coroner concluded that death had occurred as a result of carbon monoxide poisoning. Perrona Dawn was exonerated of blame, having produced the correct paperwork which included the hire agreement with instructions for the appliances on board, all signed and dated appropriately by Derek.

The promise Nora made to Annie and Derek that she would look after Rosalie and George whilst they were away now seemed like a life-long commitment. At the time, George was fairly self-sufficient, taking care of Rosalie as well as of himself, but Nora invited them both to move into The Fighting Cock after their parents' deaths so they would not be on their own.

Despite the situation, the spark of romance already between Henry and Rosalie slowly grew. They had married at the end of July just over two years after their respective losses. The wedding had, in the circumstances, been a wonderful day of celebration - even eclipsing the legendary party thrown when Woody and Nora first took over the tenancy of The Fighting Cock, the festivities then only concluding when the barbecue exploded.

But the wedding day had not been without its own drama, ending with a horrendous thunder storm. Despite this, the new Mr and Mrs Stickleback were driven to the Thrimbale, the most expensive and exclusive hotel in Cliffend, for their wedding night. They were due to start their honeymoon the following day by travelling to Inverness for two weeks.

But things had not worked out as planned. Nora had asked Henry many times why he and Rosalie parted the very next day. Henry would not tell her, he just said it was up to Rosalie to explain: Nora suspected that he did not really know the reason.

Chapter 3

Nora unfolded Alice's letter and held the thin sheets of airmail writing paper up to the light. This made them almost transparent so she lowered them again. She adjusted her glasses and read.

Dear Nora,

I expect you're surprised to receive a letter from me …

Just a little, Nora thought. But she had learnt by hard experience not to be too surprised by anything.

… but I met a couple on board who had recently been on holiday in Cliffend with Perrona Dawn and, when they realised I came from that area, they wanted to know all the gory details of Annie and Derek Tillinger's sad deaths. I was thinking anyway, that maybe I should write to you to see how everything was going now that Henry and Rosalie are married and living in the cottage opposite, and you have the pub to yourself again – except I guess that George is still with you, or has he gone back to the Old Police House? No, surely he isn't old enough to live on his own, is he?

No, he isn't, Nora replied silently. But, yes he was back in Pepper Hill, looking after Rosalie. Alice obviously did not know Henry and Rosalie's marriage had not even survived until breakfast the morning after their wedding.

Anyway, I expect you'll give me all the gossip when I see you next. Talking of which, one of the other passengers – a widow (and, if I'm not mistaken, she's on this cruise simply on the lookout for a man – and not necessarily a new husband!) has just received some news that means she'll have to abandon her trip. It's all terribly sad, her daughter has been involved in some kind of investment scandal – unintentionally, you understand. She wants to go home and help sort things out.

'Humph,' Nora sighed.

Anyway, she's got to leave the ship as soon as we reach Venice. And this is the real reason why I'm contacting you. How do you fancy joining me? Her cabin is next to mine and it'll be empty for the next three months. The holiday is transferrable, but she says she hasn't got time to bother with all the hassle of finding someone to take her place. She doesn't mind if she loses the money – honestly, some people just don't know how lucky they are to afford to leave a cruise midway through and not worry about the cost, do they? And, well, there it is. I thought of you when she asked if I knew anyone who could use the rest of the trip. I'm sure you deserve a holiday after all that you've been through - what with Woody ...

Yes, very tactfully pointed out, thought Nora.

... then looking after those two youngsters when their parents died, and all the work you put into organising the wedding. The only drawback is that you'll have to fly out to Italy next week.

Nora turned back to the beginning of the letter and saw it had taken five days to reach her. That meant she only had two days left. She couldn't even remember where her passport was, yet alone the last time she used it.

... And of course you would have to pay for the flight, but everything else will be free – apart from spending money for shore visits and the duty-free shops on board. But I'm sure you have a little put aside for a rainy day, haven't you?

While part of her mind was indignant at Alice's cheek, another was working out whether this would be possible. She quickly decided that, yes, it might indeed be.

Anyway, Alice concluded, *think about it and give me a ring on this number, it's the agent's office in Venice – just leave a message and I'll call you back. Even if you don't take up this offer, why don't you come on a cruise? The experience is utterly remarkable, I'm sure you would love it.*

Nora placed the letter on the table, removed her glasses

then massaged her brow and rubbed her eyes. In that moment, when the world was misty and blurred, she admitted to herself that she would really benefit from a holiday. In practical terms, however, she could not imagine joining Alice in a couple of days' time: that was just too soon. But sometime in the not too distant future was certainly possible. There would be a lot to organise, though. But, as she refocused her eyes, part of her felt obliged to stay and support Henry, despite his reticence. Plus, she still felt a certain responsibility towards everyone – her employees and friends as well as the youngsters.

'They are not children anymore,' she told herself sternly. But then she recalled the tears Rosalie cried after her parents' deaths. There was also the sad moment when Polly and Nora were preparing the bride for her wedding: Rosalie broke down, weeping with want for her Mum and her Dad.

And there was George. Although outwardly mature, Nora occasionally glimpsed the boy inside the teenager trying to be a man. He had a strong core of self-reliance, and part of that was to protect his big sister. But he needed to concentrate on his own future as well. To a degree he was already doing this; the reports from MaCold's, his late father's employers and the engineering company who had taken over Tasker's, were good and he no doubt would continue his training regardless of whether or not Nora was here.

That left Henry. Her son had never been gregarious or outgoing. He coped with the social side of working in the pub, but it was really his only contact with the outside world, other than his visits to the wholesalers or the bank.

Shortly after the deaths of their respective parents, and long before they were married, he and Rosalie started visiting Sunday morning car boot sales. At the first one they bought two large ceramic mugs with paintings of cockerels on them - one of which Henry still used for his special mix of both tea and coffee. These started the collection of anything cockerel shaped or depicting cockerels or chickens of any kind. It seemed to become an obsession, but it was probably simply a reason for them to temporarily forget their losses. Soon, they were combing local junk shops and charity venues. Over time, Henry filled every shelf and cranny in the pub's lounge-bar with the infernal things. Nora eventually had to *call time* and tell him no more, especially if he left other people to clean them all - the open fire tended to cause a lot of dust.

But now, Henry didn't seem to want them and, with a few exceptions such as ashtrays and the door stop, all of the cockerel-related items had been packed into plastic storage boxes and placed in the cellar. Mrs Mawberry, the cleaner who came out of retirement after Annie died, was very happy to dust clear shelves instead of having to 'move all that junk' as she went.

Nora now shook her shoulders and told herself sharply that she couldn't up and leave just like that anyway. What about the pub licence?

She stood abruptly and walked upstairs to her bedroom. As she entered, she thought she could smell the unmistakable scent her mother used to wear.

Elspeth Antworthy was a formidable woman. Nora did not believe in ghosts, but she now silently admonished Elspeth for suddenly appearing in her thoughts.

Nora opened her wardrobe door and retrieved a plain wooden box which held her most personal possessions - some precious in monetary terms, a few paper items and legal documents; the remainder being of sentimental value only. She rummaged deeply and eventually found her passport. The cover was hard and dark blue with a gold crown embossed on the front. It looked pristine and new, but the date proved it was twelve years old and two years out of date.

Chapter 4

'You can get a replacement passport quite quickly, I think,' Polly, the voluptuous, blonde bar maid, advised. 'But it'll only be a temporary one.'

Polly started to working for Nora a couple of years ago when the landlady was struggling to recover from her flu-like virus. Nora was immediately intrigued by Polly, whom she knew had a partner, Susan. Polly teased the customers, especially those who did not realise at first that she was gay: she was just a young woman who dressed somewhat alluringly. Today, she wore a very tight T-shirt-style top with a large, eye-catching jade and jet necklace, a bracelet and earrings to match and numerous rings. Nora marvelled at Polly's ability to work all day in high stiletto-heeled shoes, although she did sometimes wish that her skirts were a little longer.

Polly was originally introduced to the Sticklebacks by Max Podgrew, who said she was his niece. It transpired that they were not actually blood-related but their respective families were friends.

The Reverend Quintin Boyce, Quinny, was sitting on the other side of the shiny brown-topped bar. He cleared his throat before imparting his advice.

'If it's a proper renewal you're after, you need to go to the passport office. But you'll have to get there really early and queue up.'

Quinny was rector of St Jude's Church, situated midway between the communities of Pepper Hill and Ashfield and served the combined parish of PepperAsh. Quinny, as he preferred to be called, was a regular in The Fighting Cock and would contribute to any conversation around him, usually whilst absentmindedly fiddling with the rubber bands he always wore on his wrists.

'Where's the passport office?' Nora asked in general. She had decided that, if it were at all possible, she would take up Alice's offer – eventually, if not immediately.

Max had grunted when she told him Alice's news. He now turned his back and walked away from the bar.

'Huh! If Alice wanted company, why didn't she send for me?' he muttered loudly.

'You wouldn't have gone,' Polly countered.

'Maybe not,' he shouted back, having chosen a seat near the fireplace. 'But it would've been nice to be asked.'

'Are you really thinking about going then?' Polly later enquired of Nora, the repercussions of her boss saying *yes* running through her mind. The money from the extra shifts would be useful; Susan had just been made redundant and was trying to keep herself busy by redecorating their home. Polly had forgotten how expensive paint, equipment, new curtains and carpets and everything were. Whilst trying to prevent extravagance, she couldn't really restrain the spending, especially as it gave Susan a purpose in such bleak circumstances.

'Possibly, but not right now – not soon enough to warrant a special trip to the passport office, anyway. You see, there're a couple of things I need to sort out. One is the pub licence. Henry was twenty-one in September and, although he could probably have taken over before now, I think the old *coming of age* is a good bench mark for that kind of responsibility.'

'That's true, I hadn't thought of it like that,' Polly said, smoothing down her hair then wiping a flake of ash from just below her cleavage.

Nora knew she was several degrees less glamorous than Polly and did not try to compete. She thought low-cut tops and short skirts, which might be perfectly attractive on Polly, who was in her late twenties, would be an unwelcome sight on her. She gave herself a mental shake and straightened her shoulders. She maintained a moderately slender figure, mostly as a result of hard, physical work - and not quite eating enough, if she was absolutely honest.

And sometimes a tall glass of cold tonic water with a good measure of gin gave her just enough energy to finish whatever job or shift she was doing.

One of the reasons she had been unable to completely condemn her husband's behaviour was because she realised exactly how easy it was to just have another drink to help, then one more to be sociable, plus a nightcap at the end of the evening to relax after a long, exhausting day.

'So, I'll speak with Henry and see what he says,' said Nora.

'Right. And what's the other thing?' Polly prompted.

'Well, it's been a couple of years now - more than that - since Woody died, but his grave doesn't have a headstone yet. They - the funeral directors, that is, Maude and Griffin, not sure which one I actually spoke to - said to leave it at least six months before going back to discuss it.'

'Oh,' Polly said thoughtfully. 'I didn't realise.'

Although Polly had been employed after Woody's death, several customers told her of his drunken exploits. She empathised with Nora rather than joining in the criticism. 'To be honest,' Polly continued, 'I don't know what you're supposed to do. D'you just pick one, like, from a catalogue, or can you design your own?'

'Bit of both, I presume,' Nora replied. 'But I think there are restrictions as to the type of stone you can have in some graveyards. I guess Mr Maude-Griffin will tell me.'

'What does Henry say about it?' Polly asked.

'I haven't mentioned it to him yet. But I don't expect he's given it much thought either - not really the sort of thing a young man whose marriage has just broken up would think about, I guess.'

'No, maybe not,' Polly agreed.

Nora noticed the hesitancy in her tone.

'Has he said anything to you about what happened - what *really happened* - between him and Rosalie?' Nora probed.

'No, not a word,' Polly confirmed. 'Have they finished completely then? Or is this just some kind of blip?'

'Oh, I don't know. Maybe they just shouldn't have got married in the first place. But they seemed so happy. I know the circumstances were a bit unusual and, yes, they were very young. Perhaps they should've just lived together. That seems to be the modern way, doesn't it? And I know Henry loved - loves - Rosalie, but perhaps it was just infatuation; after all, he hasn't had any other girlfriends, not that I'm aware of anyway. And part of me used to wonder sometimes if Rosalie wasn't just playing with Henry's feelings - you know, aware that by using her *feminine charms*, she could make Henry do anything for her.'

'Yes, but we were there,' Polly reminded Nora, 'helping her dress for her wedding. There were doubts and anxieties as well as excitement ...'

'That's nothing unusual, every bride has doubts,' Nora stated.

'Yes, I suppose so,' said Polly. 'And Henry must've been missing his Dad as well.' She paused before looking directly at Nora. 'So, on the basis that he misses Woody, I think he would want to be consulted about the headstone as soon as possible, don't you?'

'Yes, you're right. As usual.' Nora smiled as she spoke. 'It's a very annoying habit, you know, to always be right.' Polly grinned in return and shrugged her shoulders. Nora continued, 'I'll have a word with him as soon as I get a chance - and when the moment is right.'

Polly nodded in response. Her face then became serious. 'Nora, there is one thing that I wanted to ask you about.' Her voice was hesitant and she looked around in order to avoid eye contact.

Nora frowned before saying, 'Yes, go on.' It was unlike Polly to be reticent.

'Well, can you remember their wedding day when we were helping Rosalie to get ready?'

'Yes,' Nora replied. The vision entered her mind of a beautiful young bride whose unruly blonde hair had been captured in a clasp under her veil and her eyes brimmed with unshed tears.

'Well, I lent her my watch as the *something borrowed* for her wedding outfit. But she hasn't returned it as yet. I guess she's just forgotten. I wondered if you could perhaps remind her, please? It was a birthday present from Susan and, although she didn't seem to mind at the time, she has made a couple of comments recently that she hasn't seen me wearing it for a while.'

'Yes, of course. I'll see what I can do for you,' Nora said.

'I'm sorry Rosalie hasn't returned it. It is very remiss of her – I think I would call it just plain bad manners, really.' An annoyed edge crept into Nora's voice.

'No, no. Don't have a go at her. She's just forgotten, what with all the other upheaval.'

'Well, it's very good of you not to be angry. And maybe if we knew what the *other upheaval* was, then we could help. But I'll make sure you get it back anyway,' Nora said, determined now to visit the Old Police House.

Chapter 5

Henry sat on his bed and removed his mother's engagement ring box from his bedside cabinet. Resting his elbows on his knees, he studied the ring. Devoid of the diamond, he thought the circle of gold seemed flimsy and insubstantial. The hallmarks on the underside were slightly worn and the band itself was no longer perfectly round.

But his eyes were drawn to the empty setting, a hollow receptacle destitute of its treasure. The four corner claws, one slightly more twisted than the others, had been stretched wide, as if relinquishing the gem was painful and filled with resentment.

Henry remembered his mother telling him that Woody's income at the time of their engagement was quite modest; she had chosen the ring simply because it was very pretty. She said she could not remember the cut or the carat, but the stone's attraction was its lustre and the beautiful colours it reflected.

When Nora gave the ring to Henry for Rosalie, the idea had been for the diamond to be a token of continuity, a thread running through the family. And if they, in turn, were lucky enough to have children - especially a daughter - this could then be passed on.

Henry had realised at the time the deception of not using that particular diamond for Rosalie's engagement ring but purchasing a replacement could cause resentment for both his mother and his new wife. But he hoped they would understand. He also knew that Rosalie had had heart-shaped photographs of her parents made for the gold locket, and that it was very precious to her. When he witnessed her burying it at Ashfield Staithe where Annie and Derek died, he thought he was doing the right thing by retrieving it.

However, he did not appreciate the importance to Rosalie of leaving the locket as a memorial to her parents, nor had he foreseen that digging it up, removing the photographs from inside and replacing them with Nora's diamond would upset Rosalie so much. He hoped she would cherish being able to wear both the locket and diamond close to her own heart: he had kept the photos safe for her. Now he would do anything to put things right.

He suddenly felt he needed to speak to Rosalie but he knew she would not listen long enough for him to explain. He had tried to write a letter, but he was not sufficiently articulate to make her understand.

The sound of laughter reached Henry's ears from the lounge-bar below. Polly and Nora were both working and Craig would be in later. Henry could take a couple of hours off, if he wanted to. But where would he go? What would he do? He didn't want to be alone, yet he didn't wish for anyone's company - except Rosalie's, of course.

Henry reached over and replaced the ring and its box in the drawer of his bedside cabinet. He stood up and stretched himself. His hands touched the ceiling, his shirt escaped the waistband of his jeans and his bare flesh experienced the slight chill of the air. He turned around to face the window and saw, hanging from the wall near one of the curtains, the plate Rosalie had bought for his nineteenth birthday which depicted a cockerel.

Henry's obsession with cockerels had, in fact, been a legacy from his father's belief in the pub being a good business and unique in its title of a single Fighting Cock. He still used his tall cockerel mug in which to make his tea/coffee concoction; it was one of an almost matching pair he and Rosalie bought in the early days of their relationship. Rosalie had the other, the perfect one: his had a hairline crack near the base.

Thinking of Rosalie made him feel restless, unfulfilled and hollow inside. Now he could understand why his father drank. At least, he thought he understood the need to do something to alleviate this ache, although he did not know the cause of Woody's pain.

Gossip in the bar said that Quinny, the rector, would ping the rubber bands he wore around his wrist in order to distract himself from some kind of compulsion, but nobody knew what this was. He certainly drank, but he didn't have a problem with it. The challenge for Henry was that Quinny never seemed to pay for his beer.

Henry realised he needed to lift his mood and not allow himself to spiral downwards into despair. He tucked his shirt back in, left his room and went downstairs to the kitchen to make a cup of his special beverage.

Henry's drink of choice was a combination of tea and coffee, very strong and equally sweet. He discovered this by accident a couple of years ago when, having returned to the pub from the sale where he'd purchased the mugs with Rosalie, he offered to make a round of hot drinks. Some wanted tea, others coffee. He had made his own in one of the new mugs. He placed in a teabag and then absentmindedly also spooned in coffee. One sip showed him his mistake, but after he supped a little more he discovered – following a few adjustments and experiments – that he actually liked the taste. As strong and revolting as it was, it was the answer to him not following his father's route of self-destruction. And, since his and Rosalie's break-up, both the taste and ritual of making it offered a form of comfort.

Henry now flipped the teabag into the bottom of his tall ceramic mug, which contained almost a pint of liquid when full. The cockerel painted on the front seemed to mock him. Next, three heaped teaspoons of instant coffee were ceremoniously strewn on top. When the kettle boiled, he lifted the spout to the rim and, as part of the routine, before the bubbles stopped dancing, he poured the water onto the coffee and teabag, briskly stirring with a dessert spoon until the swirling pool on the surface was an inch or so from the top.

Returning the kettle to its stand, Henry reached over to the fridge, brought out the milk and poured in the precise amount needed. He then finally added the sugar - two heaped dessert spoons, often using the one he'd stirred his coffee with and leaving a soggy patch in the bowl for Nora to moan about. The first sip of his special tea/coffee mix was tart, bitter and shocking. But it made him feel alive.

Polly could make a fairly decent cup of this unique concoction, but his mother refused to even try. Rosalie's attempts had been reasonable and he was sure that, with more practice, she could have become proficient.

At this point, Nora and Polly came into the kitchen. They were giggling, Henry thought, like two conspiring teenagers. Even more suspicious was the fact that they stopped when they saw him and composed their faces - until they glanced at each other and relapsed, their cheeks glowing pink and tears beginning to glisten in their eyes. Polly cleared her throat then looked from Nora to Henry.

'Oh, er ...' she began. 'Right, I'll be in the bar.' She disappeared back through, closing the door behind her, which Henry thought was ominous: the door usually remained open.

'Would you like a cup of tea or anything?' he enquired. 'What about Polly? She scarpered rather smartly just then. Is anything wrong?'

'No, nothing's wrong. You sit down and I'll make my tea. I see you're okay.' Nora nodded towards his cockerel mug. Henry blushed a little because he would've made one for everyone, he just hadn't thought to call through and ask.

'It's all right,' Nora assured him, sensing his discomfort. 'I wanted to have a word with you anyway.' After a few minutes, and with her hands warming around her cup of tea as she sat opposite Henry, she outlined her ideas for him to take over the pub licence.

'Yeah, I s'pose that won't be a problem,' Henry said, showing no emotion or enthusiasm about being left in charge on his own.

Nora then hesitated before broaching the subject of Polly's watch. Suddenly, she wasn't even sure if Henry knew anything about it. She looked down at her hands as her fingers stroked the rim of her cup and concluded that perhaps a chat with her erstwhile daughter-in-law was overdue. Then she remembered the other subject she needed to discuss with her son.

'We also need to make arrangements to erect a headstone on your Dad's grave. And we'll have to sort out the wording for the inscription.'

Chapter 6

Three weeks later, Nora and Henry were standing in the southern half of St Jude's churchyard. The sun was shining and the warm rays were welcome. Nora read aloud the pristine black lettering on the grey headstone.

Woodrow (Woody) Stickleback
Loving Husband to Nora
and Devoted Father of Henry
January, 1941 to May, 1988
Rest In Peace

The morning after Woody's headstone was erected, Henry and Nora walked across the car park towards the solid square building that housed Cliffend's Magistrates Court. They were attending the hearing to transfer the licence for The Fighting Cock public house from Nora's name to Henry's.

Afterwards, Henry said to his mother, 'I thought it would be a lot more complicated than that.'

'So did I! Good job we took our time to fill out all those forms properly. Come on, let's get home and maybe I'll make you a cup of that revolting tea and coffee mix you drink to celebrate.'

'Oh,' Henry commented as his smile faded. 'I'd rather you didn't. I'll make it myself, if you don't mind.'

'That's fine. I really don't know how you drink that stuff anyway,' Nora laughed.

A week later, Nora swallowed her doubts and finally dialled the number for the Old Police House in Pepper Hill.

'Hello?' Rosalie's voice sound apprehensive, as if she somehow foresaw problems resulting from this call.

'Rosalie? It's Nora.' There was a pause. 'How are you?' Another pause.

'I'm ... er ... okay. Thank you.' Remembering her manners, she then enquired, 'How are you?'

'I'm fine, sweetheart. Thank you for asking.'

Nora despaired; this all sounded so stilted and unnatural. She remembered the time they had made a Christmas cake together in the kitchen at The Fighting Cock. Although she knew Rosalie shouldn't have tried any, they both had a good taste of sherry before adding it to the mix. After enjoying that day so much, Nora was now saddened to think they were speaking almost as strangers.

'Look, Rosalie,' Nora suddenly gabbled. 'Can I come over and have a chat? I've got a couple of things I want to speak to you about and I'd rather do it face-to-face than on the phone.'

'Well, er ... Okay.' Rosalie was surprised. And a little wary. 'When?' she asked.

'Now, if it's convenient. I could be there in about ten minutes.'

Rosalie did not reply immediately. Her mind raced to think of an excuse for not seeing her mother-in-law. She didn't want a confrontation. The reason she had left Henry was not Nora's fault, nor was it her business. But she realised she missed Nora, both as a friend and a mother figure. She still mourned the loss of her own parents so much. Nora had been very kind to her during the first two years after their deaths, despite the fact that she had her own grief to deal with. Eventually Rosalie relented.

'Okay. Ten minutes or so. I'll put the kettle on, shall I?'

she asked.

'That would be marvellous,' Nora stated warmly. 'I'll see you in a bit.'

Nora could see a significant change in Rosalie when she opened the front door. She hadn't exactly lost weight, but she did not look in particularly good health. Her skin was pale and her wiry, blonde hair needed a wash. She wore jeans and a baggy jumper but no shoes or slippers.

Nora was aware that George was supposed to be looking after his older sister, but she realised there was a limit as to how much he could intervene - or interfere, as she was sure Rosalie would see it. She thought perhaps Rosalie was simply wallowing in her own misery. Part of her wanted to shake her and tell her to grow up; the other part felt sorry for her. She fought the urge to hug her.

'Come in,' said Rosalie, unaware of the conflict battling inside Nora. She leant forward and reached up to kiss her cheek.

Nora suddenly felt very emotional: she was not expecting such familiarity. She thought the meeting would be guarded, if not hostile. She had forgotten how young Rosalie was - still just eighteen years old.

Rosalie tried to smile, but she suddenly placed her hand over her mouth and turned away. She ran down the hallway, through the kitchen and off to the left - Nora presumed to the toilet beyond the utility room.

Frowning, she shut the front door and followed, but discreetly remained in the kitchen. Rosalie had not closed the doors; it was obvious she was vomiting. It was ten-thirty in the morning.

After a few minutes, Nora heard the cistern being flushed

followed by the sound of water running into the hand basin. Rosalie emerged holding a piece of tissue to her lips. Nora tweaked her head to one side and looked quizzically at her daughter-in-law.

'Yes, Nora, I'm pregnant. But please don't tell Henry.'

'He has a right to know,' Nora said, hiding her surprise. 'It's his baby, too.' Then she added, 'It is, isn't it?'

'Of course it is!' Rosalie snapped. 'What d'you take me for?' She glared angrily at Nora before her face crumpled and tears began to fall.

'Come here,' Nora said as she stepped forward and held out her arms.

Nora was surprised at how comparatively small Rosalie felt; standing in her bare feet, the top of her head hardly reached Nora's shoulder. There seemed little flesh on her ribs and her weight was insubstantial as she relaxed into the older woman and sobbed. Murmuring soothing words, Nora rubbed her back and reassured her that everything would be all right.

'But you have to tell Henry, you know that, don't you?' she asked.

Rosalie nodded her head. Her crying was diminishing, so Nora stepped away to pull a sheet of kitchen tissue from the roll fixed on the wall.

'Here.' She handed it to Rosalie. 'Come and sit down,' she said, indicating to the chairs around the kitchen table. 'I'll make us a cup of tea and we can chat. You don't feel sick anymore, do you?' Rosalie shook her head and started to move towards the nearest seat.

A few minutes later they each held a mug of tea in their hands. Nora noticed Rosalie's fingernails were uneven and unkempt; her own were self-manicured, trimmed sensibly short and polished with a light pearlescent varnish - she left the garish red for Polly.

Eventually, Nora said, 'Well, I guess we know how many weeks gone you are.'

'It must have been the wedding night,' Rosalie admitted, her voice still thick with tears. Nora smiled at the thought of being a grandmother - until she remembered the complications.

'You will speak to Henry, won't you?' she enquired tentatively.

'Yes, I promise,' Rosalie answered. 'But not today.'

'Okay, but soon. I don't want him to think I've been keeping something as important as this from him.' Nora's tone became serious. 'He deserves to know. And you both need to think about your future - and the baby's.' She took a sip of tea before continuing. 'Anyway, besides wanting to see you and find out how you are, I wondered if you still have Polly's watch.' Rosalie's forehead furrowed. 'You remember, she lent it to you as *something borrowed* on your wedding day?'

'Oh yes,' Rosalie said with sudden realisation. 'I'd forgotten all about it. I'll go get it for you.' She stood up and swiftly padded her bare feet out of the kitchen. Nora heard her footsteps as she made her way up the stairs. Nora smiled to herself as she thought that at least the sickness had worn off.

Whilst she waited, Nora looked around the kitchen. The work tops were strewn with various things: half-full packets of biscuits that were softening with exposure to the air; crumbs that had spilled from an empty bread bag; several cereal cartons occupied an entire corner, and the fruit bowl held a pack of playing cards in a scruffy cardboard box plus a few odd keys, paperclips and a hair grip. Nora's hands were almost itching to tidy up. Nowhere was dirty, but it lacked the daily cleaning routine necessary in her own commercial premises.

As she continued her inspection, she heard the gentle swooshing to and fro from the washing machine. Through the porthole glass door she could see white laundry sloshing around in soapy water.

The sound reminded her that she still had a load of bar towels in the machine at the pub. She didn't expect Henry to take them out and peg them on the line when the programme finished - he dealt with the glass-washer in the bar and that was enough for him. Soon though, she reminded herself, he would have to do it all.

Henry didn't know his mother was visiting Rosalie; Nora had decided not to say anything. She now hoped Rosalie would phrase the news of her pregnancy carefully and not mention her having been here.

Rosalie returned holding the watch out in front of her for Nora to take. 'The hotel staff packed up all my stuff and sent it over to me the next day in a taxi.' Rosalie suddenly became silent, her face lost its animation and a cloud of hopelessness descended. Her wedding dress was crumpled in the bottom corner of her wardrobe, underneath the ridiculous teddy bear that Henry had given to her. The tears threatened again. She gulped and swallowed, then looked up at Nora.

'Please tell Polly *thank you*, and that I'm sorry I kept it so long. It hasn't caused a problem, has it? I seem to remember she said Susan gave it to her for her birthday.'

'No, no. Not a problem as such,' Nora fibbed as she carefully tucked Polly's watch into her jacket pocket. 'I think she was just anxious to have it back. It has a lot of sentimental value.'

Rosalie sat down at the kitchen table and picked up her tea again.

Nora smiled at her. 'So, how are you in general then, Rosalie?'

'Okay, thank you. Bit confused. Tired - I'm not really sleeping very well.' Rosalie stopped speaking. She had already confided more than she intended. She felt Henry had betrayed her and, by association, Nora was capable of just as great a treachery. She could trust no one. Except George. But he wasn't here.

'Where's George?' Nora asked, as if reading her thoughts.

'He's away until the weekend. He's gone up to Aberdeen with Mr Boston - you remember him, don't you? Dad's old mate from Tasker's - MaCold's it's called now. George did tell me what it stands for, but I've forgotten now. Maintenance and construction of offshore and on land direct, I think.'

'Oh, that's a mouthful. And yes, I remember Mr Boston. He dealt with Mr Morsley, your old head teacher, about taking George on straight from school, didn't he?' Nora asked and Rosalie nodded. 'But what've they gone to Scotland for?'

'Their main offices and fabrication yard are up there, and George's been assigned there as part of his apprenticeship. They've got a new contract for maintenance on a new generation of gas platforms. Plus - and this could be well into the future, but MaCold's seem quite hopeful it'll come to something - they're talking about building some kind of windmill turbine things out at sea to generate electricity from the wind. George showed me some photographs; they look like giant propellers on very tall poles.'

Nora smiled at the picture forming in her mind. 'Well, if they do build anything like that, it'll do George good to be involved at the beginning.'

'Yes, but I'm not sure if they'll actually be built at their base there, though.'

'Anyway, changing the subject,' Nora said after a few moments. 'Or at least returning it to you, Rosalie. Is there anything I can do to help matters between you and Henry? I mean, I could set up a place and time for you two to meet and talk.'

'No, I don't think so. Thank you anyway. I'll ring him soon, I promise,' Rosalie said as she shrugged her shoulders and clutched her hands to her opposite elbows.

Nora allowed a moment to elapse before speaking again.

'Well, you know if you have a problem, even if it is to do with Henry - or it's Henry himself - I'll do whatever I can to help. I know he's my son and you probably think I'll automatically take his side, but I do know that he isn't perfect. None of us are. And you can tell me anything, if it helps. I'm quite unshockable, especially after listening to all the confidences punters share with me at the pub.' She smiled again, but Rosalie remained serious.

'It would sound so silly to you that I can't. You wouldn't understand.'

'You could try me,' Nora suggested. 'I might be able to help.'

'No, no! No one can help!'

'Not even Henry?'

'He knows what he did wrong and he can't put it right. Not now.'

Nora jumped on the reference that Henry had done

something wrong and was about to continue probing when the telephone rang.

'Excuse me,' Rosalie said politely. She looked relieved at the interruption.

'Hello?' she said into the receiver with trepidation equal to the tone Nora heard earlier. Then Rosalie's face broke into a broad smile. 'George? How's it going?' There was a pause and Nora heard the muted voice travelling down the line all the way from Scotland. 'No, I'm fine. Honestly.' Another few moments of silence passed while Rosalie listened. She turned and grinned at Nora, then mouthed her brother's name.

Nora nodded acknowledgement and looked down to where she had laid her handbag at her feet.

'Nora's here, she called in to see me. Yes, yes, everything is all right.' Nora wondered if George knew about the pregnancy.

'No. Well, I was sick a little while ago, but I'm okay now.'

Nora realised her question had been answered.

Rosalie continued to talk into the telephone receiver and seemed to forget she had company.

Nora thought perhaps she ought to be returning to the pub to help Henry anyway. She finished her tea, stood up, picked up her bag and indicated to Rosalie that she should be leaving.

'Just a minute, George. I think Nora has to go.' She moved the receiver away from her mouth and said, 'I'll let you know how things go with Henry. And, thanks for calling in.'

'Well, you know where I am if you need me. Just ring, or come over if you want anything, even if it is just to talk.' But Nora felt Rosalie's attention slipping and simply kissed her goodbye on the cheek. 'Please give George my love,' she whispered.

As she drove back to Ashfield, Nora realised she had forgotten to mention that she might be going away to join Alice Childs on a cruise in the near future.

Chapter 7

The end of October brought the usual mix of shorter days, cold winds and rain followed by bright sunshine. Still reeling from the results of her scan that morning, Rosalie felt the need to escape the silence of the house. She walked across the road to Poskett's shop and post office.

The school-children were on their autumn half-term holiday and three local youngsters were standing at the sweet counter near the till. They were carefully choosing their purchases, in the same way Rosalie and her brother George had when they were children.

'Good afternoon there, young Rosalie,' Poskett greeted her as he gave change to one of his young customers.

She frowned at him, wondering why he was always so cheerful. Outwardly, he was a bachelor, with no hobbies or interests beyond his business - or at least none that anyone knew of. The shop opened just after five o'clock in the morning when the papers were delivered and closed at an indeterminate time in the evening.

There seemed to be a steady flow of customers all day, many being commuters between Mattingburgh, twenty or so miles to the west, and Cliffend which was only a few miles east. Vehicles used the convenience of the lay-by directly outside the premises. Poskett had paid to have this installed in order to ensure highways regulations were not infringed by his patrons, especially those in a hurry. The lay-by accommodated three cars comfortably if the drivers were considerate towards other users; however, the delivery lorries would often block the entire length, which then forced others to park on the road. The new area police officer, PC Owen Yates walked into the shop before Rosalie had a chance to reply.

'Oh, good afternoon, Constable. What can I do for you?' Poskett asked, now completely ignoring Rosalie. She quietly took a couple of steps around to the other side of the shelving. She had come in to buy crisps, any flavour as long as they were not prawn cocktail, which reminded her of her school days when all the girls in her class fancied Henry. True, he was the tallest and best looking of all the boys in Cliffend High School, but he was three years older than Rosalie and her contemporaries. And he was always giving out bags of crisps, mostly prawn cocktail-flavoured.

'I bet they're out of date, or his Mum can't sell them at the pub,' Rosalie remembered saying spitefully. She was jealous because Henry had given her friend Maureen a packet before Rosalie arrived that morning.

'No,' Maureen had replied with her mouth full, spraying Rosalie with crumbs as she held up the bag and inspected the *Best Before* date. 'No, it says May 1990 on here. Want some?' She had thrust the crisps towards Rosalie.

'No, thank you!' Rosalie managed to convey disdain into her response. Although she couldn't remember the taste, and despite her mouth watering slightly as she spoke, she added, 'I don't like prawn cocktail.'

'Gosh, why not? They're brilliant!' Maureen replied incredulously.

And that was why Rosalie still thought she didn't like prawn cocktail crisps, although the two new little lives inside her were screaming for their spicy, salty tang, pink tinge and greasy feel.

Rosalie suddenly felt very sick again, but she wouldn't be able to leave the shop without an inquest from Poskett as to why she hadn't bought anything. He would ask if she wanted something that she couldn't find and, if he did not stock that particular item, would anything else do? Turning away from the garish King's Krisps display (*Krisps with a 'K'* she thought angrily to herself) in front of her, she picked up a packet of chocolate biscuits from the shelf behind.

'So, if you could have a word with the delivery drivers please, Mr Poskett. I'm sure they can park in such a way so as not to block all the space in the lay-by.'

'Well, I'll speak to them, of course, PC Yates. But, as you know, they are a law unto themselves.' Poskett's face remained impassive; an innocent shine glinted off his wire-rimmed spectacles.

'I can assure you they are *not* a *law unto themselves*, Mr Poskett. And please remind them of that when you have a word,' PC Yates responded sharply.

'Of course, Constable. I'll make it perfectly clear. Now, is there anything I can get for you whilst you're here? Tea, butter, bread - maybe a box of chocolates for Mrs Yates?' Poskett indicated towards a promotional stand by the side of the cash register.

'No, thank you, Mr Poskett. And, for your information, there isn't a Mrs Yates. Good day.'

Rosalie was so engrossed watching PC Yates' receding uniform that she jumped a little when Poskett spoke to her.

'Now, young Rosalie. Is that all for you? Just a packet of chocolate biscuits? Are you sure you wouldn't like something a little more nutritional now that you're eating for two, my dear?'

Rosalie glared at him, wondering why her condition was everyone else's business when really it was only hers and Henry's.

Her talk with Henry last week had not gone smoothly. They'd met up in Cliffend, at the café opposite the post office. When she arrived, he was sitting in the window seat. Everything started off well. Henry was unable to have his favourite tea/coffee drink and was sipping from a can of cola with a dark scowl on his face. He was overjoyed at her news but, when he asked what he could do to help, she ended up shouting at him.

She felt shame rippling through her now. She had arrived at their encounter having armed herself to fight with him whatever he tried to say or do. It was embarrassing: the café was almost full and some of the other customers laughed at her as she flounced out. And now there was the latest news that she was carrying not just one baby, but two.

Poskett cleared his throat and repeated his last comment.

'No thanks, this will be fine. And, anyway, I'm eating for three. The doctor said this morning that I'm expecting twins!' Rosalie retorted, without thinking through the consequences of divulging the information.

After leaving the shop, Rosalie waited for several cars from both directions to pass before crossing the road again to go home. She realised that she would have to telephone Henry immediately. Her intention had been to drive to Ashfield and tell both Henry and his mother together. But foolishly, she'd wanted to score a point over old Poskett, who always thought he knew everything. And he would, in turn, pass this news on to all his customers.

'Henry?' Rosalie said into the phone when he answered.

'Hello, Rosalie. It's good to hear from you. How are you?' Henry knew he had to enquire about Rosalie's health because he had previously made the mistake of asking after the baby first. It was the time following their meeting at the café; his ears still hurt at the memory of the ensuing tirade.

'Oh, I'm fine,' Rosalie stated harshly. 'It's just that, well, I had my first scan this morning and the doctor confirmed that I'm - we're - having twins. Around the end of March next year. But she said that twins, and first babies - and these are both, obviously - are prone to arriving a couple of weeks early. Anyway, there you are.'

'Oh,' Henry uttered. 'Oh,' he said again. 'Well, I, er … Is everything okay with them, then?'

'Yes, as far as they can tell. I've got to wait for a second scan then they'll be able to see more clearly.'

'Right, okay. Is there anything I can do? D'you need a lift to the hospital?'

'No, I can get there myself!' Rosalie said defiantly. 'Anyway, I haven't got the date and time yet.'

'Okay,' said Henry. 'Right, well. I'll tell Mum.' He paused before asking, 'Er … is that all right? I mean, for other people to know?'

Rosalie suddenly realised how unkind she was being; after all these were his babies as well.

'Yes, of course. I'll be over to talk to you both soon anyway. When does she leave to join Miss Childs - Alice? I still think of her as a teacher at Cliffend High and want to call her *Miss Childs*.'

'Yeah, I know,' Henry smiled into the phone. 'But I'm not sure exactly when Mum is going. She seems rather secretive about the whole trip, to be honest. I kinda got the impression it's been postponed again. Anyway, I've got to go. There's still a lot to do before we open up and Mum's really taking a back seat now - she wants to see that I can cope with everything on my own.'

Chapter 8

Christmas was approaching and, six months into her pregnancy, Rosalie already felt heavy, bloated and clumsy. George was due home from Aberdeen in three days' time.

'I've finished your room now,' Rosalie told him during their last telephone conversation before he left Scotland. She thought to herself that she seemed to be forever on the telephone, talking with everyone but not really communicating.

George was lodging with a rather strict landlady in her house a couple of miles away from his works. He was not yet eighteen - over a year away, in fact. Although legally old enough to leave home, MaCold's took it upon themselves to be responsible for his digs and welfare whilst he was assigned away from Cliffend. He was quite independent for his age, sensible and hardworking, and didn't seem to mind being on his own. Rosalie realised she was desperate for company and was looking forward to seeing her brother over the Christmas and New Year holidays.

But George seemed reticent. She wondered if she had forgotten a vital arrangement, but she could dredge nothing up from the bottom of her brain. Unfortunately, she found retaining anything in her memory increasingly difficult. She had struggled earlier in the week to remember which day she needed to put the bins out for the rubbish collection; then there was the constant problem of which medical appointment to attend, where, and at what time.

Yesterday, as a mental exercise and just to keep up practice, Rosalie tried to write out her shopping list in shorthand, as suggested by Mrs Handly, her old shorthand tutor from her Clifftech secretarial course days. But she couldn't remember the outlines for sausages or toilet rolls so she gave up, dreading what she would bring back from Poskett's if she took in a slip of paper covered with indecipherable squiggles.

Rosalie wanted to preserve her skills because she would have to find a job at some point in the future. Her parents' legacy would not last forever, especially with two babies arriving in less than three months' time - not that she would be looking for any other work for a long while with twins to take care of.

Henry helped financially of course, and George gave her a proportion of his salary as his contribution for the upkeep of the Old Police House. Their parents left the property to them jointly. Although he did not earn much, George took his responsibilities seriously. Rosalie needed a home, which the house provided, but she could not manage all the costs involved herself, especially as she was not actually working. In fact, she had not held a job since she and Henry married.

The plan had been for Rosalie to assist Henry in the running of The Fighting Cock after the wedding. They were to live in the smallholding, Tidal Reach, opposite the pub whilst Nora remained as landlady in residence. And they would all earn a living from the profits - after they paid Polly, Craig and Mrs Mawberry their wages, if they decided to keep everyone on, of course. Perhaps if she and Henry had still been together, her mother-in-law would not be intending to 'run away to sea', as Quinny so quaintly summarised the other week when the subject of Nora joining Alice on the cruise ship arose again.

'Rosie?' George's voice cut through her thoughts.

'Don't call me Rosie,' Rosalie snapped.

George was tired. He closed his eyes then opened them again quickly when he recognised the descending, sinking feeling. He'd heard of people falling asleep on their feet but had not, until now, realised it might actually be possible.

And Rosalie exhausted him. Sometimes she tried to behave like a grown up and be responsible for him, maybe in some way thinking she had to take their parents' place; at other times she just seemed to act in a very childish manner.

George had worked fourteen-hour shifts for the past month. Most evenings he had stumbled back to his digs, eaten the meal provided for him then either studied or fallen asleep. He didn't join in his colleagues' drinking bouts, mainly because he was not old enough. And getting drunk did not really appeal to him. He was embarrassed by their behaviour sometimes. Also, of course, the spectre of Woody Stickleback was always in the back of his mind. George now yawned audibly into the phone.

'Am I boring you?' Rosalie asked, catching the sound. 'I only rang to let you know that I've cleaned and prepared your room.'

'I know, I know. I'm just tired at the moment. Didn't you also say you wanted me to help sort Mum and Dad's things so you can re-arrange the rooms and leave one spare for the nursery?'

'Yes. And I'll need two rooms eventually,' she replied.

'Yeah, but not yet, will you? Won't the two babies be better together? I mean at least in the same room, not the same cot. Oh God, I'm knackered. Listen, I need to get some sleep. I'll ring you again before I leave to come home.'

Rosalie walked through to the kitchen. The chat with George had unsettled her. She drew her cardigan around her tightly and folded her arms above her swollen stomach. She felt restless. She walked to the back door and opened it. The weather was damp and chilly, and mist hung around the trees at the bottom of the garden. She shivered.

She was glad she had cut the lawn for the last time a few weeks ago; she didn't think she would be able to drag the mower out of the shed and work it around the garden now. Most of the leaves had fallen from the trees and now lay soggy and brown on the grass. She'd managed one session gathering them up, but the remainder would have to either blow away in the winter winds or slowly be turned into mulch. With sadness, she realised the grass would die, the moss would grow and her Dad's prize lawn would be no more.

Tears sprang to her eyes. She knew Derek and Annie would be disappointed in her achievements - or lack of them. Maybe they would have been pleased to become grandparents, if not preferring to wait a couple more years.

She wondered if she and Henry would have married if all their respective parents were still alive. Not at quite such a young age, she was in no doubt about that. But if Annie and Derek hadn't died, so many things would be different. Or so she thought.

Rosalie closed the door. The kitchen now felt as cold as the outside. She moved towards the sink to fill the kettle.

Turned upside down on the draining board was the large ceramic mug decorated with a cockerel. It was the partner to the one Henry still used for his tea/coffee concoction.

Being the wrong way up, the cockerel was skilfully balanced on one of the points of the orangey-pink comb on his head. His open beak looked as though he was squawking in surprise rather than holding the expression of supreme conceit he managed to portray when the mug was standing properly. His scrawny little legs were scissored aloft, his claws looked sharp and malevolent.

When the two mugs were together, it could be seen that they were subtly different. The wing feathers on the cockerel on Rosalie's mug were a lighter shade of peacock than Henry's, closer to turquoise with a slightly silvery shimmer. She wondered at the time of purchase if this mug had been left in the sunshine and the picture faded. For a fleeting moment, she felt the excitement and apprehension of that damp morning in Cliffend Town Hall with Henry at the sale when they discovered these treasures.

This event had seen the start of Henry's collection of all things cockerel-related and the beginning of his obsession with the disgusting coffee/tea beverage he now drank. For a few hours that day, these activities and the excitement they brought plugged the awful gap in Rosalie's soul caused by the death of her parents. Henry seemed happy as well. As those initial sparks ignited, they thought they would be okay and have a future together. Later that morning, when they were back at the pub and talking to George and Nora, they felt secure in a unit with those who remained from their respective families.

The picture of the cockerel became unclear as Rosalie remembered she and Henry were now expecting a family of their own.

Chapter 9

George's train was due into Cliffend at eleven-twenty-nine. Rosalie planned a casserole lunch, but George rang from London to say there was a delay and he may not reach Pepper Hill until tea time. He told Rosalie to go ahead with her lunch as he would buy himself a meal.

She finished tidying the kitchen and placed the cockerel mug on the window sill, the larger of the two pictures facing her. This reminded Rosalie that she wanted George to look through their parents' personal possessions with her during his time at home. At the moment these were in their bedroom, the largest of all the rooms upstairs.

Rosalie had tried to sort through her parents' things, but it proved too painful. Over eighteen months ago, however, she'd had to rifle through their safe box to find her birth certificate in order to complete the paperwork before she and Henry could marry. Her marriage certificate was now ensconced in there.

Rosalie had also dumped the big, ugly teddy bear in the wardrobe during one of her frantic clearing out and tidying up sessions in her own bedroom, having first found a plastic bag large enough to keep it dust-free. The locket was still around its neck, with the stupid diamond glittering away to itself in the dark - or whatever sparkly objects did when there was no light for them to reflect. Whenever Rosalie thought about it, the resentment against Henry increased a little more. She was glad the gem was out of her sight.

'Hi,' Rosalie greeted her brother later when he arrived by taxi. 'Would you like a cup of tea?'

'Yes please, Rosie. That would be great. Just let me get these in,' George replied. He carried his bag through to the kitchen.

Rosalie followed him, checked there was enough water in the kettle, pressed the switch and laid out the mugs. She looked at George who was unpacking his bag and stuffing his dirty laundry straight into the washing machine.

'Hadn't you better check there's nothing in the pockets before you put them in there?' She couldn't prevent her irritation sounding.

'Oh, stop nagging, Rosie, and just let me get on with it,' George replied harshly. He saw his sister's face crumple and softened his voice. 'You could make me a sandwich or something to go with that cup of tea, if you wanted to do something useful. I'm starving.'

Ten minutes or so later, as they sat at the kitchen table, Rosalie adjusted her bump so she could actually reach the surface. She sighed whilst trying to make herself comfortable.

George glanced at Rosie again. She looked as if she hadn't brushed her hair that day and her eyes were weary. He knew she was lonely. But she didn't have to be on her own; she could be with Henry. Instead, she stubbornly remained here.

George alternated between wanting to be on his own and needing company. He stared at the table top as he chewed his ham sandwich. Unable to prevent himself falling into despair for a moment, he wished he was back in Scotland – or, more urgently, that he could return to the time before his parents died and prevent the tragedy from happening.

Chapter 10

Two weeks before Easter, on Friday 15th March, 1991 Rosalie was attending a prenatal clinic at Cliffend Hospital. Whilst awaiting her appointment, her waters broke and labour began.

Rosalie telephoned Henry before being taken to the delivery suite, but had to leave a message on his answer machine. She then tried to contact George at his place of work. The lady who answered the phone promised to put a call out for him on the tannoy. He was somewhere in the fabrication yard, but she explained that she couldn't just go and fetch him to the phone, no matter how urgent the news.

Henry walked into the kitchen at The Fighting Cock public house and saw the red light flashing on the answer phone. As soon as he listened to Rosalie's slightly anxious voice, he ran through the lounge-bar and out of the main door to the car park, shouting the news to Polly as he left.

Within four hours of the start, Rosalie gave birth to a little boy, then three minutes' later a little girl arrived.

Rosalie was mesmerised as they each cried with the shock of birth. She held them both together, one in each arm, and was filled with a love she never imagined existed. Their warmth, their movements, their substance fascinated her. They were heavy, and she felt they must weigh more now that they were outside her body than they could possibly when still inside. Their being was beyond her comprehension and, although she'd always thought the sentiment a cliché, she suddenly believed that babies really were miracles.

The blue-clad midwife, short and plump and very

efficient, explained the importance of colostrum and breast-feeding as she carried out an intimate examination of the new young mother. Rosalie felt that no part of her body was private anymore and wondered if she would ever regain her dignity.

'The twins have a very auspicious birthday,' the midwife joked as she removed her latex gloves and replaced the sheet over Rosalie.

'What d'you mean?' Rosalie asked, her voice harsher than she intended.

'Beware, the Ides of March!' the midwife replied dramatically.

'Sorry?'

'It's a quote from the Shakespeare play we did at school. Can't remember which one now, though - so much for studying text books, eh? Talking of which, well done, my dear, they were text book deliveries. And you were very brave, for your first time.'

And my last, Rosalie thought to herself. She missed her own mother so much. There were a hundred and one questions she wanted to ask her. But the midwife mistook Rosalie's tears for those of joy at the two new arrivals.

Henry had not been present for the actual births. He arrived just after the little girl was born and had to wait until the delivery of the placenta. He was allowed to see them after everything necessary had been carried out and mother and babies were moved to a quiet room just off the main ward.

Rosalie smiled at Henry as she sat up in bed, leaning against a cloud of pristine white pillows. She was nursing the baby boy whilst the baby girl wriggled restlessly in a clear plastic cot beside her bed. An empty one stood on the other side. To Henry, these looked like two fish tanks.

At six pounds, their son was nearly fifteen ounces heavier than his little sister, and Henry could see the difference in their sizes. He picked up his daughter and held her tentatively but protectively in his arm - cradling her head with his other hand, as shown by the nurse before she discreetly left the room.

He had never held a baby before, let alone a new-born. The feeling of her warmth and solidness was imprinted into his memory so deeply that he knew he would never forget these first few moments. He was fascinated as he watched her uncurl her fist and, with miniature pink hands and fingers that tapered into tiny pearl nails, she clung onto his little finger with such strength and determination that he felt a bond forming which nothing could sever.

As Henry stared at her closed eyes and bright pink wrinkled face, he recalled how characters in television programmes always talked about the smell of new-born babies. He was not sure which aroma belonged to her and which to the general atmosphere of the hospital. *Perhaps women are better at identifying scents than men,* he concluded. Maybe that's why they have such expensive tastes in perfume. To distract his thoughts, he fiddled with the hospital tag around her wrist.

There was a book of baby names lying open on the blanket between Rosalie's feet.

'The nurse lent it to me. Apparently they keep a couple of copies behind the desk,' Rosalie replied to Henry's query.

'Have you got anything particular in mind?' he asked.

Rosalie shook her head. She had tried and tested all sorts of combinations since discovering she was carrying twins but had made no decisions, nor had she asked Henry for his preferences. Until their birth, she hadn't known if she was having two boys, two girls or - as in fact happened - a boy and a girl.

'I wondered about Annie for her,' she said thoughtfully, indicating to the baby in Henry's arms. She suddenly felt the need to move her legs, but this brought a flash of pain. She winced before settling again. 'But she doesn't look like an *Annie*. I wondered what you thought of Sarah?'

'Sarah,' Henry said softly as he looked down at his daughter. She had released his finger and seemed to be trying to swat something from her head. Under the blanket, her little feet were kicking and she generally seemed fidgety. Perhaps she was registering the space she now had in which to move, in contrast to her previous constrictions.

'Yes, *Sarah* sounds perfect.' The baby gave a tiny mewling sound and Henry smiled down at her. 'What about a middle name?'

'Well, for Sarah, we could have Rose. Or Rosanne, a combination of my name and Mum's. But definitely not Rosie! What d'you think?'

'Perfect. Absolutely perfect,' Henry agreed. 'Sarah Rosanne Stickleback!'

'And for this one …' Rosalie smiled fondly down at the baby sucking at her with great vigour. There were no problems with either baby latching on and, although breast feeding at the moment was an alien feeling, she knew she would become accustomed to it. 'I would like to use your middle name, if you don't mind - *Thomas*. I quite like it. According to the book,' she nodded towards the paperback, 'it means *twin*. I wouldn't want to be so obvious as to have it for his first name but, as a middle name, it would be fun. What d'you think?'

'Yeah, that sounds okay. What about *Duncan* for his first name? Duncan sounds solid. Duncan Stickleback!' He thought he would look up the meaning later.

Rosalie agreed with a smile before re-adjusting the newly named Duncan Thomas in her arms and gently wiping his cheek with a muslin cloth.

'Is your Mum coming in?' she asked suddenly.

Henry had been dreading this question. He swallowed hard and took a deep breath before replying.

'Mum left late this morning before you called. A taxi took her to the rail station. She's catching the two o'clock train to London, then another to Southampton where she's joining Alice for a cruise to the Caribbean. But she said to give you this.' Still holding baby Sarah, he leant his weight over onto one cheek and delved into the opposite back pocket of his jeans. He pulled out a white envelope. Rosalie managed to free one of her hands, struggled to undo the envelope then held up the hand-written letter.

Dear Rosalie, she read. Nora was obviously trying to sound kind and affectionate, expressing regret at the fact that she would be away by the time the twins were born. Rosalie smiled at the irony of her only just missing them. Nora had enclosed a generous cheque for Rosalie to purchase anything she wished for the new arrivals.

And if there is anything else you need, please let me know and I'll see what I can do. I'll forward contact details as soon as I'm on board. Also, please don't mind me for saying this, but if there is any way you and Henry could put aside your differences for the sake of the babies, then please do so. You know I still think of you as my daughter and, although I don't know what happened to split you and Henry up, you know you have my full support.

Yes, except now I need your help you're not here, Rosalie thought angrily to herself. She glanced up from the page and saw Henry watching her. She quickly read the last paragraph, which reminded her that the top tier of their wedding cake had been kept in an airtight container at the pub, to be used at the reception after the twins' christening ceremony. She handed the letter to him.

'You'd best read it as well, that way we both know where we stand,' she stated.

Rosalie sighed as Henry's eyes scanned the note. She too wished they could live as a happy family, but she planned to continue to make her home at the Old Police House with the twins and her brother, George.

Rosalie looked down at the baby in her arms and adjusted his position slightly in an attempt to alleviate the ache in her muscles. A feeling of awe clenched her chest; she hardly dared to believe that the babies were hers. She smiled at Duncan, memorising each part of his face, his chubby and dimpled hands with their four miniature fingers and a thumb each. He finished suckling and his eyelids fell.

Sarah was beginning to grizzle as she lay in her father's arms. He tried to rock her, jiggle her and, in the end, said, 'I think she needs her nappy changing.'

'Well, be my guest. You'll have to get used to doing it - I can't cope single-handedly with two babies.'

Henry's heart sang at this, he didn't even hear Rosalie's explanation of what to expect inside the nappy. He thought his mother's words had softened her resolve, hoping this was a truce of some kind. He wanted Rosalie and the babies to move into the pub with him. And then maybe there could be a new start to their marriage.

But of course, there was to be no second beginning for Rosalie and Henry. Rosalie and the twins were discharged from the maternity wing of Cliffend Hospital on Saturday morning. Henry arrived with two baby carriers for the car in which they would travel back to Pepper Hill, where George was due to arrive later to meet his nephew and niece.

George had originally been due to return to Pepper Hill the week before Easter, Easter Sunday being the last day of March. However, when he received the news that Rosalie had gone into labour, he was given leave immediately and made arrangements to travel on the overnight sleeper train.

Chapter 11

The talk after the service at St Jude's the following Sunday morning was all about the Stickleback twins and their parents.

Quinny was in the vestry whilst Mrs Ervsgreaves bustled around the small room taking robes off the hooks behind the door and placing them on hangers before rehanging them. The cool air wafted a crisp breeze as she moved; the wattles of flesh dangling between her chin and neck reminded Quinny of the cockerel picture on Henry's mug. He wished she would stand still for a moment.

'Good news about the Stickleback babies,' he commented, smiling to himself. 'I'll get myself over to see them as soon as I can.' He pinged the rubber band on his wrist. 'And Henry, of course,' he added.

Quinny felt true pleasure at the news. He did not have any children of his own - nor was he likely to now at his age, but he could rejoice in others. Sadly, he saw his life as a satellite: alone and inexorably moving in circles around everyone else until one day it would end. And then?

'And then?' the voice in his head asked, echoing his own words.

Mrs Ervsgreaves was too busy with her own thoughts to hear the rector talking to himself. She did not even notice when he quietly left the vestry via the small outside door.

The telephone was ringing when Quinny walked into the rectory.

'Hello, Reverend Quintin Boyce here,' he said. He usually quoted his nickname, but something warned him to be a little more formal on this occasion.

'Hello. It's Bishop Patrick Clement from Mattingburgh.'
'Oh,' Quinny replied with trepidation.
'I'm in Cliffend tomorrow morning,' the bishop advised cordially. 'And I thought we could have a chat.'
Quinny grimaced. Time spent with the bishop never ended well, especially after Quinny had inadvertently been caught relieving his bladder against a yew tree in the churchyard some years ago.
'What say I meet you at the pub in Ashfield - what's it called now, something to do with fowl?' The bishop laughed; it was an ominous sound.
'The Fighting Cock,' Quinny replied belligerently, ignoring the attempt at humour. 'I'll be there lunchtime, bye.' He replaced the telephone receiver onto its cradle and sat down at his desk, groaning out loud and vigorously twanging the elastic bands on his wrist.

Lunchtime the following day found Quinny walking due east from the rectory to the pub. The sun was shining but, rather than cheering Quinny, it made him hot and irritable.
There was no pavement along this part of the road and cars travelled at speeds the rector considered far too fast. He knew he ought to pray for the drivers' safety, instead he swore furiously at them, especially those whose slipstream seemed to pull him out into the carriageway.
Quinny was beginning to think he would have to walk the entire distance of about half a mile between the rectory and the pub when he heard a familiar diesel engine approaching from behind. He could usually rely on someone from either Pepper Hill or Ashfield to stop and offer him a lift.
He did not drive: taking lessons in his youth had proved

traumatic, both for him and for his unfortunate instructors. Each one lasted only for a single lesson and they returned to the driving school with horrific descriptions of Quinny's antics behind the wheel. They all vowed never to take him out again, so he was eventually persuaded to give up.

This morning, Quinny turned around and saw the late morning bus approaching. Its route from the city of Mattingburgh to the seaside town of Cliffend included passing through Pepper Hill and Ashfield. He wondered if he should treat the driver to a cheery smile. As he did so, his toe caught a chipping that had worked loose from the road surface. He promptly lunged forward and cursed profusely as he steadied himself.

'Enjoy your trip?' the lady driver asked facetiously.

Quinny actually managed to force a grin as he stretched his arm out. His hand gripped the rail, joining him to the bus and making him judder violently in time with the engine.

'You going up the other end?' she eventually asked when she finished laughing at her own joke.

'Yes, but I've come out without any change,' the rector managed to say above the hacking throb. The smell of diesel fumes was beginning to make him feel queasy.

'Oh, that excuse again! They tell me you never pay at the pub either,' she stated, then flicked her eyebrows for him to get on.

'Funny you should mention the pub,' Quinny said as he hauled himself unsteadily aboard. 'That's exactly where I'm heading.'

Chapter 12

Bishop Clement was already sitting at a table mid-way along the wall between the open door and the fireplace in the corner. He stood up as Quinny entered. As they shook hands, Quinny noted the half-empty pint glass on the table, the accompanying tray already containing ash and a stubbed out cigarette end.

'I see you arrived in style,' Bishop Clement said, nodding towards the road along which the bus travelled after Quinny disembarked.

Henry approached their table before the rector replied. He was carrying a pint of beer perched on a tray; it had a good head and was dribbling froth down the outside of the glass. He placed it in front of Quinny.

'Just to keep you two level pegging,' he said with a smirk as he straightened his back and shoulders.

Henry was several inches taller than the rector and towered almost a foot above the bishop when he was standing. He seemed particularly pleased with himself today too. Quinny did not immediately notice; he had momentarily forgotten about the births.

Quinny sat down opposite the bishop.

'Cheers,' he said to Henry before taking his initial sip.

'What can I get you two gentlemen to eat?' Henry asked. 'I recommend the shepherd's pie. It's made with fresh lamb mince - possibly from Max's boss, old Goldwin's own sheep. The mint is from Mrs Ervsgreaves' garden, and I bought the potatoes and other vegetables fresh from Poskett's shop.'

'Oh. Is that your idea of supporting local business?'

Bishop Clement asked as he looked over to the bar for a specials' board. Finding nothing on display, he asked, 'Could I have a look at the menu?'

'Sorry, no menu today. I had to go out early, and Polly's just managed to do the shepherd's pie. So it's that or I could make you a cheese and pickle sandwich,' Henry informed them.

'What would you like then, Quinny? My treat, of course.'

'Oh well, in that case, I'll have both,' Quinny said enthusiastically. 'Thank you. Wrap the sandwich up, will you please, young Henry, and I'll take it home for supper. You are doing some sort of pudding as well as the shepherd's pie, I take it?'

As Henry walked away, Bishop Clement said, 'I really don't know how you get away with cadging off everyone - including me.' There was mild admonishment in his tone which Quinny thought was probably hiding a more serious point.

'Well, I guess it's because people let me,' he replied seriously. 'And it's usually because they want something in return. Or they feel guilty for not supporting their local church and rector. Maybe the odd pint makes up for the local landlord never crossing my collection plate with silver - or gold, or notes of any denomination, come to that.'

'So, what did His Bishopness want?' Max asked Quinny at the bar later as they enjoyed a final pint.

'Not much. He called it a social call, checking to see if everything is okay in the parish.' Quinny placed his glass carefully on a beer mat to protect the brown wooden bar surface.

'Oh, I thought perhaps he was making you retire.' Max

sounded disappointed.

'Shame *you* don't retire. You could go and join Alice. Er, how is she nowadays? Quinny taunted. 'Fancy that timid little Miss Childs being a wizard at the gambling tables.'

Max grunted.

'Still can't see why she wanted Nora on board the cruise ship with her rather than you, Max,' Quinny continued dangerously before swiftly changing the subject. 'Anyway, the bishop reminded me that the repair work to the church tower can start soon. Remember, I told you it was flagged up in the last quinquennial report, along with repairs to the rectory. And that's starting in the autumn, so I'll be living on a building site for a few months. No wonder the old bugger wanted to soften me up with a meal before telling me that.'

Max smiled in reply while Henry returned to the bar carrying his large cockerel mug, the end of a dessert spoon rose out of the top which he held with his thumb as he drank.

'Gentlemen, please keep it civil, will you? I don't want you two scaring my customers away,' Henry warned.

'Oh, yes. Sorry. I meant to say, congratulations, young man,' Quinny said brightly as he extended his hand to Henry.

Henry set down his mug and shook the proffered hand.

'Yeah,' Max added. 'Me too.'

'Thank you.' Henry smiled, his entire body relaxing. 'We'll have to come and talk to you, Quinny, about the christening. But we'll leave it a few weeks, I expect. That reminds me, I'll have to check with Mum where she put the top layer of the wedding cake that she told us to use for the christening party.'

'Well, come on then, what are their names?' Max asked

with more enthusiasm than he was feeling. Quinny's jibe about Alice had stung him, but he thought there might be a free pint if he showed an interest in the new little Sticklebacks.

'Duncan Thomas and Sarah Rosanne Stickleback,' Henry announced proudly. 'Mother and babies are all doing well and safely at home in Pepper Hill.'

'Oh, so they aren't coming to live here, then,' Max enquired tactlessly. He immediately regretted this as he realised his lack of diplomacy had probably scuppered his chance of a free drink.

Henry grunted; his good mood of two seconds before had evaporated. He scowled as he picked up his cockerel mug and returned to the kitchen.

Chapter 13

Rosalie was coping very well with looking after the two babies, mostly on her own. She was nursing them herself as much as she could, supplementing them with artificial milk if they were still hungry when they finished her own.

On the Monday before the christening on Sunday 23rd June, Rosalie was writing a shopping list, definitely not using shorthand. She did not need too many things and had neither the time nor the energy to drive to the supermarket in Cliffend, unload the twins into one of their special double-baby trolleys and fight her way around the shelves with trays and boxes standing in front of the products she wanted. Then there would be the hassle of placing everything onto the conveyor belt and trying to quickly pack and pay in order not to hold up other shoppers.

She had experienced the helpful *packer* service the supermarket offered a couple of weeks ago, but found when she returned home that a three-pound bag of potatoes had been placed on top of a loaf of bread and a packet of tomatoes. Needless to say both were squashed to the point of being beyond use.

She placed the twins in their double pram after their feeds and changes. They obligingly fell asleep quite quickly, their long eyelashes resting on chubby cherub cheeks. Their needs were constant and she considered herself no longer a person in her own right but a slave to them. But she felt a glow of contentment and love enfolding her, somehow giving her stamina and patience when she thought she had neither left.

Rosalie swung her bag onto her shoulder and checked

that she had everything she needed - even a quick trip up the road to the village shop and post office was a logistical nightmare.

There was only one other customer in Poskett's when she arrived, an elderly lady who was wearing a thick woollen overcoat and winter boots despite the relatively warm weather. Rosalie managed to gather most of her groceries whilst manoeuvring the pram around the shop, but she was stumped near the end of the aisle by an A-frame advertising stand.

Poskett came over to move it aside.

'You look tired, young Rosalie. Here, let me help you.' He relieved her of her basket and list.

'I know I'm very lucky, compared with some,' Rosalie stated wistfully, fighting the tug into oblivion that lack of sleep gave. 'They have their moments - like when one is settled and the other disturbs them and they both have a scream together. But, on the whole, they're good. I hear horrendous tales from some mothers at the Babies and Toddler group I go to in Cliffend.'

'Perhaps as there's two of them, they keep each other amused,' Poskett stated sagely.

Rosalie presumed he was quoting hearsay from other customers as she didn't think he had personal experience of babies or children.

'It's the christening soon, isn't it?' he enquired.

'Yes, next Sunday. You are coming, aren't you? I mean, the shop will be shut on a Sunday, won't it? Apart from the papers first thing in the morning, I suppose.'

'Well, that's very kind of you to invite me, young Rosalie. And yes, I'll try to get over to the church. What time is it?'

'Eleven o'clock - during the normal morning service.

There's a celebration for St Jude on Wednesday, so the church'll be decorated with lots of flowers. I hope it isn't an omen that the twins will be lost causes after the patron saint.' Rosalie added that last sentiment quietly. Poskett pretended not to hear.

'Oh,' he said, whilst hovering near the chiller containing cheese, butter and other dairy products. 'You've just got six yogurts on your list. D'you want one of the packs containing two each of strawberry, raspberry and vanilla? Or would you like six individual ones?' Rosalie hesitated. 'Individual pots are bigger, but the packs work out cheaper,' he added.

'Um, I'll have two packs of six. I like them whatever the flavour and will probably eat two at a time anyway; with this greedy pair feeding off me, I need to keep up my input.'

'Right.' Poskett decided to change the subject. He'd had to avert his eyes rather quickly the other day when a young mother sat on the chair by the till, pulled out a breast and began to feed her baby in front of everyone. And the shop had been full of people. He did not know what to say; he tended to agree with the people who tutted and disapproved, but he then reminded them that it was perfectly natural - and the baby was obviously very hungry because the teat had been the only thing that stopped its ear-piercing screams.

Still, it did seem a strange thing to do quite so publicly. On the other hand, the family were a long way from home. The bus wasn't due for another ten minutes and the mother had spent a lot of money in the shop. He gave a couple of sweets to the toddler who stood stock-still staring at his Mum and sibling for the duration of the feed.

Poskett now pushed his round-lensed spectacles onto the bridge of his nose. 'So, who have you chosen as godparents?' he asked.

'Sorry?' Rosalie queried. Her mind was concentrating on timings for the babies' next feeds; she had momentarily forgotten about the christening.

'For the christening. Who have you asked to be godparents?'

'That reminds me, Quinny keeps telling me off if I use the word *christening*. Apparently, I should say *baptism*.'

'Oh, right. Of course. Yes, he would, wouldn't he?' There was a pause before Poskett questioned, 'Why?'

The sound of the bus drawing away from the side of the road opposite the shop distracted them. Rosalie had pushed the pram over to the till and was rocking it back and forth so the twins would think they were still moving. The shop bell pinged as the door opened and the rector walked in.

'Ah, Reverend Quintin,' Poskett said pleasantly as he placed Rosalie's laden basket on the counter. 'Good morning, we were just talking about you.'

'Were you, indeed?' Suspicion echoed in the rector's voice. 'Was it anything to do with the forthcoming baptisms for these two?' he asked, bending down and peering into the double-width pram.

Poskett opened his mouth and was about to ask, for the third time, who were going to be the godparents. But he decided not to; he didn't want the job himself, and he would find out eventually anyway.

'Right, Rosalie, is there anything else?' he enquired instead.

'Nappies. I need more nappies. Just a minute, I'll fetch them.'

'Okay, then. I'll start totting up. D'you think you'll get home again while these two li'luns are still asleep?'

'Hope so,' Rosalie stated, thinking how nice it would be to sit down and have a cup of tea in peace before another round of changing, feeding, burping, mopping dribble and worse, then changing, bathing, changing, feeding and changing began again.

Chapter 14

A crowd of people gathered inside St Jude's Church. The day was warm and the atmosphere friendly. The sun shone through the beautifully bold-coloured stained glass in the arched windows, creating vivid rainbows on the stark, white-washed walls. More subtle shades were added by extravagant flower arrangements and echoed further in ladies' outfits.

The congregation's muted chattering accompanied the quiet organ music played by Mrs Ervsgreaves. She wore a loud floral-patterned summer dress suit topped by an enormous scarlet hat with a wide yellow ribbon, neither of which picked out any of the other shades in her clothes. Her dewlapped chin wobbled as she nodded her head in time with the music.

Delilah Ervsgreaves' face was pinned into a smile which, although genuine, was shadowed with disapproval.

'It's such a shame that the mother and father of those two poor little mites don't even live together!' she had announced to the early arrivals, none of whom wished to become embroiled in the Sticklebacks' disagreement. Luckily her back was now turned to the congregation as she sat on her organ stool, the fabric of her dress pulling tightly across her ample bottom. Her fingers followed their routines, moving smoothly over the keys, her feet dutifully pressing the appropriate pedals and lingering on the dominant and tonic, the vibrations from the lower making the pews quiver.

'Has anyone seen Quinny?' Mabel enquired of the group now waiting around the font at the back of the church. She and Mr Ervsgreaves, the two church wardens, were handing out hymn books and attempting to shepherd the growing multitude into vacant pews, despite their general reluctance to be seated.

The main party were yet to arrive. Speculation grew as to whether or not the parents would appear together. One or two regulars at The Fighting Cock, led by Max Podgrew, wondered if Rosalie and Henry could manage a whole hour without arguing. In Max's mind, all church services, no matter their content and intention, lasted that almost unendurable sixty minutes. Polly had banned actual bets being placed inside the pub itself; she had no control over her so-called uncle's gambling away from the bar.

Polly fidgeted. Although used to wearing high heels, she felt uncomfortable in St Jude's and could not stand still. She had bought a modest outfit last week for the occasion and visited her hairdressers for her hair to be cut, re-tinted and styled. She also modified her make-up for today and, as a result, felt forced to be someone she wasn't. She was not sure now about accepting Rosalie and Henry's invitation to be godmother to the twins. George, although he was their uncle and despite his young age, had been chosen as godfather.

At that moment, George Tillinger walked apprehensively into the church, fearing the change of temperature as an omen: the interior was distinctly chillier than outside. Poskett had offered him a lift earlier, and he'd happily left Rosalie and Henry at the Old Police House to bring the twins together.

He was officially on two weeks' holiday, but he planned to leave in the morning and return to Aberdeen because Rosalie was being unreasonable with Henry and he didn't want to take sides.

George nodded to Polly and then glanced around. He could just about recognise most of the people from both ends of the village, even though today they wore their best outfits, had polished their footwear and neatened their hair.

Stan and Vera were standing next to Max Podgrew's boss, Fergus Goldwin. George stared at one elderly woman in particular. Although he was certain he knew her, he could not think of her name. Then he suddenly realised it was Mrs Mawberry, Henry's cleaning lady. She looked smart in a navy outfit and matching hat that were very different from the clothes she wore for work.

'Ah, it's you, George. I nearly didn't recognise you,' Mr Ervsgreaves' words echoed George's earlier thoughts. He extended his hand and was listening to exclamations of how much he'd grown when a hush swept down from the people sitting near the front of the church to those at the back.

Everyone turned around and saw Quinny standing at the top of the nave, near the chancel entrance. He had crept into the church through the small door into the vestry. He had robed and now appeared resplendent in a plain cream alb, almost hidden by his chasuble made from rich ivory silk embroidered with gold.

Quinny was feeling happy with the world, so much so that he'd almost forgotten to wear his rubber bands this morning. He was looking forward to today.

Suddenly, there was a clatter from the main door, after which the congregation heard voices in a heated discussion. One baby started to cry. Then the other joined in.

'Oh, God,' they all heard Rosalie curse before they could even see her. 'Duncan's just been sick all down my dress!'

Chapter 15

Quinny was disgruntled at the disruptions caused by the renovations taking place to the rectory during the autumn following the twins' baptism. In the end, he was persuaded to take a long holiday. He chose a retreat at an abbey many miles away which promised rest and restorative meditation, plus optional study on an obscure subject which he had no intention of taking up. He was sure no one would question him too deeply about either the intellectual content or activities.

When he first arrived, his primary concern of course was the location of the nearest pub. After that was established, everything else fell into place.

Upon his return to PepperAsh, the good ladies of the parish had prepared the house for him. The redoubtable Mrs Ervsgreaves collected him from the station at noon one Saturday in late November. During the short journey, she was keen to describe the changes to his home.

'The house is completely different now, very bright and airy. All mod cons installed, central heating - oil, there's a new tank hidden behind the fencing near where the bins used to be. The bins are still there, but a bit further along. They've re-plastered the walls inside and painted them - just that awful magnolia, but you can always cover it over.'

'Thank God it isn't beige,' Quinny commented heavily.

Mrs Ervsgreaves ignored him. In her opinion, there was not much difference between the two shades.

'And the woodwork has been stripped of that dreadful brown paint, and sanded and varnished up,' she continued. 'The carpets are a bit plain, but they're all that heavy-duty serviceable wear, especially in the hall and study - not very cosy, but they're okay, I suppose. The kitchen and bathroom have been tiled, and you've got new kitchen cabinets, sink, cooker and fridge. There's a new bath and a shower unit too. They've just hung plain curtains everywhere, but I'm sure we can provide something a little more to your taste in due course. We've stocked up your fridge and there isn't too much admin outstanding in the parish. Bishop Clement has taken the last three Sunday services, but the congregation numbers were quite low.'

Quinny grunted at the end of Mrs Ervsgreaves summary.

'I bet he'll soon close us down. He's already tried to get me to retire.'

'No, no, he wouldn't do that, would he? I mean, they've just done all that work on the rectory.'

'That doesn't mean anything. It'll be easier to sell the house now it's been modernised.'

The closer they drew to St Jude's, the greater Quinny's trepidation became. He fiddled with the elastic bands around his wrist and suddenly felt very thirsty. Mrs Ervsgreaves was approaching Ashfield; The Fighting Cock was around the next bend.

'Can we stop at the pub, d'you think?' he asked. 'I could really do with a drink.'

The kindly lady tutted heavily, but obligingly indicated and turned off the road into the car park.

Henry stood in his usual place behind the bar, clutching his cockerel mug which Quinny could see, even from a distance, was full of his disgusting tea/coffee mix.

'Well, look who it is,' Henry said as the rector strode in, followed by an agitated Mrs Ervsgreaves. Her remit from the bishop was to collect the rector from the train station and deliver him safely back to the rectory before he could cause any trouble.

The pub was quite crowded for a Saturday lunchtime. Various customers greeted Quinny with 'Hello,' or 'Good to see you back'. He smiled in acknowledgement, happily twanging the elastic bands on his wrist as he hoisted himself onto his usual his seat at the bar, by the end near the door to the kitchen area.

He then turned and looked around the lounge-bar with the eyes of the recently returned viewing old haunts with renewed appreciation. Even the scuff marks and cigarette burns on the carpet, the chipped edges of tables and the sad emptiness of shelves and nooks were comforting. The fire roared in the grate and the hearth showed signs of recent arced brush marks through spilt ashes. He could taste the wood smoke in the atmosphere and it made his eyes water. It felt good to be back.

Quinny noted a Christmas tree stood in its customary place in the corner of the room. It was as yet undecorated, and looked shy as if acknowledging it was really a little too early for its presence.

'Thought I'd make this my first port of call,' Quinny grinned to Henry then glanced back at the customers. 'What, no Max? Don't tell me he's finally gone off to join Alice on board the HMS Revenger.'

'RMS Vaguaries,' Henry corrected him. He then explained, 'no, no, he's just late. I expect he'll be in soon.'

'Well, it's good to be back,' Quinny confirmed. 'Talking of which, is Nora home yet, or is she still gallivanting around the world as well?'

Henry hesitated before replying. 'She's still off enjoying herself. And good luck to her!'

At that moment, Polly appeared through the open door from the kitchen, smiling broadly. Quinny - not usually one to notice fashion - saw that, despite the rather cold weather, she was wearing a very low-cut top. When she moved her head, the dangling earrings glittered with sparkling stones. She wore a garishly bright gold chain made up of very large links around her neck from which hung a pendant in the shape of a sea horse with a pearl for its eye. The curl of the tail dangled into her cleavage and, like the earrings, glistened with her every movement.

Quinny smiled, despite trying to make his face disapprove. He thought perhaps Polly ought to be adorning the Christmas tree, not walking around the bar. This prompted him to ask the next question.

'How're those two nippers of yours, Henry? Are they coming over later? I expect they'll enjoy seeing that decorated.' He pointed towards the naked tree, again attempting to show disapproval. But he could not prevent himself from smiling. It really was good to be home.

'Yes, they'll be here this afternoon. Rosalie as well. She and I need to discuss some proposed changes to Tidal Reach. Shaun, that's Stan and Vera's son, is taking over the tenancy and I'm keen for him to make a go of things. He wants to start up a septic tank emptying business, but one or two residents are raising objections.'

'And I'm one of them,' Mrs Ervsgreaves stated emphatically, her head alternately nodding and shaking to emphasise her point. The movements made the loose layers of skin under her chin wobble, reminding Quinny of a turkey gobbling to itself as it walked.

'Right,' he said slowly, not wishing to be embroiled in conflict quite so soon after arriving home. He avoided eye contact with both Henry and Mrs Ervsgreaves. Instead, he glanced around the lounge-bar again.

He suddenly realised the cockerel ornaments were no longer displayed – not even Morris and Mortimer, the two bookends that used to sit on the mantelpiece. He knew the majority had been packed away shortly after Henry and Rosalie's wedding, but some had remained. Now even these had disappeared. He wondered if this was permanent, or if they'd just been removed to make way for the Christmas decorations.

Mrs Ervsgreaves interrupted his thoughts. 'Imagine the smell that comes from disposing of such effluent.'

'Yes, but everyone in the two villages has septic tanks, Mrs E. The mains sewer doesn't come out this far,' Henry said as Polly stepped around him. She picked up a glass and drew a pint for the rector. 'And everyone needs to …'

'Yes, thank you, young Henry. I know that we all … er …' One or two of the people listening sniggered as they wondered how the stout and imposing Mrs Ervsgreaves would continue. 'Make waste, shall we say. But there are ways and means of disposing of it.'

'Yes, but at the moment we have to ring Cliffend council and, if they feel like it, they'll eventually send a tanker out. And it costs a fortune, especially for me because I'm *commercial waste*, according to them. If we had someone local, it would all be much quicker – and I dare say, cheaper,' Henry explained.

'Well, you would say that, wouldn't you? You'll probably get yours emptied free, if they're allowed to start it up!' Mrs Ervsgreaves snapped and turned her head away, immediately regretting voicing her unfortunate opinion.

'Good to have you back, Quinny,' Polly said in the

ensuing silence as she placed his beer on the bar in front of him. 'This one's on Henry.'

'They're all on me, I think,' Henry added with a grin, glad of the distraction. He knew there would be opposition to the proposal but he hoped the majority of residents in both hamlets would see the sense of the idea.

'Cheers,' Quinny said as he took a sip. 'Anyone would think I've been away for years, the way you're all carrying on, instead of – what was it – a couple of months.'

'It's felt like years,' Max said as he approached from behind; he had managed to slip in without anyone noticing. He extended his hand to his old adversary, a smile creasing his brown and weather-worn face. 'And I'll have a pint as well,' he directed at Polly.

'And you can get this lady a drink for ferrying me back from the station.' Quinny nodded towards Mrs Ervsgreaves, conscious that she was still suffering indignity from her earlier observation.

She now simpered shyly and asked for an orange juice.

'I still have to take the rector home,' she explained when pressed to have something stronger. 'And then I want to start collecting signatures for a petition against this – this cesspit-emptying business opening up.' She indicated towards the door beyond which, across the car park, stood Tidal Reach.

'Well at least the place will be being used,' Max stated. 'Not just left to rot.'

'The cottage *has* been lived in,' Henry said defensively. 'It's just that no one has had any ideas of what to do with the buildings or land.'

'Well, they still won't be making use of the barns and sheds and things, will they?' Mrs Ervsgreaves interjected, her previous indiscretion forgotten. 'They'll just empty the contents of the tankers into holes in the ground.'

Polly raised her eyes to the ceiling and shrugged her shoulders, making her jewellery glisten. This matter had been the subject of debate for a few weeks now and she, personally, was bored with it. But Henry was determined to expound the benefits of the scheme, without drawing too much attention to the fact that it would be of detriment to him if the council refused the application.

'There's a natural soak-away feature in the soil between there and the marshes and then down to the river,' he explained for what felt like the hundredth time. 'By the time the water reaches the Potch, all the sediments and bacteria will have been filtered out and neutralised in the ground. Besides which, the buildings will be needed to house the tractors and tankers when they aren't being used.'

The door opened and a voice from the other side of the lounge-bar bellowed across the room.

'Just look who's turned up again! Quinny, how the devil are you?' Stan asked as he came in, followed by Vera.

'Well, come and join us,' Max said mischievously. 'We were just discussing your son's new enterprise.'

'Yeah, you lot aren't going to put up any objections, are you? Especially after someone's already been belly-aching to the council that they don't want a sludge wagon-emptying service there.' Stan glared at those gathered around the bar.

Quinny supped. Max stared at the brown polished top; he thought of Alice on board the cruise liner and wondered how they disposed of their waste at sea, beyond the obvious, that is. Henry straightened his shoulders ready to defend any challenges. Polly decided that maybe they really ought not to squabble amongst themselves. Delilah Ervsgreaves wanted to usher Quinny out of the pub and deliver him to the rectory as soon as possible because she needed to go home to start cooking dinner. Then she could rethink her strategy for fighting this planning application.

'Well, it's going to be discussed at the council meeting in Cliffend next week,' Stan said defiantly. 'Then, if we get the go-ahead, Shaun'll start up as soon as he can.'

Chapter 16

On New Year's Day 1999, there was a tangible excitement; it was the first day of the last year of the old millennium. There were now only twelve months, three hundred and sixty-five days, before, to quote the popular phrase, *the zeros lined up*, beyond which it was felt all would change.

Rosalie Stickleback, however, did not share the anticipation of a new and electrifying world to come. She could not foresee her circumstances improving. She was still living separately from her husband, and neither she nor Henry dared broach the subject that divided them.

The large brown teddy bear was still hidden at the back of the wardrobe in Annie and Derek's bedroom at the Old Police House in Pepper Hill. It wore the locket proudly, defiantly around its neck; the diamond inside the heart stored its brilliance until such time as it was revealed again.

Saturday, the second of January, was a dismal, grey day in Cliffend. A cold wind blew straight off the North Sea into the main street. Rosalie had left Sarah and Duncan with Henry at The Fighting Cock public house in Ashfield while she came into town to look through the January sales.

She entered the brisk and bustling Moorland's department store and immediately felt the energy of the hot, white lights overhead, the noise of customers searching for bargains and the urgency of the untidy atmosphere. Staff, not quite refreshed or recuperated from their festivities, struggled to keep order. Herds of shoppers, bored from enforced time with families, appeared to have been unleashed on the stock and were scrabbling through clothes, shoes, household linen, electrical goods and luxury items as if today was the last opportunity they would ever have to buy them.

Rosalie walked towards a group of ladies jostling around racks of coats and jackets that had just been wheeled into a central area. She took a deep breath as she too lunged forward and fought to inspect the goods.

It was the same every year; items she hoped would be reduced were still full price, whilst others she had never seen before were marked half price or less. And the garments that were supposedly reduced were not the ones she wanted anyway.

She sighed as she discarded a thick winter coat. It was more the style her late mother, Annie, would have worn than anything suitable for anyone under thirty. She looked around at the ill-mannered snatching taking place, and then watched as two ladies set off in an undignified race towards the queue for the changing rooms, both carrying a large assortment of clothes to try on.

Rosalie suddenly felt very foolish as she admitted to herself that she had been caught up in the sales frenzy. Within reason, she could afford to pay the original prices if she really needed anything new.

She turned away from the central racks and walked slowly across to the children's section, telling herself harshly that she was supposed to be shopping for the twins, not for herself.

Sarah and Duncan were now seven years old - seven and three-quarters; they would be eight in March. Duncan, born three minutes before his sister, was very similar to Henry in colouring with his dark hair, fair skin and blue eyes. She guessed that when he was old enough to shave, his beard would have his father's reddish tinge.

Sarah, on the other hand, was almost a clone of Rosalie, with her straw-blonde hair. She was not thin, but not fat either; her cheeks blushed pink easily and, also like her mother, she had blue eyes that were a slightly different shade to Duncan's. Rosalie could see traces of her own father, Derek, in Sarah's face, especially along her jawline and chin: these were absent from her son.

Sarah needed a new coat for the start of the new term in a few days. By the time school had finished before Christmas, the buttons were straining across her front. And she had complained that the sleeves - which even Rosalie could see were suddenly not long enough -cut in under her arms. Sarah had started to cry when she told Rosalie that the coat was too small: the little girl seemed to think it was her fault, and that she had done something to make it shrink.

'You ate too many mince pies at Christmas,' Henry unhelpfully joked when he had been told earlier that day. In truth Sarah was in the phase of growing outward before her height caught up and brought her back into proportion. Duncan was taller and thinner, wiry and adventurous. He seemed content when spending time with either parent, whereas Sarah sometimes clung to her father and wanted to stay with him at the pub when Rosalie arrived to take them home.

And this added fuel to the unending feud between Henry and Rosalie, both of whom were struggling themselves, especially with no parents of their own to seek advice from: three of the four grandparents died on the same day, and the fourth, Henry's mother, Nora, was still on her never-ending holiday on board Alice's infernal cruise ship. Nora had not even returned for the twins' christening.

The month of May this year would mark eleven years

since Annie and Derek Tillinger, and Woody Stickleback died; the end of July should have been her and Henry's ninth wedding anniversary.

Huh! Rosalie thought to herself, we didn't even make it through the first twenty-four hours of marriage, never mind nine years.

Rosalie was unaware of Nora's hurt that she obviously wanted to remain on her own and not try to repair her marriage to Henry. Nora felt she did not wish to return home and be embroiled in their warfare. So much so that she and Alice took jobs they were offered on board the RMS Vaguaries cruise ship. She still played the bountiful grandmother when she briefly appeared back at The Fighting Cock between cruises, then - without real explanation - she soon became absent again.

Rosalie and Nora corresponded regularly. Nora had telephoned on Christmas Eve to wish everyone season's greetings. She told them how alien it still felt to eat roast turkey in gloriously hot sunshine. Rosalie couldn't remember exactly where Nora said she was, but concluded somewhat churlishly that no doubt a brightly coloured postcard would soon arrive describing the wonderful time the widow and spinster were having.

On her way to the shops this morning, Rosalie dropped George off at the railway station; he was returning to Aberdeen. He still worked for the engineering company MaCold and seemed to move location with each new assignment. Although he no longer lived permanently at the Old Police House, he still used it as a base - some of his mail was sent there which Rosalie dutifully posted on as and when necessary.

George had given his sister money to buy her and the

twins' Christmas presents. Rosalie saved hers and, thinking that the children already had more toys than they appreciated, decided to buy something more practical for them.

Two weeks before Christmas, Henry had asked her to purchase something for the children from him.

'That's rather a lot of money, Henry,' Rosalie said when she accepted the cash.

'Well, if you see anything you would like for yourself, please feel free to …' The image of a gold locket with the shining diamond sparkling inside hung invisibly between them.

'That won't be necessary,' she almost snapped. Then, regretting being the cause of the hurt expression on Henry's face, she added, 'I think I have everything I need, thank you. I'll half whatever is left and deposit it in Sarah and Duncan's savings accounts.'

Henry also insisted that he would buy *a little treat* for the twins - a token present for them to open from under the tree on Christmas morning - or, as it transpired, the afternoon when Rosalie took them over to Ashfield and joined them for their tea.

Rosalie suspected that Polly had actually purchased the gifts - a kit for making jewellery, complete with nylon thread and plastic beads of every colour imaginable for Sarah, and a building set for Duncan. But, after all, Polly was their godmother, and she'd also bought a gift for them each from herself.

Rosalie watched the pleasure on the children's faces as they unwrapped and played with their toys. Suddenly she didn't mind whose choice it was - a secret part of her even wondered if her husband and his barmaid were romantically involved. But she soon shook herself back to sensibility and reminded her imagination that Polly was gay, and that she had a partner, Susan.

Now browsing through the girls' section of the children's wear in Moorland's department store, Rosalie picked out a coat. It was purple with a matching satin-finish lining. She imagined it would be warm, and the buttons were big enough for Sarah's little fingers to manoeuvre them through the buttonholes. She checked it was for a seven-year-old, then replaced it on the rack and chose the next size up, thinking it would possibly be of some use next autumn and the beginning of winter if she bought the bigger one.

Rosalie collected a few more mundane items on her way to the cash till - warm tights for Sarah, a new pair of gym shoes for each of them and T-shirts for Duncan. When she had paid, the items filled three carrier bags.

Chapter 17

It was almost dark as Rosalie left the shop at four o'clock to drive back to Ashfield. Although still closed to customers, the lights were on in the pub when she arrived. The curtains were open and she could see the twins running around inside the lounge-bar, seemingly happy and carefree. She wondered if this would change when she walked in. However hard she tried, she didn't think she would ever stop being angry with Henry and she knew her animosity was having a negative effect on the children, especially Sarah.

As Rosalie pulled the key out of the ignition, she saw another vehicle's headlights approaching. It turned into the car park and, as it passed under the light over the entrance, she recognised the post van. The driver did not switch off the engine, but the passenger's door opened.

Quinny hailed a cheery 'Thanks' to the postman, whom everyone called Postman Jim the Second because his predecessor was Jim and his own name was Paul James. On seeing Rosalie about to leave her car, Quinny altered direction and walked across towards her, his footsteps scrunching in the gravel.

Rosalie thought Quinny seemed a lot happier since his holiday and subsequent return to his newly refurbished rectory. He had been missed, and many of his ladies now fussed around him so much that anyone would have thought he was an exemplary man of the cloth instead of the moody and often grumpy old so-and-so who never, as Henry regularly complained, paid for his drinks.

'Is everything all right, Rosalie?' Quinny asked as she

stood up out of her car. Even in the relative gloom on this side of the car park, she could see he was tugging at the rubber band on his wrist.

'Yes, fine, thank you. I've just done a bit of shopping in town. New stuff for the kids, had a look around the sales, you know.'

'Oh. Twins not with you, then?' Quinny stooped down and looked into the back.

'No. Henry's had them today. I need a break sometimes, you know!' Rosalie snapped.

'I wasn't saying you didn't,' he retorted before feeling one of her *well don't ask stupid questions then* glares.

Quinny hummed to himself as he turned from Rosalie and glanced over towards the smallholding on the other side of the road.

Although there was an occasional residual smell from the waste disposal business, if the wind was from the west, it had caused little impact on the residents, other than lowering the cost of emptying their septic tanks. The number of tractors towing tankers entering and leaving the premises each day was barely noticeable and, so far, there hadn't been any problems.

'Right, if you don't need a hand, I'll leave you to it,' Quinny stated, the scorn in his tone sounding out of character.

Rosalie swallowed then spoke in a quieter voice.

'Sorry, Quinny. I'm just a bit tired after the last week or so. Come on in and have a pint.'

'Bit early, isn't it? Pub isn't open for another couple of hours or so.'

'Don't worry, Reverend,' Rosalie responded with a smile. 'No one's going to ask you to pay for your drink!'

'Oh, so Henry hasn't made a New Year's resolution to try and get money out of me then?' He laughed as he held out his elbow for the lady to take.

'No, he isn't that brave,' she replied as they walked towards the door. The handle groaned as Quinny twisted it.

'I haven't come for a drink anyway,' he advised her as the warm fug of stale smoke, beer, and something sweet that neither of them could recognise, met their nostrils.

'Oh? Well, may I enquire as to the nature of your visit?' Rosalie asked ostentatiously, unable to disguise her suspicion.

Quinny did not have a chance to reply before two very excited children tumbled out from behind the Christmas tree screaming in genuine delight.

'MUM! Mum, look what we've got!' Their outstretched hands held slabs of home-made toffee and their lips were sticky. Sarah smiled, revealing the gap where she had recently lost one of her front teeth.

'Well, I hope you don't make yourselves sick!' Rosalie exclaimed in an irritated tone. The smiles instantly fell from both Sarah and Duncan's faces. But Rosalie didn't notice, instead she sighed heavily. 'And don't think you're getting into the car in that mess. Go and wash your hands and faces.'

Instead of relishing the wonderfully interesting time the twins must have had making the toffee, she immediately thought of the problems she would now be facing, and wanted to berate Henry for causing these.

Henry stood in the doorway between the lounge-bar and the kitchen, holding his cockerel mug which was now only half-full of his tea/coffee mix. He felt extremely dismayed at Rosalie's outburst; he thought she would be pleased that

Sarah and Duncan were enjoying themselves so much.

'Come on, kids,' he said kindly. 'Let's get you cleaned up.'

He glared at Rosalie. She scowled back, widening her eyes as if to challenge him to defy her.

'Then you can give her *her* present, can't you?' he added.

The twins did not reply, they just looked bewildered. Their excitement was visibly deflated as they filed past their father and almost crept into the kitchen. Their faces were drawn in disappointment and confusion.

Quinny, who had walked across to the bar and heaved himself up onto a stool, slowly shook his head.

'They wanted to make something for you, Rosalie,' Henry stated with controlled anger. 'And Polly remembered her Mum's toffee recipe. So that's what we've been doing all afternoon. There's a plate of toffee for you on the kitchen table. I hope you enjoy it!' he informed her before turning away and joining the children.

'Huh!' Quinny said from behind her as if to confound Rosalie's rejection and loss of dignity. 'How to graciously accept gifts - now there's a topic for tomorrow's sermon. And while you're waiting for them to get cleaned up, Rosalie, you might as well make yourself useful and pull us a pint.'

Chapter 18

Rosalie's outburst towards the twins at the pub haunted her for the journey home. She hadn't meant to sound so harsh, but she was tired after shopping and the sight of Duncan and Sarah in such a sticky state filled her with dread. Their fingers were still tacky despite having washed their hands, and their clothes were covered in dollops of brown sugar, butter and syrup. Sarah's hair, which always seemed to attract her food, was matted together in several places with hardening, glutinous globs.

Rosalie admitted to herself that she could not remember her own Mum ever being so angry towards her and George, and she felt deeply ashamed. But then, Annie had Derek's help in bringing up her and her brother, whilst Rosalie felt she had no one to share the burden. Everything Henry did for the twins seemed to make more work for her to deal with.

She sometimes dreamt of a holiday – just her. She would leave the children with Henry as he was *so good* at parenting. Maybe she could join Nora and Alice on the cruise ship. But then she remembered her parents and their trip away, which turned so quickly into the nightmare she was still living.

As soon as they arrived home, Rosalie forced herself out of her bad mood. After a few minutes, she was immersed in their story of toffee-making. She listened intently as she marshalled Duncan and Sarah, still wearing their coats, into the bathroom. She removed every item of clothing with toffee stuck to it and placed them all in a heap ready for the washing machine. She then showered them both thoroughly.

Throughout this, though, Rosalie realised how selfish she was being. She would never want to discourage the twins' creativity, and she was pleased they had been thinking of her when she was not actually with them. She gently soaked as much of the toffee out of Sarah's hair as she could manage; she responded with kindness to the little girl's writhing when she pulled with the hairbrush.

'I'll have to cut the rest out - perhaps we can hide the shorter bits by brushing the longer ones over them.'

Sarah did not seem convinced that this would work. She fingered her scalp then worried the gap where her front tooth had recently fallen out. She began to test all the others to see if any more were loose.

'Right, I'll take you to the hairdressers as soon as I can,' Rosalie stated quietly.

'Will it be before we go back to school?' Sarah asked hopefully.

'Yes, I expect so.'

'Good,' Sarah replied.

'Why d'you say that?' Rosalie questioned.

''Cause there's some girls who say my hair's like a straw stack,' Sarah confessed. She then slapped her hand over her lips as if she had said something she shouldn't have.

Rosalie was shocked. Her own hair was the same texture and approximate colour. It too was a little unruly at times; perhaps that was why she did not always notice that Sarah's was untidy.

'Well, don't worry about what some silly girls say, Sarah. You have beautiful hair. I expect they're just jealous because theirs isn't as nice as yours,' she said as she stroked back a lock that had fallen onto Sarah's face and was heading straight for the jam in the cake she was devouring.

'And they said I can't eat properly because I always end up with half my dinner stuck in it,' Sarah whispered.

'But, you do, don't you?' Duncan added. 'Look, you've just got jam in that bit!' He jabbed at her head with a straightened index finger.

Rosalie could see a smidge of red near one of the shortened tresses; Sarah had obviously been prodding the area to feel the spiky ends.

'You must've touched it when you had jam on your fingers. Here …' She moistened a sheet of kitchen tissue then gently rubbed away the jam. 'There, all gone. Now, finish your cake and we can all have a piece of the toffee you made me. Would you like that?' she asked.

Both Duncan and Sarah smiled, all miseries apparently forgotten.

But the revelation did not slip Rosalie's mind. She dutifully chewed the over-sweet toffee and made a mental note to speak to the twins' teacher to see if Sarah was being bullied.

Later, after she supervised the children cleaning their teeth before going to bed, she returned to the bathroom to brush her own. As she looked at herself in the mirror, she could see a frown line deepening between her brows. She vowed to try not being so bad-tempered in future.

Chapter 19

Mothering Sunday in 1999 fell on 14th March, the day before the twins' eighth birthday. The children had made Rosalie a Mother's Day card each, and she couldn't help noticing that Duncan's handwriting was neater than Sarah's, although overall Sarah's artwork and presentation was better and more colourful. Henry had arranged for them to present her with a bunch of flowers and a box of chocolates. He had also invited them all to The Fighting Cock for Sunday lunch.

The following morning, Rosalie was still thinking about the meal when she heard Sarah creeping out of her bedroom, which was next to her brother's and opposite Rosalie's. Sarah was still fresh from sleep, with tousled hair and pink cheeks. She stood quietly in her bare feet wondering who to go to first, Mummy or Duncan.

Even at her young age, Sarah realised Rosalie tended to favour Duncan over her. His toys always seemed better, it was noticeable at meal times that he was given his plate first and his portions were slightly bigger. Their Daddy, on the other hand, put Sarah first. He would listen as she chattered, whereas Rosalie always seemed too busy, or too tired, or just too irritable to bother. But Sarah still loved her brother just as much as she ever had.

Sarah shivered. Although she did not realise, the back of her nightdress was tucked up into her knickers, exposing her legs to the chill of the morning. The house was silent, except for the gurgles and knocks from the pipes and radiators where the central heating had clicked on.

Then suddenly the alarm on Rosalie's bedside clock sounded. It made Sarah jump and she felt like crying. But she didn't want to be unhappy, not on her birthday.

'Sarah!' she heard her brother shout. 'Sarah, come on, wake up.' Duncan's feet sounded on the floor and he burst through his bedroom door. 'Wow, you're up!' he exclaimed. 'It's our birthday! We're eight today. Come on, let's go see Mum and get our presents.'

Rosalie realised that Duncan had stopped calling her Mummy some time ago. Although she could not pinpoint exactly when it happened, it pulled at her heart to hear her son becoming more formal. Sarah, on the other hand, still said Mummy - and of course Daddy for Henry. She wasn't sure how Duncan referred to his father.

It had been a tradition for a couple of generations in the Tillinger family for the children to receive a watch on their eighth birthdays; Rosalie thought this neatly solved the problem of the twins' presents this year. For Duncan she bought a boy's digital watch with a ridged plastic wristband. It was thick and black, and had many functions - alarms and a calculator, amongst other things - that Rosalie neither understood nor thought Duncan would need.

Sarah's watch, on the other hand, was petite with a pink faux-leather strap. The black numbers were sharp against the pearlescent face around which whirred a second hand with a heart shape at the tip. The hour and minute hands were thicker and terminated in arrowhead points, which Sarah found a little unsettling, as if they were reprimanding her for being late.

'Cor, thanks Mum,' Duncan enthused as he discarded the wrapping paper and box before struggling to fasten the watch around his wrist.

'You can both learn to tell the time on each other's watches as well as on your own,' Rosalie said softly as she helped Sarah disentangle hers from its presentation packaging. She also surreptitiously untucked her daughter's nightdress. 'Look, Sarah, yours has got a round face with hands that point to numbers.' She held the watch for her to study. 'And Duncan, yours tells the time with just figures, so you'll have to learn the twenty-four hour clock too.'

'What's the *twenty-four hour clock*?' he responded, feeling proud of his new acquisition at the same time as being a little wary of something new. When he looked at it, however, he handed it back to his mother and stepped away.

'It hasn't got a face. And there's no hands. Why doesn't it point like the clock?' His voice had risen above the normal, comfortable level to a near whine. Rosalie could clearly hear his distress.

She felt despair, as if all her efforts were inadequate. She wanted the twins to have a special, traditional present but again felt as if she'd failed.

Henry had bought a separate gift for each of them. Rosalie told him her intentions and warned him not to be too extravagant. They had agreed not long after Duncan and Sarah's births that they would not compete for their children's affection with money.

'Daddy knows the twenty-four hour clock, I think,' Sarah informed her brother without removing her eyes from her watch.

'Does he?' Rosalie asked. 'How does he know that?'

'Because Granny Nora writes it on her postcards when she's telling him about places she's visited and times they have to be back to the boat and things … like when they sail away and arrive,' Sarah replied disjointedly. Rosalie smoothed her daughter's straw-like hair and Sarah automatically moved closer for a cuddle. 'D'you know the twenty-four hour clock, Mummy?' she asked, directing piercing blue eyes at her.

'Yes, I do. And if you like, I'll teach it to you both - after breakfast.'

'But what about my watch? Will you teach me to tell the time on mine as well?' Sarah suddenly seemed agitated.

'Yes, of course I will, sweetheart.'

'Will you do it first, Mummy? Before you teach us Duncan's watch?'

Chapter 20

At the end of February in the millennium year, George was travelling home to Pepper Hill. In three days' time, he would be twenty-six years old.

George was not prone to dwelling on the past but, as the journey trailed from Scotland, with a vicious wind hammering rain onto the side of the carriage, he felt a little nostalgic. He had changed trains at Mattingburgh and this last twenty-five miles was the most uncomfortable part of the entire five hundred and fifty-mile journey.

The carriage was dimly lit and overcrowded; he had to look past the smeared and smudged marks on the windowpane to see the outside world. The ledge where he wanted to rest his elbow was covered with a semi-dried sticky brown liquid mark, which he assumed was spilt coffee. Despite this being a non-smoking coach, somebody had lit up a cigarette three seats in front and was ignoring the very loud coughing and tutting around him.

As George tried to relax, thoughts of PepperAsh - good and bad - gently flowed into his mind. He closed his eyes and a slight smile came to his lips.

He missed Rosie and Duncan and Sarah. His sister had sounded excited when he telephoned yesterday to confirm that he really was now on leave.

The twins, apparently standing on the other side of the room, shouted across 'Hello, Uncle George. See you tomorrow.' Sarah added, 'Happy Birthday,' as an afterthought. Sunday 27th February was George's birthday; he was looking forward to being with his sister and the twins.

As children, Rosalie used to tease George that he was actually born on 29th February and could only commemorate his birthday every fourth year. George did not worry too much about this, especially when he was old enough to realise that 1974 was not a leap year. He didn't tell Rosalie that he knew this, however, and turned the teasing back on her when she'd tried to give him a gift on his seventh birthday.

'But, it isn't my birthday,' he told her with a stern expression and a shake of his head. 'I don't have a birthday this year, do I?'

Rosalie had been surprised. At almost nine, but in reality still eight until April, she thought she could outwit him. In the excitement of present-giving, she momentarily forgot her previous joke.

'What d'you mean?' she asked.

'Well, you said I was born on the twenty-ninth of February, not the twenty-seventh, and that I only got a real birthday every four years. I had one last year so the next one isn't for another three years, is it?' he explained patiently with a shrug.

At that moment Annie, their mother, had entered the room. Rosalie was still holding the present she had so carefully selected, saved for, bought and wrapped for him – a square box that contained a toy crane painted green and black. It had string wires that carried a hook at the end of the boom and wheel-winding mechanisms that could lift up a load.

When Annie saw George's serious face and Rosalie's bewildered expression, she knew one was tormenting the other.

'What's going on here?' she asked.

George took a deep breath and spoke very quickly.

'Well, Rosie is trying to give me a birthday present ...'

'My name isn't Rosie, it's *Rosalie*!' she had exclaimed indignantly. And from that moment onwards he would use this shortened version to irritate her. Sometimes she would ignore him, sometimes she would pretend to object and other times she would be very angry. But the more furious she became, the more he taunted her with it. He was the only person who dared to use the name *Rosie*; he saw it as a sibling endearment.

George often wondered if his fascination with finding out how things worked, the first steps towards becoming an engineer, started with that toy crane. The open mechanisms were so inviting that, when he started to play, he realised he wanted to dismantle then re-assemble it. Of course, when he did take it apart, it never quite went back together properly again. Perhaps that should have been a warning for him to choose a different career. But following his late father's footsteps into Tasker's had seemed an easy escape from his bereavement. He smiled again to himself now as he remembered the crane.

Memories of that gift reminded him of the presents he'd brought home for them. Although he was looking forward to seeing them, he did not want to become embroiled in the constant fighting between Henry and his sister.

He shivered and tried to tell himself that the chill was caused by the draught from the perished fitting around the train's window, not by his own apprehension. George tried to shake off thoughts of family antagonism and his non-birthdays. He stared at his own reflection in the glass as the scenery dashed past outside, but even in this distorted reflection he looked tired.

It was now seven weeks into the new millennium; the preparation work leading up to the event had been relentless. A rumour circulated within his company that a bug had been programmed into certain computers which would bring all MaCold's operations to a standstill on the stroke of midnight.

George had thought it was nonsense, but the chief executive of MaCold grew more and more paranoid with each news report. Then, after a rival firm made a bid to buy MaCold's, the CE was embroiled in a bitter battle to prevent a hostile takeover.

Although not management, George was caught up in the frenzy to fight this off. He felt as though he hadn't slept properly for many weeks and was now totally exhausted. He also felt foolish because he prided himself on not becoming involved in ridiculous fights and arguments at work. But this matter was too serious to ignore. Everyone within the organisation had been drawn in, however aloof they wished to remain. In fact, the less concerned an employee appeared, the more suspicion fell on them that they were spying for the opposition.

Over the years, and as part of his ongoing training, George made sure he was keeping up with all the evolving information technology. He could not understand how this glitch was supposed to switch all their computer programmes into a parallel system and alter stock ordering, organising the work shifts, payroll, equipment use and billing, and take away all operational control.

In reality, nothing untoward happened as the clocks boomed midnight and fireworks erupted across the country. The initial seconds of the year 2000 ticked by and moved inexorably into the first minute. Drinks were raised, toasts proclaimed, people hugged and kissed, and new resolutions were made. The first hour past and revellers treated the initial signs of sobriety with more alcohol then continued their parties on the streets. Outside MaCold's main offices, voices could be heard singing *Auld Lang Syne* in multi-coloured harmonies.

At nine o'clock George finally left the boardroom, returned to his office and sat down at his desk. He laid his head on his arms and started to doze. He was rudely awoken precisely seven minutes later by the sound of the fire alarm. For a moment, he thought the nightmare of a millennium bug had actually come true, but it was only someone having a quick cigarette beneath a smoke detector which had accidentally triggered it.

It had been lunchtime when George eventually arrived home to his flat. He climbed straight onto his bed and fell into a deep sleep. During the early evening, he woke feeling confused and grimy; he was fully clothed and still wore his shoes.

For a few moments George listened to the silence inside his flat. He felt bewildered and thought he ought to get up and find something to eat. But he decided he would do that later. He then rolled over and slept solidly for another twelve hours before finally rousing himself.

Today, the rocking motion of the train was lulling him back into slumber. He was glad he'd decided not to drive home; he wasn't sure how safe he would have been for such a long journey, and he could always borrow Rosie's car if he needed transport whilst in Pepper Hill.

He felt the train slow down; the gravitational pull dragged his body forward as the brakes screeched the vehicle to a halt. George opened his eyes. Darkness had fallen and the lighting inside the carriage was dim and dirty. The passenger in the seat beside him stood up and stepped out into the aisle without a word of farewell.

George ached and wanted to stretch his limbs, but there wasn't enough room between his and the seat in front. He settled back into his former position and ignored the sound of other passengers alighting and disembarking.

'Excuse me, is this seat taken?' a voice asked.

George opened his eyes again. A young woman with long dark hair and an enormous rucksack was standing in the aisle obstructing other people's passage to the vacant seats beyond. Although he smiled, he really did not wish anyone to sit next to him. But she looked as tired as he felt.

'Yes, it's free,' he said. 'Let me help you.' Despite his heavy and aching limbs, he stood up, took her rucksack and stowed it in the luggage rack above their heads.

'Thank you,' she replied as she slid in beside him and sat down. 'My name's Tina.'

'I'm George. How d'you do.' And in a very formal gesture they shook hands.

Chapter 21

Poor old St Jude was, as his advocacy indicated, a complete lost cause. Despite there being two opportunities every year to celebrate his saint's day, each was overshadowed by a more popular and, one could say, secular event. Even so, Quinny usually dedicated an entire sermon to St Jude on the closest Sunday to each.

The first of Jude's days, 17th June, often coincided with Father's Day which had grown in favour during the last decade or so.

The second, 28th October, came a poor second to any forthcoming Hallowe'en festivities.

Throughout October of the millennium year, Cliffend shops were stocked with fancy dress outfits, including ghostly sheets with hidden fluorescent patterns, vampire headdresses and capes for the boys; witches gowns for the girls; and devil, skeleton or spider costumes suitable for either. And to complete the horror, there were also available pink plastic masks with hooked noses, protruding eyebrows and hairy warts, or tusked false teeth and dripping blood.

Cliffend's Junior School, which Sarah and Duncan attended, as had Rosalie, George and Henry before them, was a Church of England school. None of the team of rectors in the various Cliffend parish churches was free this year to give a talk to the children on the true meaning of Hallowe'en, so Bishop Clement volunteered Quinny. This was scheduled to take place on the Friday afternoon before the half-term holiday began.

The head teacher was, in Quinny's opinion, an extremely

young man. He introduced himself as Dick Vincent.

'Yes, my name *is* Dick, not Richard,' he expanded as they shook hands. Quinny nodded his head in response.

At the appointed time, Quinny found himself in the school hall, which doubled as the gymnasium. As he stood in front of the stage, the unmistakable smell of bulk-cooked meals and floor polish reached his nostrils.

These instantly returned him to his own school days, with all their distant horror and glory. A sickening loathing from PE lessons filled him. He recalled the ill-fitting singlets and shorts that began too big then seemed to shrink as he grew. The memories of clambering over climbing frames and shimmying up ropes brought a second wave of nausea. He swallowed hard against this as he relentlessly pinged the rubber band on his wrist.

The panic passed and he planted a serene smile on his face. He nodded, hoping he was exhibiting encouragement. Some of the young faces in front of him were adorned with the remnants of chocolate pudding from their lunch.

He recognised only two of the multitude - the little Stickleback twins being in the Year Five group. He could see shadows of both parents in their inquisitive expressions.

Quinny's stomach rumbled; he'd only had time for a sandwich and a cup of tea. Being hungry made him extremely grumpy, as his parishioners knew to their cost. Only the promise of a home-cooked Sunday roast kept his Sunday sermons short and to the point. Mrs Ervsgreaves, whose husband was one of his church wardens as well as PCC treasurer, now kindly extended invitations every second week. This left alternative Sundays free for other good people to do likewise.

Chocolate pudding with custard was on the Ervsgreaves'

menu last Sunday, but Quinny hadn't yet received an invitation from anyone for this week. He now felt both hungry and irritable. Although he was salivating, his mouth was dry and the inside of his lips stuck firmly to his teeth.

As his discomfort increased, Quinny clasped one hand over the other wrist behind his back. This hid the fact that he could finger and worry at his elastic bands but still appear serene.

Talking to school children - or people in any great number - was not one of his favourite pastimes, although most seemed to think that, because of his vocation and weekly sermons, it was quite natural for him. But the elastic bands were not working, and he feared he wouldn't be able to speak a single word in his present distress.

Luckily, he remembered the breathing exercises he had learnt during the relaxation sessions on his recent retreat.

He stood up straight and as tall as his height would allow, his hands still behind his back.

He thought about the air, its soothing, life-giving qualities.

He inhaled deeply through his nose, keeping his shoulders level and extending his diaphragm downward by pushing out his belly to expand his lungs to full capacity.

He counted to three, slowly.

He exhaled back out through his mouth, pulling his tummy in to squeeze his lungs entirely empty.

He counted to three.

The noise in the hall was fading and his nerves jangled less.

In … One, two, three. Out ... One, two, three.

In … One, two, three. Out ... One, two, three.

When his breathing was smooth and natural, he felt

calmer and his imagination no longer contained the vicious sharp edges that tore at his mind. His thoughts returned to the hall and he looked straight ahead above the bobbing heads. He was now able to mentally scan through the talk he was about to give. He did not notice that the noise from the chattering children had crescendoed to a deafening level until Mr Vincent quietened them.

The head teacher then introduced Quinny as the Rector, Reverend Boyce from St Jude's at PepperAsh. Quinny was so unused to people addressing him by his proper title and name that he almost looked around to see if another cleric was about to usurp him. He twanged his elastic band again and made himself jump in surprise then took a deep breath in.

'Right, boys and girls, who can tell me what the word "Hallowe'en" means?' Quinny raised his eyebrows as he asked and smiled his most welcoming smile.

Frowns immediately descended upon the young faces in front of him.

Everywhere seemed to stock pumpkins. Until this point in time, Rosalie could only ever remember them being grown for garden shows or displayed at harvest festivals. After fame and adoration, they were invariably made into pumpkin soup. Now it seemed they were widely available as party costume accessories. Their hardened outsides - ridged, plump and orange - seemed to invite people to gouge out the innards, carve the thick rinds into grotesque, stylised faces and place candles inside to make lanterns.

Earlier in the day, Rosalie shuddered as she looked at the display of slightly lewd pumpkins Poskett had procured in bulk from Fergus Goldwin, the local farmer for whom Max

Podgrew worked. Rosalie could not pinpoint why she thought they looked more than a little obscene, unless it was just the way the shopkeeper had stacked them, complete with a carved example of a grinning face on the top. She declined to buy any.

Checking her watch, she realised it was time to collect Duncan and Sarah from school. She thanked Mr Poskett who, with a little rancour at his loss of sale, closed the door behind her. Ignoring his attitude, she walked back past the empty lay-by, along the pavement and across the road to where her car was parked on the driveway of the Old Police House.

Chapter 22

At nine years old, Duncan and Sarah usually travelled to and from school on the bus, but today Rosalie collected them in her car. It was Friday 27th October, the last day of the first half-term.

As she helped the children to secure their safety belts, she noticed Sarah had chocolate in her hair, as if she had dragged the ends across her dessert dish at lunchtime. Sighing to herself, she settled into the driver's seat and glimpsed the clock on the dashboard which showed it was nearly half-past three. She started the engine and, as she set off, used the interior mirror to engage the children's attention whilst asking about their day at school.

'We learned about …'

'Learnt,' Rosalie corrected. The twins ignored her.

'… *Hallowe'en*.' They chorused the word: neither was musical, and the sound distorted and clashed within the confines of the car.

'Can we go Trick or Treating?' they then asked, for the hundredth time. 'Pleeeeassee!'

Duncan took the lead in explaining.

'We can dress up in scary clothes …'

'And where are you going to get those from?' Rosalie asked pointlessly.

'The shops sell them!' Sarah stated, her voice slightly higher than Duncan's, especially when she was excited. 'Daddy'll buy them for us.'

I bet he will, thought Rosalie, but she chose not to say this.

'Or we could just get a white sheet and put it over our heads …'

'What, both of you under one sheet?' Rosalie asked incredulously. 'I can't see that working for long, can you?'

But neither heard her because Duncan was making 'Booooo' noises behind her and Sarah giggled in a helpless, hapless, high-pitched nine-year-old way.

'Please,' Rosalie emphasised the word. 'Can you two just calm down? If you tell me a bit about this Trick or Treating then I can say whether or not you can do it.'

Rosalie was fully aware of the ritual - waiting until after dark, dressing up and wearing ghoulish make-up (even Duncan wanted to paint his face!) then traipsing around the village, banging on doors, ringing bells and asking unfortunate residents the nonsensical question 'Trick or Treat?'

'No,' she stated at the end of the children's explanation. 'I don't think that would be a good idea. Besides which ...'

'Witch,' Sarah shouted, bursting into helpless giggles again. 'You said *witch*, Mummy!'

Rosalie could hear her daughter drumming her heels against the front of the rear seat.

'Yes, besides *which*, what will you give people if they knock on our door?'

'We won't be there, will we? We'll be out knocking on their doors!' Duncan countered smartly.

'Well the answer is still no.'

'Can we go if Daddy says it's okay?' Sarah added quickly.

Rosalie sighed again. This was a constant trick her daughter employed. Luckily, Henry's stock response to any such requests was *'Ask your mother if it's all right first. If she says yes, then it's okay.'* At least in that respect Rosalie knew she could rely on Henry's support.

'The rector came into our assembly this afternoon and told us all about "Hellowe'en",' Sarah stated.

Rosalie smiled when she heard the single nod of satisfaction in her daughter's voice.

'*Hallowe'en!* It's *Hallowe'en,*' Duncan piped. 'Not *Hellowe'en.*'

'So, what did he say?' Rosalie asked.

'He said,' Duncan replied, 'that the *e'en* part of *Hallowe'en* stands for eve or evening – the day before ...'

'Like Christmas Eve is the day before Christmas Day. So why don't we say Christmase'en?' Sarah queried.

'I was going to ask that!' Duncan was furious at being upstaged. He nudged his twin sister in the ribs. This induced a loud and indignant 'Ow!' from her.

'All right, you two, no fighting,' Rosalie said as she noticed an oncoming car with its headlights on. She reluctantly flicked her switch as well. She knew the clocks would have gone back to Greenwich Mean Time and the afternoons would be dark when they finished school after the half-term holiday. Today, however, the sun was shining through the gold and red tree leaves. A moderate autumnal breeze sent some scurrying from the twigs above to roll and tumble along the road ahead.

As they approached Ashfield, Rosalie anticipated a request from Sarah to see her Dad.

'So, what else did the rector say?' she asked as a distraction. 'Or weren't you two listening?'

'I was listening,' Duncan stated indignantly.

'I was listening too,' Sarah added quickly.

'Not all the time,' her brother challenged.

'Yes I was!'

'Not when you were sucking the chocolate out of your

hair, you weren't.'

Rosalie smiled.

'I was still listening!' There was a sulk in Sarah's voice.

'Okay, Sarah. You tell me what he said then. And don't interrupt her, Duncan. You can tell me next time.' Rosalie consciously favoured her daughter on this occasion.

'Well the *hello* part …'

'*Hallow*,' Duncan corrected.

'Mum, you said I could tell you. Tell him not to tell!'

Rosalie groaned audibly. She was driving through Ashfield and could see the lights on at The Fighting Cock ahead. She knew Sarah would also spot them and silently predicted her next question.

'Can we go and see Daddy?' There was a pause before she added, 'Please.'

'Not today, sweetheart.'

This induced a disappointed 'Ahhh!' which sounded as if it would end in a whine if Rosalie didn't quickly cut it off.

'But you'll be spending time with him tomorrow, won't you? I expect he's busy tonight preparing everything for you.'

'Is Daddy taking us Trick or Treating then?' Sarah asked, quickly regaining her composure and aware of every chink in her parents' defences.

'Dad said we had to ask Mum,' Duncan reminded.

'And Mum has already said no!' Rosalie stated.

'Anyway you'll get bats in your hair if you go out after dark on Hallowe'en,' Duncan stated confidently. 'Max said that if little girls go out in the dark on Hallowe'en, bats come flying down and get all tangled in their hair,' he explained for Rosalie's benefit.

'No they don't!' Sarah bellowed. 'And anyway, if they

did, they'd get in your hair too.'

'No they wouldn't. Max said they only go in girls' hair.'

'Why?' Sarah's voice now contained the dangerous cry that usually preceded tears.

''Cos girls' hair's longer.'

'Not all girls!' Sarah retorted.

'Will you two stop arguing!' Rosalie finally yelled into the mirror. As they passed St Jude's, she spoke in a calmer voice. 'You didn't finish telling me what else the rector said about Hallowe'en.'

Sarah was now happy to let Duncan take up the narrative.

'He said that *Hallows*,' he started, enunciating the word his sister mispronounced earlier, 'means, er ...'

'See! You've forgotten, haven't you?' Sarah jibed triumphantly.

'No. I know. It means dead people. People who have gone to heaven. Hallowe'en is the day before all the saints are remembered. Quinny ...'

'Reverend Boyce to you, young man,' Rosalie admonished. 'Or you can call him Reverend Quintin.'

'Everyone else calls him Quinny. Why can't I?' Duncan taunted.

'Because it's disrespectful for children to call adults by a nickname,' Rosalie explained. She decelerated as they entered a length of the road known as The Tunnel. At the lowest point a path led down through the woods, across the marshes and eventually out to Ashfield Staithe. Rosalie shivered as she thought of this. At that moment, a shower of acorns pounded the car roof from the oak trees overhead. The children gasped at the suddenness and violence of the noise.

'That sounded like a bomb!' exclaimed Duncan. He had recently watched a film on television about the Second World War and was now fascinated with guns and explosions.

'It was just a twig or something falling from the trees,' said Rosalie.

'Could've been a gun firing!' Duncan stated excitedly as he imitated a gun with his hand. 'Uh, uh, uh!' he cried as he enacted the part in the film where a lone sniper swept the plains in front of him, peppering all objects, still and moving, without discrimination.

Then he aimed the pretend pistol at his sister. 'Bang! You're dead, Sarah!' Sarah screamed as he blew smoke off the end of his barrel fingers in triumph.

'Stop it, please. I am trying to concentrate on driving!' Rosalie stated firmly as her nearside wheels dropped into a deep pothole. Duncan fell towards Sarah, who screamed again.

'WILL YOU TWO BE QUIET!' Rosalie bawled, trying to regain control of the steering wheel. Setting off again and focusing on her driving, she was unprepared for Duncan's next question.

'Did Granny and Grandad Tilly go to heaven?' The twins had adopted this shortened name for Rosalie and George's parents when they were too young to pronounce 'Tillinger' properly.

Rosalie was momentarily stunned. She hadn't thought about where her parents actually *were,* other than inside her own memory and, more importantly, not physically with her anymore.

She had held their images on the tiny, heart-shaped photographs fitted inside a golden locket that she buried at

Ashfield Staithe on the first anniversary of their deaths. After that, she had visited there in order to talk to them, drawing comfort from the last vestige of their beings. But that was before she realised Henry had removed the locket containing the pictures. Her Aunty Shirley had insisted her parents were cremated not buried; Rosalie and George, both being underage at the time, were not asked their opinions. Even so, she still envisaged her parents near the place where their souls left their bodies.

'And what about Grandad Woody? Did he go to heaven too?' Sarah asked, sensing this question would lead to trouble. Then to ensure her Mum did not ignore her, she added, 'Max said he was an old devil, and devils don't go to heaven, do they, Mummy?'

Duncan took a deep breath in and intoned, 'Uuuuuummmmm!' Feeling the tremolando on his closed lips, his voice started relatively low, but rose in pitch and then fell again. He added, 'Sarah called Max *Max*, not Mr Podgrew, and you said we shouldn't call grown-ups by their nicknames.'

Rosalie silently screamed to herself before vowing to agree to Henry's suggestion that the twins spend the whole of their half-term holiday with him at The Fighting Cock.

Chapter 23

The following day, Saturday, Rosalie dropped Duncan and Sarah off at the pub. Henry was working behind the bar, wiping a batch of wine glasses that had just been washed. The washer had been set up on its next cycle and hummed quietly in the background.

'They're very excited,' Rosalie told Henry. Although she was looking forward to a few days' peace on her own, she now didn't want to leave the twins here. 'Hello,' she said pleasantly to Polly who, dressed in a black skirt, sparkling gold top and very tall heels, was holding a box containing packets of Hallowe'en decorations.

'Hello, Rosalie,' she replied and then called out to the twins. Duncan and Sarah rushed towards her, shouting her name in return and scrambling for whatever she was carrying.

'Come help me put these up,' she said, leading them to the table nearest the corner fireplace and entering whole heartedly into their entertainment as usual.

Although Hallowe'en was on Tuesday, Henry decided to hold a themed party that evening and had bought an assortment of decorations from the wholesalers several weeks ago.

Together Polly, Duncan and Sarah threaded cotton-wool cobwebs around the corner nooks and hung black plastic spiders in the middle of the lounge-bar. They placed small, plastic but vividly orange pumpkin-shaped lanterns on various shelves - empty now because Henry no longer displayed any of his cockerel ornaments. Vampire and ghost posters hung drunkenly from hooks where pictures or plates previously hung.

When evening arrived the lights were dimmed to allow customers to enjoy the anonymous atmosphere. Max and Quinny sat at their usual seats at the end of the bar by the door leading through to the kitchen.

'So, what d'you think of all this palaver?' Max asked Quinny as he waved to indicate the room. 'You being a vicar …'

'… Rector,' Quinny corrected.

'Whatever. Isn't Hallowe'en supposed to be a religious festival?'

'Yeah well, if you want to see what people make of a *religious festival,* just look at Christmas,' Quinny stated as he finished his beer. 'Or Easter, coming to that matter.' He nodded towards Henry. 'Another, when you're ready, lad. And I'll raise my glass to old St Jude, seeing's as everyone else seems to have forgotten him!'

Reluctantly, Henry pulled a pint for the rector.

'Me too,' Max agreed as he followed Quinny's example and pushed his glass towards Henry. 'Don't the clocks go back tonight?' he asked, completely forgetting about the saint. 'Or is it forward?'

'Back,' Henry advised. '*Spring forward and fall back,* as the saying goes.'

'Fall?' Max queried, wrinkling his face with distaste.

'Yeah, you know, as the Americans say, "fall", meaning autumn, when the leaves fall from the trees. Fall back - when it's one o'clock we turn the clocks back to midnight and gain an hour. Spring forward - turn the clocks forward to two o'clock when its one o'clock and we lose an hour.'

'Smart-arse,' Max grumbled, frowning deeply in the direction of the beer that was not being poured quickly enough for his liking.

'Well, it's all the same in the end - you can't really gain or lose time,' Quinny stated. 'Doesn't make any difference either way. Didn't change things much when they just left the hour forward for about three years - end of the sixties, early seventies, I think it was.'

'I wasn't around in the sixties or seventies,' Henry said as he carefully set the first pint in front of the two men. Their attention was momentarily distracted when they heard a scuffling noise behind them; they looked around.

'Henry, why is Sarah sitting on the windowsill with the curtains drawn round her?' Max asked, suddenly noticing the fabric moving.

A face framed by straw blonde hair peeped quickly through the gap and looked fearfully around the room. Then the image was gone, hiding again.

'I've said I'll give the kids a fiver if they can see a witch flying across the sky on her broomstick. But now they have to stay indoors because some *idiot* ...' and he looked directly at Max, '... told them that if they went outside after dark on Hallowe'en, bats would fly into their hair and they would have to have it all cut off to get them out!' As he handed the pint over to the rector, he said to Max, 'I guess that puts you in the chair, seeing's you set the fear of God into them.'

Max grinned. His father used to tell him the same tale; it hadn't done him any harm. He handed over a note and waited for the change, which Henry drew out of the till. He pretended to step back towards Max but instead turned and placed the coins in the charity box next to the ice bucket on the bar.

'Your generosity will be rewarded in heaven,' Quinny advised sanctimoniously. 'And cheers to St Jude!'

'It bloody well better had!' Max snarled. He picked up his glass and carried his drink towards a vacant table near the hearth, the one Polly and the children used earlier. He called back, the viciousness stark in his voice. 'By the way, Henry, the only witch the kids are likely to see'll be your missus!'

Chapter 24

The Hallowe'en party at The Fighting Cock passed without any witches being sighted or war breaking out in the bar. Everyone's attention then turned to the bonfire and Guy Fawkes firework event.

Unfortunately, 5th November fell on Sunday. When the matter was discussed at the PepperAsh Village Hall Committee meeting, there were loud protests against celebrations taking place on the Sabbath. Quinny remembered many conversations, mainly at the bar of The Fighting Cock, about which day of the week constituted the *Sabbath*. He said he had no objections to the bonfire and fireworks display on the Sunday. But other, more vociferous, members of the committee had won and Saturday, 4th was the chosen day. Quinny smiled as Mrs Ervsgreaves, the main protagonist, preened over this victory: she had recently lost the battle for Tidal Reach not to site Shaun's septic tank emptying business, so this was a small compensation to her favour.

The half-term week leading up to the weekend was bright with clear skies, which led to chilly evenings and ice-cold nights. On the Wednesday morning, the first day of November, a crystal-white frost glittered everywhere. A small congregation, comprising mainly pensioners, stood valiantly in St Jude's Church singing *For All The Saints* whilst Mrs Ervsgreaves, huffing and puffing and insulated by all her rolls of fat, attempted a complicated accompaniment on the bad-tempered organ.

Reverend Quintin Boyce gauged that a short sermon was in order – his mind being mainly on the *order* he would place at the bar at The Fighting Cock for a pint. This made his sermon a little disjointed.

'We are all saints if we try to live by the Word of God,' he preached staring serenely at an imaginary being somewhere in the middle distance. 'And we are not sinners if we fail but try again. We are only not saints if we don't try. But if we don't try for most of our lives, then in that final moment we confess and try, we may be saved. We may become saints. Somewhere along the line we are all sinners, but that doesn't mean we won't all end up saints.'

He snapped his book shut, pulled his eyes back into focus and glanced around his congregation.

Three people looked up aghast, obviously expecting more words of wisdom to follow. Two others had their eyes closed and could possibly have been asleep. The remainder were either fiddling with something or allowing their gazes to drift vacantly around the church.

Mr Ervsgreaves, who was standing at the back, smiled at his wife. The organ was opposite the pulpit and she suddenly became aware that Quinny was about to announce the next hymn. In her haste to prepare the page, she knocked the music book off the stand. The spine hit the keys and lower Eb sounded, reminding Quinny of the gloomy note emitted through misty nights by Cliffend harbour's foghorn.

After the service ended, a regular attendee said 'Thank you,' to the rector. 'That was uplifting,' and then piously drifted away.

'Will you be at the bonfire and firework night this Saturday?' Mr Ervsgreaves asked Quinny later as he tidied the hymn and prayer books away.

'Wouldn't miss it for the world,' Quinny chuckled before catching the front hem of his cassock with his toe as he stepped forward. He flicked the garment impatiently away.

He didn't usually like fireworks. This wasn't because the loud explosions reminded him of the bomb that dropped on his family's home during the war when he was a child; he simply did not enjoy being out in the cold. But this year's party promised to be different. 'Henry's doing the catering, isn't he?'

'Yes, but there won't be a bar, just soft drinks, possibly cups of tea, coffee and someone mentioned hot chocolate,' Mr Ervsgreaves said. 'And a barbecue. No beef burgers, though, only baked potatoes with butter and some sausages, I think. And something sweet for the kids - cakes, I shouldn't wonder. I expect the missus'll be busy baking on Friday. She wants me to drive her to the new supermarket that's just opened up in the retail park outside Cliffend.'

'Did I hear my name being mentioned?' the indomitable lady herself asked as she approached. She was carrying the unfortunate full-music hymnal which had fallen earlier. Without waiting to hear her husband's answer, she sighed and said, 'Oh dear, I shall have to take this home and repair it.' She was pressing the edge of the spine back into place where it had ripped away from the cover.

'Yes, my dear,' crooned her husband. 'We were talking about the bonfire and fireworks event.'

'And very pleased I was when they decided to hold it on the Saturday night instead of the Sunday!'

Quinny nodded sagely but said nothing. He was a very reluctant member of the Pepper Hill Village Hall Committee, the hall itself serving both communities of PepperAsh. The folk of Ashfield were often aggrieved that their rivals hosted all the interesting events; football and cricket matches, parties and jumble sales. Smaller *do's* were often confined to The Fighting Cock which, of course, had the advantage of being a licensed premises, but the only outside grounds available there were the car park and a small area of grass with picnic tables. The village hall had a proper playing field.

'I saw Henry up at the field yesterday morning,' Mr Ervsgreaves commented. 'He was there with the twins, helping to lay the foundation of the bonfire.'

'*Lay the foundation of the bonfire*?' his wife scoffed. 'Anyone would think it was a matter of structural engineering.'

'Well,' Quinny broke his self-imposed vow of silence. Checking his rubber band was in place, he was disturbed when his fingers found the beginnings of a tear. 'If it's anything technical, he'd do best to ask that brother-in-law of his to help.'

'Where is George Tillinger these days, anyway?' Mrs Ervsgreaves questioned, making it sound more like an order than a simple enquiry.

'I believe he's working offshore on an oil rig up near Aberdeen at the moment, but I'm not sure of the exact location. Now, if you'll excuse me.' Quinny did not want this lady and gentleman to witness the betrayal when the rubber band snapped from his wrist. 'I have to get back to the rectory. You'll lock up behind you, won't you?' He walked away before either could reply.

'It's come to something when you have to lock the church door every time you leave,' Mrs Ervsgreaves muttered. She started shaking her head and the many chins around her throat rippled.

'Well, we'd best just do it, my dear,' her husband soothed. 'We can go straight into town from here.' He sighed as he removed the enormous key from the lock in the massive church door. His wife caught a whiff of communion wine on his breath.

Chapter 25

At the beginning of October, Henry dragged Woody's old barbecue out from the back of the garage and managed to repair the damage caused by the petrol explosion all those years ago at the pub's opening event. With the barrel cleaned, the grid shining and the metal frame repainted, it was almost as good as new.

Early on the Saturday morning, Henry loaded the barbecue and other equipment onto the trailer attached to his car. He then raided his stock of soft drinks, and crisps. He remembered to take plenty of packets of prawn cocktail flavour - the latest batch were a new brand - King's Krisps, spelt with a K. These supposedly had more flavour than their rivals - or so the salesman claimed. Henry studied the picture of a crown on the front of the packs. He shook his head; the capitals on the decorated columns that encircled it reminded him of the cockerel's claws in the picture on his favourite mug.

Over the past few years, Henry felt as if his world had shrunk. It now consisted only of the pub, the wholesalers, his bank, quick visits to the Old Police House when collecting or dropping off the children, and occasionally popping into Poskett's for groceries and to use the post office facilities.

Long gone were the days of browsing the makeshift stalls and benches of car boot sales with Rosalie, or visiting charity shops in Cliffend and sometimes Fenstone, and on rare occasions even Mattingburgh, in search of cockerel items for the pub. Most of the collection had been packed into boxes and stored away. They represented Henry's life before

Rosalie left him. Life after their separation was very bleak; clear shelves, blank surfaces and bare walls reflected this.

Henry whistled as he secured the load under a tarpaulin; he realised that he was looking forward to the evening's events. Rosalie had taken the children back to the Old Police House yesterday and, although they had only been gone for a day, Henry smiled at the thought of seeing them again. He wished he had more free time to spend with them but it was difficult sometimes for him to take any meaningful breaks. Tonight, though, Craig and Polly had agreed to manage the bar at The Fighting Cock and forgo the fireworks in return for an extra evening off during next week.

Henry walked through the lounge-bar and nodded to the usual Saturday customers on his way to the kitchen. The smell of onions from a large saucepan gently boiling on the cooker and potatoes baking inside the oven met his nostrils. With his eyes slightly watering, he prepared a mug of his special tea/coffee brew. He also made a couple of sandwiches as a late lunch. Still eating these, he returned to the bar and caught a conversation taking place.

'Bugger that bloody policeman,' Max said to Quinny. 'Boss was hoping to lose a few old tractor tyres on the bonfire. As it is, Yates objected when I turned up with the second pile of broken pallets.'

'Well, you shouldn't use Guy Fawkes Night as an excuse to burn up and get rid of all your old rubbish, should you?' Quinny retorted.

'Isn't me, is it? It's Fergus frigging Goldwin. He told me to load up the trailer with all the old garbage and take it up there - I've been clearing up fly-tipping all year and this's usually as good a way as any to get rid of the stuff. Bloody councils make it so difficult for people to dispose of their rubbish that they'll pay any old Tom, Dick …'

Quinny couldn't help smiling; the image of the head teacher Mr Dick - not Richard, Dick - Vincent from Cliffend Junior School came to mind and, in his imagination, he saw the man unloading refuse onto the village bonfire.

'… or Harry …'

'… Or Henry!' Craig added.

'Henry?' Quinny called.

'What?' Henry replied. He was standing at the other end of the bar, but could still hear most of Quinny, Max and Craig's conversation. He now walked over and towered above the group as he joined them.

'Are you a *Henry* or a *Harry*?'

'I'm a *Henry*. You should bloody-well know that by now!'

Craig and Max sniggered. 'I hope you don't use that kind of language when your kids are about,' Quinny stated.

Henry glared at him. Rosalie had reminded him a couple of times recently not to swear in front of Duncan and Sarah. They had both been heard using the odd profanity, normally after returning from a visit to The Fighting Cock.

'Well, they hear nothing from me that they don't hear from you,' Henry countered, remembering how Max embellished his boss's name a few minutes earlier. 'Anyway, it's time I was off back up to the village hall.'

They all glanced up at the clock behind the bar. It was three pm.

'I hope you're taking those bloody onions with you,' Max said, nodding through to the kitchen. 'The smell of them is giving me indigestion.'

'You're always moaning about something,' Henry replied. 'And, yes, I'm taking everything with me now.'

Craig decided he'd better look busy; he didn't want to

help with transportation, especially if it involved carrying onions.

Henry gathered up the batch of jacket potatoes and placed them on an industrial-sized tray. When he tried to lift it up and manoeuvre it out to his car, he found it heavier than he thought it would be. He then returned for the onions. He fixed the saucepan lid on tightly then carried it carefully to the trailer where he secured it amongst some old sacking to absorb the heat. He decided they could travel *al fresco* as he did not want the smell to contaminate the inside of the car. He collected the chilled containers of uncooked sausages from the fridge and wedged them into a space on the back seat. Finally he walked around the rear of the vehicle, checked the tow bar and trailer then climbed into the driver's seat and set off.

It was a relatively short journey from Ashfield, past the rectory and St Jude's Church, through the tunnel of trees to Pepper Hill. The sky was bright with only a few white clouds blowing across. The sun was low and shone fiercely into Henry's face as he drove. He folded down the sun visor but, in certain places, he still needed to use his hand to shade his eyes. The strength of the sunlight was not equal to the temperature it gave, however; the air was cooling considerably and he wondered if there would be a frost later.

Henry glanced towards the Old Police House on his left as he reached Pepper Hill, but he could see no movements inside or out. Poskett's shop was just beyond this, immediately to the right. The lights were on and there were three cars parked in the lay-by; Henry assumed business was brisk.

The village hall stood at the top of the hill not far from the shop; the car park held four other vehicles. Henry steered off the tarmacked area and onto the field, thankful that the weather had been good recently and the grass was not too soft. He drove in a wide arc and parked close to the back wall of the building, his pitch having been marked out near the door. This meant that, as it grew dark, he would have adequate light from the security lamp on the gable end. He could see the ladies were already busy inside the kitchen. There were plastic cups set out for teas and coffees and the water urn was coming to the boil.

Henry quickly unloaded the barbecue after persuading Stan, a regular at The Fighting Cock who happened to be nearby, to help. On one of the tables they placed the cutlery, packets of napkins, paper plates and plastic glasses, as well as condiments - sauce, ketchup, tubs of margarine, salt cellars, pepper pots and various jars containing three different strengths of mustard.

Henry set up a small gas ring cooker on the end of the table nearest to the barbecue. When this was alight, he retrieved the saucepan of onions and placed it on the stand on top to keep hot.

'You'll have to make sure the individual plates are weighed down when you start taking them out of the packets, Henry,' Stan stated. 'This wind doesn't seem very strong, but it'll easily blow them about.'

'Don't worry, Stan. As soon as I put anything on them, they won't move far,' Henry chuckled. 'Can you get that roll of black plastic sacks out and stick one onto the other end of the table - put another over by the seats and anchor it down.' Henry pointed to a group of fold-away chairs stacked beside the door. 'And, if you still want a job, just stand the chairs out, please.'

Stan puttered and Henry heard the words 'Slave labour.'

'You'll have a free feed as soon as the barbecue's up and running,' Henry promised. 'Mrs E said she'd be bringing cakes and things for the kiddies, so leave that end …' and he pointed '… of the table clear to put them on.'

The bonfire was built a sensible distance from the hall at the far end of the field. The area had been cordoned off with a thin line of red plastic tape threaded through the insulated coiled terminals of a line of electric fence spikes.

The police officer, PC Owen Yates who seemed to have appointed himself in charge, had taken a great deal of care in organising the site. Henry could see him wearing his fluorescent yellow jacket over by the bonfire talking to someone.

Henry was a little wary of Yates but, as he strictly observed his licensing hours and checked identities of anyone who appeared under-age - either by looks or behaviour - he felt he gave no cause for the officer to worry him. They were not even on first-name terms.

After a while, Henry looked up from his work and saw Yates walking towards him. Underneath the startling yellow, Henry could see the policeman's uniform.

'Good afternoon, Mr Stickleback,' Yates said as he extended his arm.

'Please, call me Henry,' he replied as he shook the proffered hand.

'Right, well, er, I'm Owen when I'm off-duty, and PC Yates when I'm on.'

Henry's frown deepened. 'So, as you're wearing your uniform - hidden, mind you, and you're directing proceedings at what is meant to be a social event. Are you on or off duty at the moment?'

Owen smiled, reminding himself that, despite Henry's reticence and measured movements, he was not to be underestimated.

'That depends on what happens in the next few hours, doesn't it?' he replied.

Chapter 26

The bonfire was due to be lit at dusk. Luckily there was a light breeze blowing away from the village hall and the main cluster of houses along the road. Accelerants were strategically placed within the mountain of wood, paper, cardboard and other combustibles. Owen, or PC Yates, depending who spoke to him and how, had inspected it to prevent opportunists camouflaging the disposal of their rubbish. He now set light to the taper and, as soon as a healthy flame caught, he tossed it as far into the central summit as the wind would allow. After a shaky start, orange flames licked around the materials. They crackled and sparked for a few minutes then roared, sending up puffs of smoke. These quickly became towering billows, which filled the air and announced the opening of the festivities.

At the barbecue, the potatoes were being kept nice and hot, and the smell of the onions mixed with the bonfire smoke. Henry hoped it would bring the customers to his stand in a steady flow. He arranged a batch of sausages onto the barbecue grid above the red glow from the briquettes.

Crowds of people were arriving on the field. Some were milling around the bonfire, others followed the aroma of food and made their way towards the barbecue where a rowdy queue was forming. Stan stood next to Henry, who was flicking over the sausages then stirring the big saucepan of simmering onions which still made his eyes water each time he lifted the lid.

'Could you do me a favour, Stan?' Henry asked. 'Can you take the money? I didn't think we'd be so busy this early. The float's in an ice cream container under the table.' He indicated with his head; he held a paper plate in one hand and a long fork with two brown and glistening sausages speared onto it with the other.

'Help yourself to ketchup and salt, or anything you want,' Henry told his customer. 'It's all on the table there in front of Stan.' The man held out a note. 'You can pay him as well. The prices are marked up on the board at the end. All proceeds are in aid of the village hall fund - we need some play equipment for the kiddies.'

'Yeah, well, especially yours, I expect,' the man commented dourly.

'Please be generous,' Henry continued, choosing not to hear the grumble. 'Any change will be gratefully received as well. The food has all been donated by parishioners and committee members - myself included. Everyone wants to help a good cause, don't they?'

The man waved away Stan's attempt to tender his change. 'Give it to the play equipment fund,' he muttered, glaring at both of them.

'Good customer patter you've got going, young Henry,' Stan said. 'Me missus is over there - I'll ask her to come and help you here. I said I'd give Yates a hand with the fireworks. He's set most of them out now.' Stan pointed excitedly to a line beyond where the policeman was standing.

Henry wondered if Stan was secretly hoping there would be some form of drama tonight; he felt that the bonfire and fireworks might not be enough to excite the good folks of PepperAsh. Woody's antics with the petrol can and barbecue at the pub opening night over twenty-five years ago had set a precedent - now the residents had high expectations.

'Come on, Vera,' Stan called. 'Come and help young Henry here. You take the money while he concentrates on cooking the grub.'

Vera was a cherry-faced, very round and heated individual didn't look as if she needed to be too close to either the barbecue or the bonfire. Whereas everyone else wore overcoats or jackets against the chilly autumn evening air - and in Henry's case, a butcher's style apron tied over the top - Vera wore just a skirt and blouse.

Henry rarely saw Stan's wife. The last time he could remember hearing Vera speak was at the re-opening night following the pub's refurbishment shortly after that terrible day when Woody, Annie and Derek all tragically died.

Henry had built a trick inside his head to cope with his loss: whenever thoughts overwhelmed him - as they often had in the early days - he would hear the sound of a big metal gate being slammed shut, the bars resounding against the frame. This was followed by the unmistakable jangling of an enormous bunch of keys, one of which was inserted into a lock. The echo as it was turned chilled his heart. As soon as the mythical key withdrew, relief swept over Henry. The upsetting, disturbing thoughts would then recede, just as the man in a uniform of black trousers and white shirt measured his footsteps back along an empty corridor, the treads growing quieter and softer.

Slowly, Henry had become aware that this trick could be similar to Quinny pinging the rubber bands on his wrists.

Henry could not understand where his vision had sprung from, but he was thankful for it. Then, one evening as he changed channels on the television, he found an old comedy series set in a prison. During a link between two scenes, he saw and heard the very image that had instilled itself inside his head. He didn't mind that he'd borrowed this to utilise; he knew he wasn't very imaginative and was almost relieved the idea was not originally his.

He thought that too much responsibility came with brilliance. True geniuses were all too aware of this and tended to keep their own counsel; only those who thought they were cleverer than everyone else busied themselves letting other people know.

Chapter 27

The village hall was only a short distance up the hill from the Old Police House. Rosalie was standing outside her gate with Duncan and Sarah ready to cross the road to walk there. The dark sky above was clear and the weather had turned very cold. The warm glow of the bonfire in the distance looked inviting.

The twins - both wrapped up in coats, hats, scarves, mittens and boots - were fascinated with the plumes of misted breath they blew out in front of their faces. They were looking forward to the fireworks and paid little attention to their mother as she spoke to them.

'Hold onto my hands, you two,' Rosalie demanded as she saw headlights approaching from the Ashfield direction.

The road had a pavement on the side opposite the Old Police House. The children were accustomed to crossing over to the bus stop near Poskett's shop and post office, but that was usually in daylight; in the evenings the bus stopped on their side of the road.

'No!' Duncan shouted before pulling his arm back and twisting away from her. 'I'm a boy! I don't have to hold hands with *girls*!'

'I am not a girl,' Rosalie snapped. 'I'm your *mother*. Now, hold my hand.' Rosalie stood still, extended her arm towards Duncan and waited for his defiance to subside. Meanwhile, Sarah slipped her hand into her Mum's other one without Rosalie noticing. Eventually, just before the car passed in front of them, Duncan stepped sideways towards her and took her hand.

Rosalie relaxed her shoulders and softened her voice as

she addressed both of them.

'Right, look in both directions. It's clear now. Let's go - keep looking as you cross.' She marched the children across the road to the safety of the pavement on the other side. They set off towards the hall.

'We'll have to get there soon or they'll start letting off the fireworks before we arrive,' she explained then smiled when she felt their paces quicken.

As they walked onto the field, the wide open space made the darkness feel denser, despite the light from the lamp above Henry's barbecue and the sparking red and orange bonfire flames beyond.

Groups of people huddled around the fire. Two figures stood a little apart from the others, one had an implement with which to push any embers that fell from the bonfire back on. Rosalie felt Sarah's hand tighten around hers.

Rosalie steered the children towards Henry's barbecue where several people were also gathered. The smell of grilling sausages, baked potatoes and onions rose and mixed with the smoke from the bonfire. It curled its way towards them enticingly.

As soon as Sarah saw her Dad, her nervousness vanished. She started skipping impatiently and Rosalie let her daughter's hand slide from hers. A hollowness entered Rosalie's heart, as it did each time she realised that, even in her innocence, Sarah preferred her father's company to hers.

Rosalie couldn't prevent her resentful thoughts. *Where was Henry a few weeks ago when his little girl was sick all night?* Gastroenteritis had swept through Cliffend Junior School just after the autumn term began. It was suspected one of the pupils had brought a bug back from a holiday abroad and infected the entire school - probably not even succumbing themselves.

Duncan was one of the very few unaffected, but Sarah had made up for her sibling by prolonged vomiting and profuse diarrhoea. In fact, Rosalie believed she still wasn't completely over it. She had suddenly been sick several times on odd days, but usually in the mornings of a lesson she didn't like at school - although she had also been ill one Friday evening, when even the thought of not being able to spend the weekend with her beloved father at the pub did not bring about a miraculous cure.

Duncan now also pulled his hand from Rosalie's and ran towards Henry, who had moved away from the barbecue and was crouching down to talk to Sarah. Rosalie felt disappointment for a second time. She slowed her pace and swung her steps nonchalantly, hoping her hurt didn't show.

'Hi there,' Henry said cheerfully as she finally approached.

'Hello, Henry, Vera.' Henry's new helper was meting out change to a lady who was complaining that her husband had wandered away from her. The unfortunate individual suddenly appeared walking towards the barbecue with a sparkler in each hand, waving them around in opposite circles.

'You see what I mean?' the woman implored. 'Honestly, at his age, playing with sparklers!'

Rosalie smiled. Henry mistook this as being for him.

'How's it going?' he asked enthusiastically.

'Well, it took an age for me to get the kids ready. But now they're here, I guess they'll enjoy themselves.'

'Didn't they want to come?' Henry enquired with a frown.

'Oh yes, they wanted to come. They just didn't want to

wrap up warm or hold onto my hands as we walked up - or at least Duncan didn't. Just the usual stuff, you know.' Rosalie felt a little childish as she trailed off her explanation. She looked around; several people were walking across the field towards the bonfire. Sparks snapped from deep in the fire's heart then flames quickly roared with a deafening display of heat and power. The smell of wood smoke and food grew thicker. Duncan suddenly sneezed.

'Bless you,' a voice behind Rosalie said. She turned around and, in the harsh security light shining from the top of the village hall, she saw Max Podgrew wrapped up in an old duffle coat with a scarf and bobble hat representing a football team she didn't recognise.

Max then spoke to Henry. 'When you're ready, I'll have a couple of sausages and a baked potato. No onions, though. They give me gripe!'

'Right, coming up.' Henry motioned for the twins to return to their mother, he then moved back behind the barbecue.

'No sign of Quinny yet?' Henry asked as he selected one of the pre-cooked hot potatoes at the end of the grill, placed this on a paper plate, deftly sliced it in two with a strong kitchen knife and added a dollop of margarine from a catering-sized carton onto each half.

'Not yet,' Max replied as he watched Henry, who rolled two sausages with the tongs to check if they were cooked properly before transferring them onto the plate next to the potato.

'There you are,' Henry said as he handed it over. 'Help yourself to ketchup and things, and a knife and fork.' He indicated to the condiments and plastic cutlery on the table.

'Right,' said Max and proceeded to smother both

sausages and potato with shiny red ketchup. Picking up one of the sausages with his fingers, he took a large bite and chewed noisily.

'Bloody hell, that's hot,' he roared.

'Don't swear in front of the twins,' Henry snapped quickly before Rosalie could launch her own vitriol.

'Quinny said *bloody hell* the other day when he spilled some of his beer,' Sarah stated before asking, 'Dad, can I have a whole sausage?'

'Sarah, how many more times do I have to tell you not to call the rector *Quinny*? He's *Reverend Quintin* - I mean, *Reverend Boyce* - to you.' She surreptitiously looked around her to see if the rector was within ear-shot. 'And don't repeat any swear words other people use, please!' Rosalie glared at Henry.

Henry's natural red beard was highlighted in the reflection from the bonfire flames in the distance. His eyes were wide, returning Rosalie's stare and, without words he managed to convey his challenge to her statement. But because he didn't want to make things worse and, officially, the twins probably shouldn't have been in the bar at that time, he shrugged and looked away.

'I'm hungry,' Duncan whined, struggling to free himself from his mother's grasp.

Max, still standing near-by, sensed the tension building.

'I'd better get back to the bonfire,' he said. 'That young bobby hasn't got a clue about when to do things. The fire'll be well and truly done long a'fore the fireworks start.' He sauntered off and across the field.

''Ere, did he pay for that?' Vera demanded. She had been gossiping with one of her friends and forgot to take his money.

'Probably not,' Henry laughed. 'I think he's been spending too much time with Quinny! Don't worry, I'll catch up with him, either later this evening or at some time in the pub. Anyway, let's get these kids fed, shall we?' Henry asked.

Rosalie nodded in reply to Henry's question as to whether he should prepare half a potato each for the children.

'Can they manage a whole sausage each, or one between them?' Henry enquired.

Just then, Rosalie snatched at Duncan and Sarah's hands to prevent them touching the barbecue.

'Don't get too close, you two. That thing's hot!' she scolded.

'Yes, Mum, of course it's hot. It has to be *hot* to cook the sausages!' Duncan explained in Rosalie's own patient but exasperated voice.

'Hey, don't be cheeky to your mother, Duncan,' Henry chided before Rosalie had time to digest that it was her son being impudent, not her daughter; in fact, Duncan had been misbehaving quite a lot today, which was unusual.

Their reply was silenced as a cacophony of sharp snaps and cracks and shot-fire echoed across the blackened dome above them. The sounds stung their ears. Both Duncan and Sarah swung around and stared up at the indigo sky where lively silver stars scattered and fell, trailing dazzling streams behind them which disappeared almost instantly, leaving just a shadow of an image against the inside of their eyelids.

'Wow!' Duncan enthused.

'Pretty stars!' Sarah squealed as she danced up and down, suddenly holding Rosalie's hand again and jolting her shoulder. Rosalie started to silently count to ten. She reached seven when a violent bang made the ground shudder.

She had never experienced the noise of a mortar bomb being launched, but this was the same sensation as aroused by watching the news reports from war zones on the television. A *whishing* sound followed, then the loudest explosion she had ever heard ripped the night apart. It shocked the crowd around the bonfire and physically hurt Rosalie's stomach.

'Mummy!' Sarah began to wail as silver sparks formed momentarily into a flower head image before scattering outwards like a fountain. A second blast rocketed into the sky and, this time, a mass of green sparks flew in all directions, much to the satisfaction of the amassed people near the bonfire whose collective '*Ahhhs*' were only silenced by yet another loud explosion.

Rosalie leant down to pick up Sarah. But Sarah was not a light child and she struggled. Suddenly, her daughter was lifted from her arms.

'Here, give her to me,' Henry said. Having abandoned the barbecue, he bent over, hoisted Sarah effortlessly up and held her to him. Vera quickly took Henry's place, despite not wearing any protective clothing. She flashed a grin of satisfaction towards the Sticklebacks as she asked the next customer what they would like.

'That was a very loud bang, wasn't it?' Henry tried to soothe his little girl.

Sarah buried her face in the bib of the butcher's apron covering his chest as Henry swayed slightly to comfort her.

'Brilliant!' Duncan shouted. 'Are there any more?' His eager face shone pink from the distant bonfire; his smile made Rosalie's heart lurch.

Duncan's question was answered by a volley of

explosions, each seemingly more savage than the last. Sarah started to cry.

'She's such a baby!' Duncan sighed in a dramatic manner that made Henry smile.

Further conversation was futile as a barrage of rockets zoomed skyward, their whistling followed by a loud blast from each which projected more coloured stars in an outward circle against the darkened sky, the first round being silver, the second red, the third electric blue and the final one green.

'Look at the rockets, Sarah. Aren't they pretty?' Henry cajoled as he turned so that she faced the direction of the bonfire and fireworks. 'Look up.' A spray of golden stars fell gracefully and, thankfully, silently from one of the fireworks. 'It's raining drops of gold.'

Sarah lifted her head from his chest and stared upwards. She reached out and pointed to the second spray. They all then jumped as another mortar-type explosion ripped through the air.

'I hope the boss's got all the horses inside,' Max said as he returned from the bonfire area and dropped his empty plate into the rubbish bag. 'What's this, young Sarah? You aren't afraid of a few old fireworks, are you?' He grinned and rubbed his hands together.

'Come on, Sarah,' Henry said as he turned away. 'Let's go and get you something to eat, shall we?' Sarah was staring at Max. She eventually nodded. Henry added, 'by the way, Max, you still owe me for your food!'

From over near the bonfire, someone stepped forward to light a firework on a post. An unmistakable *whizz* started as the jet of sparks from the Catherine wheel spun around its central pin so fast that it looked like a circle of tiny coloured stars.

'Look, Sarah,' Henry encouraged. 'Look, isn't that pretty?' She dutifully looked but did not smile. 'No more big bangs,' he told her, just before yet another mortar-style firework was ignited beside the Catherine wheel. But, instead of a trail of sparks shooting skyward and leaving in its wake a scattering of snapped stars, it gave a pathetic *phut* sound. Figures in the darkness moved towards the site.

'Don't go near it! It might still be alight!' someone from the crowd shouted.

Luckily, the person stopped and turned back. But the explosion still knocked him to the ground.

Chapter 28

'Right then, that's a baked potato for you, Rosalie. Butter but no sausage or onions,' Henry said as he handed over the plate. 'Ketchup, salt and everything is on the table. Tell Vera I'll put the money in the till later.' He tried to smile, but Rosalie glared at him. The glow from the bonfire shone onto one of her cheeks and the flames from the barbecue flickered into her front. She was angry about something, but Henry couldn't guess what. Many things had happened this evening that she would not have liked: the suddenness of the display and the noisy explosions from some of the fireworks, the fact that Sarah had gone to Henry when she was frightened and not to her, and the children had both been rather cheeky – the possibilities were endless.

'Half a potato and one sausage for you, Duncan.' He ensured he handed the plate to his son first so as not to be accused of favouritism towards Sarah – again. 'And the same for you, young lady.'

'Thank you, Daddy,' Sarah said, her blue eyes concentrating heavily on the sausage. 'Please may I have some ketchup?'

Henry moved aside, picked the bottle up from the table, unscrewed the lid and tipped it towards Sarah's plate. Nothing happened, so he gave the bottom a sharp tap. Thick, red liquid sluggishly oozed out and dolloped on one end of the sausage.

'Here, have some butter on your potato too,' Rosalie said, growing even more furious that Sarah had said *Thank you* for her food but Duncan, so far, had not.

'Duncan, what do you say to your father for your potato

and sausage?' she eventually snapped.

'Thank you,' Duncan mumbled.

Rosalie wanted to admonish him further but felt it would serve no useful purpose. She would speak to him later though. Instead, she took a deep breath and moderated her tone.

'Right, we can go and sit on those seats to eat.' She indicated towards a group of plastic chairs by the corner of the village hall in the periphery of the security light's arc. Before she moved away from the table, however, Vera handed her three sets of plastic knives and forks, each wrapped in a paper napkin.

With exaggerated care, Duncan walked quickly in front of his sister and mother, cautiously holding his plate with both hands to ensure the sausage and half potato did not roll off. He chose the most advantageous chair and balanced his meal on his lap.

Rosalie helped Sarah to keep her plate steady as she struggled up onto another chair. Duncan complained that they were blocking his view of the bonfire.

'I'm helping your sister,' Rosalie scolded as she thrust a set of cutlery towards him. 'And, if you were a gentleman, you would've let her choose which seat she wanted instead of racing ahead.'

'She would've chosen the best seat for herself if I'd done that!' Duncan exclaimed indignantly whilst stabbing the sausage.

Sarah sensed she was in trouble but did not understand why. Suddenly she didn't want to be here watching the fireworks in the cold with her angry mother who was likely to shout at her for doing something she didn't know was wrong. But she was hungry and, having not yet received her knife and fork, she picked up her sausage with her fingers as she had seen Max do with his.

She quickly dropped it again because it was hot. She then gathered the potato, which was cooler, in her hand when her mother, having drawn up another of the plastic chairs, sat down and glanced at the twins.

'Don't use your fingers, Sarah!' Rosalie almost screamed. 'Use the knife and fork.'

'They aren't any good, Mum,' Duncan replied for his sister. 'Look, they break easily.' In order to demonstrate, he pressed the plastic fork into the sausage, bending it so far that it snapped where the head above the prongs joined the handle.

Not for the first time that evening, Rosalie forced herself to count to ten. Both twins were watching her. Duncan was defiant, but Rosalie was shocked when she detected a shadow of what she could only interpret as fear in Sarah's face.

'Just enjoy your tea, you two,' she said with forced lightness. 'Then we can go and watch the rest of the fireworks. I think they're giving out sparklers over where those people are.' She pointed towards a small group slightly apart from the crowd. She could recognise Max and Stan even from this distance, and one of the others was PC Yates. He was wearing a bright yellow fluorescent jacket; the light beam from a torch he held danced and bounced as he gesticulated.

Absentmindedly, Rosalie loaded some of the flesh from her baked potato onto her fork and transferred it to her mouth. The butter, which she really knew was cheap catering margarine, slithered like oil. Her first bite proved that the potato was only lukewarm and not cooked properly in the middle. She hacked at the remainder with her plastic cutlery but found that it was all quite hard. Then, just as her son's had, her own fork bent and snapped.

'Right you two, stay here while I have a word with your father,' Rosalie ordered as she stood up and marched back to the barbecue.

At the head of a short queue, Henry was cheerfully serving a mother with two children who both looked just a little younger than the twins. Rosalie pushed to the front and stood scowling at her estranged husband.

'Rosalie, what on earth's the matter?' Henry asked, alarmed at the fury on her face.

'This potato is bloody-well not cooked properly!' Rosalie shouted.

The young mother behind Rosalie, who had tutted when she pushed in front of her, gulped and drew her hand up to her mouth in horror. In the ensuing silence, whilst Henry tried to fathom how to handle the situation, she bent down to her children.

'Don't listen to that rude lady,' she whispered loudly.

As Rosalie turned around and glared, the woman visibly cowered. Then, suddenly mortified, Rosalie realised she had sworn. She remembered telling Henry and his regulars not to swear in front of the twins. Luckily, neither Duncan nor Sarah heard their mother's outburst.

In her peripheral vision, Rosalie caught sight of a glowing jacket walking towards the barbecue. PC Yates called out from several yards away.

'Is everything all right?'

'Yes, thank you.' Henry replied. 'Mrs Stickleback here has just brought to my attention the fact that I have undercooked one of my potatoes,' Henry said, trying to infuse humour into a tense situation.

PC Yates swallowed. Years ago, when he was first assigned to PepperAsh, the sergeant at Cliffend Police Station told him the tale of the Sticklebacks' infamous break up. The first time he'd met Rosalie was in Poskett's shop only a few months later, but before she'd had the twins. He'd always found Henry Stickleback to be a steady sort of person; he seemed one of the more responsible landlords he had to deal with. But Yates was in no mood for any more trouble tonight: there could have been serious repercussions from that idiot who went to see why the firework hadn't gone off properly a little while earlier.

'Is that right?' he asked officiously.

'She was very rude just now, Officer,' the young mum volunteered in an offended voice. 'And she swore in front of my children.'

Henry almost smiled.

Rosalie felt her heart thudding; she could see the seriousness of the situation. Thoughts of her being deemed an unfit mother and her children removed from her to live permanently with their father flashed through her mind.

Then the fatigue hit her. She was tired of squabbling. Plus, it always seemed to be her fault, no matter how hard she worked - and raising twins almost single-handedly was really difficult at times.

She heard Henry start to speak. He was saying something about replacing her potato with a freshly cooked one. He stretched over for a clean plate and offered a new one to her.

Suddenly, she was furious at his apparent casual attitude. She picked up the almost cold potato from her own plate, the margarine slithered down her fingers and made gripping it difficult. She answered his enquiry as to whether she would like sausages and onions this time by hurling it at him.

Henry didn't duck, despite seeing the missile approaching. It hit his cheek, dropped to his shoulder then slithered over his apron, down the side of his front and onto the ground. The people in the queue behind gasped as they watched the grease slide down his beard. Pieces of potato dripped onto his apron.

PC Yates drew himself up, making the fluorescent material of his jacket crackle.

'Madam, would you please modify your behaviour in accordance with the situation and the people surrounding you, or I will be forced to arrest you on a public disorder offence.'

Rosalie was not listening to the police officer who, in her opinion, was being silly and officious. Her heart was beating furiously; she was so angry with Henry that her chest hurt. She looked away from his foolish face which at one time she had loved so much, and over to where she'd left the twins sitting eating their tea.

The chairs were empty. Panic shot through her veins and pounded into her brain. She snatched her head towards the bonfire. Some of the smaller fireworks were being let off, but she knew even these were dangerous if unsupervised children crept too close. She looked desperately around her, but could see neither of them.

'DUNCAN?' she suddenly shrieked. 'SARAH? Where are you?'

'What? Aren't they with you?' Henry fired at her.

'They *were* with me until I had to come back and complain about *that*!' She pointed to the potato lying next to

Henry's boot. 'I told them to stay sitting on the chairs, over there.'

'Right, Mrs Stickleback. Mr Stickleback,' PC Yates said, switching to official disaster mode in an instant. 'Who are we talking about here?'

'Our twins,' Rosalie yelled at him. 'Duncan and Sarah. They're nine years old.'

'And you left them on their own to come over here and complain about ...'

'Oh stop being so judgemental, you fool, and do something useful, like help me find them! DUNCAN? SARAH? Where are you?'

The line of customers began to disperse. The young mother shepherded her children away, muttering to herself that it served that bad-tempered, foul-mouthed woman right and she should take care of her kids properly instead of pushing in and causing a fight over a potato.

Amidst her deafening heartbeat, Rosalie's breathing quickened until it strangulated in her throat. It was her fault. She was in charge of the twins. She was their mother. But she had left them alone while she challenged Henry. The fact that the potato was not cooked properly suddenly seemed so unimportant against her children's safety.

Rosalie frantically called their names, but her thin falsetto voice flittered away in the breeze and was quickly smothered by the bonfire crackling in the background. Henry's deeper tones carried further but brought about no better results.

'Where were they when you last saw them?' PC Yates was asking her.

She thought this was such a stupid question. They were over there, or at least they should have been. She pointed in reply, still shouting their names.

'There they are,' a woman called in a high, excited voice, indicating towards the corner of the village hall. 'Now coming out of the hall. I expect they've been to the toilets.'

Quinny stood quietly at the edge of the crowd near the bonfire. He didn't want to join in the festivities, neither did he wish to be on his own. He witnessed Rosalie march angrily towards Henry and the barbecue. He silently, correctly, predicted trouble. He watched the twins staring after their mother. Quietly, they both stood and placed their plates on their respective chairs before disappearing into the village hall. He was about to walk over to their seats and wait for them when the commotion started. He said a quick prayer for their safety and his imagination attached it to the next rocket that whooshed up into the inky night, drowning out the frantic calls from Rosalie and Henry for Sarah and Duncan.

He tugged his coat tightly around him as he sighed, ending with a cough brought on by the smoke from the fire, the sulphurous fireworks and the barbecue. When he recovered, he watched Rosalie herd the twins back to their supper.

And he wondered if the Sticklebacks would ever bury their hatchets anywhere other than in each other's backs.

Chapter 29

'So, Rosie, what exactly happened?' George asked urgently into the telephone receiver. His mobile needed recharging after a long call with his nephew, Duncan, and he was using the public kiosk at the café he favoured near MaCold's fabrication yard in Aberdeen. 'Why is Sarah in hospital?'

'It wasn't my fault!' Rosalie exclaimed. 'You're all making it sound as if I made her ill. It was more likely to be something Henry gave her to eat when the twins were staying at the pub.'

'Okay, okay.' George tried to keep his voice neutral. 'Just calm down. It probably isn't anyone's actual fault. People get ill.'

'Well, that's just it, isn't it? I'm being blamed for not knowing she was ill, aren't I? She's been with Henry most of the last fortnight - says she gets more peace and quiet there to do her homework. I ask you, George, honestly, how can a pub be more peaceful than here?'

George hesitated for a moment. He could tell his sister that Sarah didn't receive constant criticism when she stayed with her Dad. Also, her godmother, Polly, and Quinny, or whoever was around, would always try to help with her homework if they were able.

Sarah, now aged eleven, was struggling with maths and any other subject that dealt with numbers. She was still at Cliffend Middle School with another two years to go before she moved up to the High School.

The last time George visited, he had found Sarah grappling with her maths homework.

'I think I'm writing the right numbers down, but I put

them the wrong way round,' she had explained, her voice rising with panic. 'Yet when I say them, I say them right - or, if I've put them down right, then I say them wrong. Or I use them wrong when I'm doing the sums. Mr Angelis says I'm just careless.'

After a referral to a specialist, Sarah had been diagnosed with dyscalculia but some of the teachers didn't recognise this as a condition.

'Duncan always gets it right, why can't I?' In her frustration, she began to cry. 'Everyone thinks I'm thick or stupid!'

'No one thinks you're either thick or stupid,' George had said, cradling her head and shoulders. 'You just need to take your time and stay calm if you read them but don't understand straight away.'

'Mr Angelis says I'm sloppy and I rush things to get them done so I don't have to spend too much time on them! He thinks I just daydream in my head all the time.'

'Now, we both know that isn't true, don't we?' George began to feel very angry with this *Mr Angelis*; he wondered why neither his sister nor Henry had challenged him. He remembered his maths teacher, Mr Shields; he was approachable and would take time to clarify any problems individual pupils were experiencing. 'Shall I ask your Mum - or Dad - if they could have a word with your teacher? Maybe you could have a couple of extra lessons?' George had enquired.

'Mum did talk to him, but ended up taking his side, and then just got annoyed at me because I can't do the work. Dad tried to speak to him afterwards, but it was no good because of what Mum had already said,' Sarah replied.

Now, only a few weeks later, Sarah had been rushed into

Cliffend Hospital and was, as George and his sister were having this telephone conversation, being prepared for an emergency appendectomy.

'Henry is with her. *Saint Polly,*' Rosalie's words were heavy with sarcasm, 'and Craig are holding the fort at the pub.'

George sighed. 'Okay. Well, being childish isn't going to help anyone.'

'I'm not being childish! I'm being blamed for Sarah nearly dying!' Rosalie shouted into the receiver.

'Now you're just being melodramatic,' George stated flatly. Not for the first time, he was feeling more than a little irritated with his sister and brother-in-law. It would help, he thought, if Nora came home more often than she did. Her initial holiday cruise with Alice had turned into a twelve year absence. Even though he understood they were now working on board the ship, he did not know in what capacity.

'I am not making this up, George. The hospital said that they thought the appendix had burst and she would end up with peritonitis, whatever that is.'

George knew that *that* would be extremely nasty, but he was wise enough not to enlighten his distraught sister, who was now crying inconsolably into the telephone over five hundred miles away.

A colleague had been stricken with lower stomach pains while working out on one of the rigs a couple of years ago. He was too stubborn to admit he was ill and refused to return to shore, until he collapsed and the medic radioed for the emergency helicopter. He spent months recuperating after his operation, which resulted in him being unable to return to his original job. He'd had to leave MaCold and was now working in a library.

George understood that he should never ignore health warnings; he kept himself fit and limited the frequency of drinking sessions with his mates. He had gained weight between his two most recent medical examinations and was now consciously cutting back on junk food and beer.

'Look, Rosie. I know you do your best with the twins, and Henry knows it too.' *But you could help yourself by being a little less angry all the time,* he added in his mind. 'Sarah's been upset recently; all that stuff about her maths and saying she needed special tuition has really knocked her confidence.' Again to himself he thought, *and you should be more supportive.* Even Duncan spent time with her trying to help. He had devised a way for her to write down numbers and say them back. This worked to a point, but problems arose when tackling figures such as fifteen, or any of the teen numbers, which sounded as if the five or whatever should be written before the one.

George knew Rosalie would listen to advice from very few people; it reminded him of the months after their parents' deaths when she had confided in him. She could also talk to Henry then, but that did not lead to anything good - except the birth of the twins, of course. And George's niece and nephew were very precious to him.

'Yes, well,' Rosalie began defensively, sniffing back her tears. 'I wasn't that brilliant at school so maybe she just takes after me. The teachers bother more now than they did then because they have results' tables which we didn't have. Anyway, I'm making an appointment with the school as soon as Sarah is better to see if we can sort something out.'

'Good! Well look, as soon as we finish talking, I'll clear up a few outstanding bits on my desk and come home to help.'

George was due several weeks' leave and the project he was working on was progressing ahead of schedule. The deputy engineer, Bexley, was capable of handling things for a while; he was eager to prove himself and was already looking to be in charge of an imminent new contract.

George arrived at the Old Police House late the following evening.

'Duncan is staying with Henry at the pub,' Rosalie explained as she prepared grilled pork chops, baked beans and mashed potatoes for her brother. Although she did not understand why, this meal reminded her of the unfortunate incident with the jacket potato at the one and only Bonfire Night event organised by Pepper Hill's Village Hall Committee. She added hastily, 'I've been at the hospital with Sarah most of today. Duncan was okay visiting for a while, but it isn't good for him to spend too long there. And anyway, Sarah will be coming home the day after tomorrow.'

'It's okay, Rosie ...'

'Don't call me *Rosie,*' she snapped.

George smiled. He had been using her nickname ever since she'd told him Sarah was ill, and she hadn't objected. Now that her daughter was recovering, Rosie - Rosalie - began to notice.

'Rosalie,' he corrected himself. 'No one is blaming you - despite what you think. Anyway, you said she had spent most of her time recently with Henry. Why didn't he notice she was ill?'

'Well,' Rosalie said as she sat down opposite her brother and picked up her coffee mug. 'He did say that she looked pale and wasn't eating much. But he thought it was ...'

Rosalie wasn't usually embarrassed when she talked with her brother, but now she blushed on Sarah's behalf. 'He thought that perhaps ... at her age, you know.'

George frowned. Then he realised.

'Oh, right. Teenage girls and stomach aches.' He shuddered as he remembered Rosalie's gaunt face when she first started her monthly periods. The stomach cramps, the lethargy, the headaches and bad temper. But Rosalie had been at least two years older than Sarah was now. 'Isn't she a bit young?' he asked.

'Well *that* obviously wasn't what was wrong. And no, not really. It can happen any time from now onwards. She is quite well developed, you know.'

It was George's turn to blush.

'Well, I don't really look at Sarah in that way. I know she's growing up, but ...' He trailed off, remembering a recent scandal in the media of a young girl taking her own life because her uncle had molested her - worse than that, the post mortem had shown she was pregnant. Entries in her diary detailed a rape and the new DNA paternity testing proved it was likely to be the uncle, or another close family member. George stopped eating and placed his knife and fork onto his plate.

'I hope you aren't going to waste that food,' Rosalie said somewhat harshly, pointing towards the remaining half-eaten pork chop.

George suddenly felt very angry, an emotion he was not easily aroused to. The last time he felt this furious was when his Aunty Shirley, their Mum's sister, tried to organise who accompanied whom as they walked into the crematorium chapel behind their parents' coffins. That outburst resulted in Shirley and Terence Pessham scampering back to

Australia immediately after the service without even attending the wake. They had not contacted either Rosalie or himself since.

Breathing down his bad temper now, George composed himself before speaking.

'Just give it a rest, please Rosie. I've been driving all day, you know.'

'Don't call me *Rosie,*' she responded, but her anger had dissipated. 'And, yes, I know you've had a long journey. Thanks for coming home.' She sounded sincere.

Chapter 30

George walked out of the front door at the Old Police Station as Rosalie parked in the driveway. The passenger seat was empty; Duncan had elected to sit in the rear with his sister for the journey back from Cliffend Hospital.

George walked to Sarah's door and opened it for her.

'Well, what have you been up to?' he asked, holding out his arms. He was rewarded by his niece smiling and moving tentatively towards the edge of the seat.

'Hang on a minute, I'll undo your seat belt,' Duncan offered. He guided the buckle across her front as the strap retracted.

George bent into the car to lift Sarah out. He caught her intake of breath as he took her weight.

'Still hurts a bit, does it?' he asked when she was safely in his arms. Her pale face and ruffled hair peeped out of one end of the blanket wrapped around her, and her seemingly tiny bare feet from under the other. She held her hands clasped behind his neck and he could see the dressing on her forearm covering the wound where the cannula had recently been removed.

'Yeah. It isn't too bad though, not compared with how it was before the operation,' she said.

Duncan bustled in front and opened the doors for George to convey Sarah to the sofa in the living room. Her face then crinkled with discomfort as she tried to arrange the cushions behind her to lean against. George noticed Duncan was standing anxiously watching.

'And how are you, Duncan?' he asked.

Duncan looked surprised that anyone should enquire as

to his well-being.

'I'm, er, okay, I think, Uncle George.' Remembering his manners, he asked 'How are you?'

'I'm fine, young man. Thank you for asking,' George replied with a grin. 'Are you glad to have your sister back home?'

Duncan smiled and looked enthusiastic. He then realised he didn't want to sound too pleased.

'S'ppose so. It's been a bit quiet without her.'

George understood this sentiment exactly. If Rosie wasn't at home when they were younger, the house always seemed peaceful, which was nice to begin with but grew unsettling after a while. *Can't live with, can't live without,* he thought, then chuckled at the irony when applied to Rosie and Henry.

'She's got loads of school work to catch up on,' Duncan volunteered brightly. 'Shall I go and get her books?'

Sarah groaned.

'No Duncan,' George replied. 'Not today. Maybe in a couple of days' time.'

'What are you plotting to do in a couple of days' time?' Rosalie asked as she carried Sarah's hospital bag in from the car. She took it into the kitchen, placed it on the floor by the washing machine and began to load in the clothes.

'Mum, can we have a puppy, please?' Duncan suddenly asked.

Surprised, Rosalie stopped sorting the laundry and walked slowly into the living room. When Sarah gazed up hopefully, she could see a slightly out of kilter focus in her daughter's eyes which she attributed to the painkillers combining with the lingering effect of the anaesthetic.

Duncan's face was now downcast, as if he were searching

the floor for something, desperately trying not to look directly at his mother.

George, as usual, was impartial. When Rosalie's expression asked if he knew anything about this unexpected request, he shrugged slightly and almost imperceptibly shook his head.

'Puppies take a lot of looking after, you know,' George stated, realising Rosie might need support if she didn't want a dog. 'And you and Sarah will be at school during the day so that would mean your Mum having to take care of it.'

'And what about when you go and stay with your father, would you be able to take it with you?' Rosalie added, sounding more abrasive than she intended. 'To begin with, you'd have to be there with the puppy all the time to look after it, take it outside when it wanted to go to the toilet – preferably before it made a mess indoors. You'd have to take it for lots of walks, and you know, Sarah, that you don't like going out in the rain. Well, a dog would need plenty of exercise regardless.'

'I knew you wouldn't let us have one,' Duncan said, defeat evident in his voice. Sarah began to shuffle around on the sofa then tried to stand up. George stepped forward to help.

'It's okay, don't get upset,' he said.

'I'm not upset,' Sarah retorted. 'I want to go to the toilet!'

'A puppy might be a good idea, you know, Rosie,' George stated later that afternoon. He promised the twins he would try to talk with their Mum and was keeping his tone gentle and reasonable, hoping to avoid an argument. Sarah was upstairs in her room having a nap and Duncan had gone to meet up with his friends to play football on the field beside the village hall.

'Yes, but you know who'll end up clearing up after it, don't you?' Rosalie complained. 'And don't call me *Rosie*, especially if you're trying to get round me, even if it is on the kids' behalf!'

George smiled at this.

'You really are the most awkward and stubborn person I know, *Rosalie*,' he said, emphasising her full name.

'Yes, well, I'm the person you've known the longest, aren't I?'

'But wouldn't you like a puppy - a dog - to keep you company during the day?' George asked. He could appreciate an animal would be a tie but not necessarily a burden. After all, Rosalie worked hard with the children, and mostly on her own; one more creature to look after wouldn't add much to the daily routine. Or so he thought, from his unencumbered, carefree bachelor point of view.

'It might be nice. But what would I do with it if I wanted to go out?'

'Have a kennel and run outside and put it in there?' George suggested.

'It would bark and annoy the neighbours. I might not know much about keeping a dog, but I do know they don't like being left on their own.'

'What about Henry? Wouldn't he help? I'm sure his regulars at the pub would be willing to lend a hand.'

'Don't drag Henry into this. But if the kids want a puppy, they can keep it there,' Rosalie said.

'But they're here most of the time, aren't they? Although I suppose they could take it with them when they spend weekends there. What do other people do?'

'Don't really know,' Rosalie replied. 'We never had a dog

when we were growing up, did we?'

'No, but we had rabbits and hamsters. Mum said not to have cats in case they went on the road. D'you remember old Poskett's moggy being run over?'

Rosalie nodded. Poskett couldn't have been that old when they were children, but he'd run the shop and post office for as long as they could remember. At some point, he had acquired a cat, a ginger tom, to keep the mice at bay. Inevitably Winston, she thought it was called, roamed at night and was unfortunately found dead one morning in the lay-by outside Poskett's premises.

'Goldfish,' Rosalie continued. 'We had three of them in a bowl on the sideboard, I seem to remember - one of them was a lot darker orange than the other two. They had some plastic seaweed in with them.'

'It wasn't plastic, it was a proper plant to help aerate the water,' George explained.

'Didn't stop them dying, though, did it?'

'Perhaps we should've cleaned them out more often; the water got really cloudy, didn't it?'

'Yes, and Mum had to take over looking after them. Which is exactly my point, George!'

'Well, you could help! After all, it isn't like you go out to work every day, is it? They shouldn't be expected to do everything for the dog themselves, anyway. They aren't quite old enough for all the responsibility. You could help them train it, encourage them to look after it. And it might help take Sarah's mind off her problem with numbers.'

'Oh, I see how you're hoping to manage this little scheme,' Rosalie snapped suddenly. She stood up and turned to the sink to wash the few mugs, plates and cutlery they had used at lunch time. 'Well, George, the answer is

NO!'

The hot tap hissed angrily and, after a few minutes of knocking and banging during which Rosalie seemed to be trying to break every item of crockery not safely tucked away in the cupboards, George silently stood up.

'I'll go and watch the boys' football match up at the village hall,' he said. Then he left the house.

Chapter 31

Henry was aware that the twins wanted a puppy. They had asked him, but he told them their mother would have to agree. They argued that they could keep it at the pub, but Henry said it wouldn't be practical.

'For a start, you know I often leave the front door open to clear the air in here. It could easily escape and get onto the road,' Henry explained. 'And you wouldn't want it getting hurt, would you?'

'No, but it could be a guard dog, if we got a big enough one - a German Shepherd or a Rottweiler,' Duncan suggested hopefully.

'A Jack Russell would be more useful at fending off intruders,' Quinny intervened, as ever at the bar listening.

'Well, I definitely don't want one of those here!' Henry stated. 'It would probably end up biting all the customers.'

The subject of a puppy arose every so often, but Rosalie staunchly refused. Sometimes, however, when the children were at school or at The Fighting Cock with their father and she was on her own, she wondered if it might be nice after all to have something to keep her company.

About six months after Sarah's appendectomy, Rosalie received a letter from her doctors' surgery summoning her for a routine cervical smear test.

'I have an appointment to see Dr Thorne,' she told Henry on the telephone. 'Nothing's wrong, just - you know - er, women's things.' She paused then added, 'It's tomorrow afternoon. I thought Duncan and Sarah would still be at school, but they brought a letter home yesterday to say that there was a teacher training day. Would you believe it, eh? Such short notice, and on a Friday too. So I was wondering if I could drop them off as I go through to Cliffend and then collect them on my way back. It shouldn't be for too long.'

'Well, normally, you know I'd be happy to, but we've got a big do on,' Henry said hesitantly. He felt guilty at having to say no; he enjoyed the twins being with him.

'They aren't tiny children now, you know, Henry. They're twelve - nearly thirteen. You don't have to watch them all the time. Anyway, they've got homework to do. They can sit through in the kitchen and get on with it.'

'Yes, but the kitchen'll probably be in use until early evening.'

'Well, they can go upstairs to their rooms, or they can help you,' said Rosalie, sighing impatiently.

'But it's a party for one of Owen Yates' colleagues and I don't think it's a good idea to have the kids in the bar when there's a load of police officers there, do you?' Henry regretted the harshness in his tone as soon as he had spoken.

'Oh, please yourself!' Rosalie shouted down the phone before slamming the receiver onto its cradle.

'Is anything the matter, Mum?' Duncan asked tentatively, sensing trouble.

'No, not really.' She took a deep breath then forced herself to relax.

Duncan frowned and looked much older than his actual years. His voice occasionally squeaked when he spoke. Rosalie knew Duncan was growing up. However, both he and Sarah were still officially too young to be left on their own, no matter how sensible she thought they were. But she was angry with Henry for not helping her when she asked.

Now, it was too late to find anyone else without having to go into great detail.

Half an hour later, she had changed her clothes and was ready to leave. The twins' geography homework was strewn across the table, but they were watching television.

'Right, you two, listen a moment.' She found she was addressing the backs of their heads. They were sitting quietly side by side on the sofa, engrossed in a science fiction series that all the youngsters seemed to be talking about.

Rosalie despaired. She couldn't believe they were watching such rubbish. But then she wondered if she really knew her children at all, particularly Sarah.

Sometimes Rosalie was totally flummoxed by her daughter's behaviour - one minute she seemed so childish and the next sophisticated far beyond Rosalie's own experience. She had no idea of Sarah's inner thoughts, hopes, ambitions or dreams.

Rosalie's confusion often manifested itself as irritation and, as much as she tried, she could not prevent this happening. She despaired that, without realising, she was morphing from a young, modern woman and mother into a permanently scowling middle-aged frump. She silently thanked her children for this. Then she blamed Henry.

'Right, you two, I have to go and see Dr Thorne.' Sarah looked up, alarm registering momentarily on her face. Then she tried to glance sideways at the television screen.

Rosalie sighed. 'Will you switch that rubbish off for a moment, or at least lower the volume.'

'Ahh, Mum,' Duncan and Sarah whined in unison, but at least they did turn around and look at her.

'I just want to tell you that I have to go out for half an

hour - an hour at most. Can you look after yourselves for that long?'

''Course,' Duncan said, uninterested in anything this may entail. The programme lasted another thirty minutes and he could easily find something to do after that until his mother returned. Then he would get on with his homework, if he had to.

'Sarah?' Rosalie asked her daughter. 'Will you be okay with Duncan for a little while?'

'Yes, Mum.' She turned her head back to continue watching the television, silently seething because Rosalie assumed that Duncan, who was the elder by three minutes, would look after her instead of them being equally capable.

Rosalie sighed again. She glanced out of the kitchen window and saw that the weather had turned dull and she could detect drizzle on the glass. It would be dark by the time she returned. They would have tea, as they did every evening, she would wash up afterwards and tidy everything away whilst cajoling the children to finish their homework. Later they would settle down to watch the television again, and that would be the end of another day.

She asked herself, *is this all there is to my life now?* She looked at Duncan and Sarah and realised that, even if her days were filled only with taking care of them and ensuring their happiness and welfare, her life would be fulfilled.

With this in mind, she eventually pulled on her coat and said, ''Bye.'

The programme finished, Duncan switched to another channel and Sarah stood up and stretched.

'I'm hungry,' she declared. 'Are you?'

Duncan thought for a moment. He presumed their

mother would organise tea when she returned. But, thinking about it, yes, he was. Starving, in fact.

'Yeah,' he eventually replied. 'What's there to eat?'

'A sandwich - cheese.' Sarah walked over to the fridge. 'No, there isn't any cheese. Beans on toast?' she suggested, having migrated to the cupboard. She stood on tip-toes and stretched her hand to the back 'Mum's hidden a Mars bar in here.'

'Better not have that,' Duncan stated. 'You know how mad she was last time you nicked her chocolate.'

'You had some as well,' Sarah countered.

'Yeah, but you took it.'

'Huh!' Sarah appeared to sulk for a moment. 'Or I could do some chips,' she said in a complete change of mood. There were plenty of potatoes in the vegetable rack at the end of the sink unit.

'Yeah, chips would be good,' her brother replied.

But Sarah noted he didn't offer to help to prepare them.

Slightly annoyed, but not enough to say anything, she moved the chip pan from the back of the cooker to the large ring on the right-hand side at the front and switched it on to heat up the fat. She then picked out the largest potatoes, set them onto a couple of sheets of newspaper on the draining board and proceeded to peel them. She rinsed the now naked white potatoes in cold water and cut them up into chunky chips. She preferred something substantial rather than the fashionable skinny chips which, according to the dieting tips in her teenage magazine, held a greater ratio of surface area to innards thus allowing them to absorb more calorie-laden fat from the fryer.

Sarah was not worried about her weight - not unduly so, anyway. Some of her friends at school were fatter, some were thinner; most of them were on diets of some sort or another. Many had developed or, as in her own case, were developing figures. Some had boyfriends, some didn't but wanted them, and some, again as with Sarah, were not yet interested.

She lifted the wire strainer and loaded in the cut chips. But the red light was still showing on the fryer, which indicated that the fat was not hot enough. She tidied up the peelings, wiped down the draining board, took plates out of the cupboard and set them to warm on a low heat under the grill.

Something then happened to take her away from the kitchen. Afterwards Sarah could not even remember what it had been.

Chapter 32

Sarah returned to the cooker a few minutes later and lowered the strainer full of uncooked potato chips into the pan. But she did this too quickly. The fat was very hot by then, it spat and hissed as it engulfed the chips. As she let go of the strainer in fright, clouds of greasy steam quickly rose. She cried out as the fat roared louder; it boiled up over the sides of the pan and down onto the glowing red cooker ring.

'Duncan! DUNCAN!' she screamed. Duncan ran into the kitchen just as Sarah was trying to lift the pan off the ring, the flames were now flaring up out of it.

'Stop! No, Sarah. Put it down. LEAVE IT!' he shouted above the noise. He pulled his sister back just as she dropped the burning pan back onto the cooker. The flames shot higher into the air, which suddenly scorched their throats with thick, acrid smoke, making them choke.

Fear caused a flush of cold perspiration to flood over Duncan as he crouched forward and switched off the cooker ring. But, as he did so, he registered a painful, piercing sensation that increased in intensity as milliseconds passed. Some of the boiling liquid fat had splashed onto the top side of his right wrist.

Ignoring this, he quickly reached over to the sink, turned on both taps and snatched the towel and tea cloth from their hooks close by. When these were soaked, he opened them out and spread them over the top of the burning chip pan. The flames hissed angrily as they were smothered. But they would not be extinguished.

'Get more towels!' Duncan yelled urgently to Sarah.

She pulled a couple from the airing horse on the far side

of the kitchen and dumped them in the sink under the still running water. The smoke was rapidly filling the kitchen.

'Open the back door,' Duncan ordered.

Sarah was crying, but flung the door wide anyway. The flames were evaporating the water from the towels, adding to the steam and pungent smell.

'More,' Duncan urged.

Sarah ran into the hall, up the stairs and grabbed as many towels from the airing cupboard as she could carry. She almost tripped herself as she hurried back down. She piled them into the sink under the taps until they were drenched.

Duncan seized them and threw them over the pan, which slowly hissed and sizzled less and less, until finally just a spiral of putrid, black greasy smoke curled up towards the burnt and bubbling patch of ceiling above the cooker.

They both suddenly became aware of the stench, along with the dampened black marks on their hands and forearms. Duncan was opening the kitchen window when they heard their mother enter through the front door.

'What on earth ...?' they heard her ask before actually seeing her. The door through to the hall slammed shut as a result of the two outside doors both being open at the same time. Sarah jumped as she stood absolutely distraught in the middle of the room.

The cool air wafting in was turning the atmosphere into a cauldron of burning, steaming vapour. Rosalie saw Sarah's face was streaked with blackened fatty smoke, tears were streaming down her cheeks. Her clothes were soaked with greasy, dirty water, as were her brother's.

Duncan sensed Sarah's fear and stepped forward between her and their mother.

'It wasn't Sarah's fault. I wanted some chips and asked

her to make them. I switched the ring on under the pan and forgot to tell her.'

Duncan glared at Rosalie, daring her to contradict him. He looked confused but ready for combat: an adolescent doing a man's job.

Rosalie could see Duncan was lying. When she'd purchased the chip pan a couple of years ago, she ensured there was a way of telling when the fat was hot enough for the chips to go in.

As they faced each other, Duncan realised Rosalie knew he was defending his sister. But his unspoken words hung in the air between them - *You dare blame her, Mum. You just dare!* And in the background Sarah softly sobbed.

Seconds ticked quietly by, but they felt like hours.

In the end, Duncan spoke first.

'I'm going to 'phone Dad.' His voice squeaked on the last word. He knew this action would annoy his mother, but it was the only thing he could think of to say and do. He held out his hand to Sarah and guided her to the telephone with him.

'Dad?' he said into the receiver as soon as the call was answered.

'No, it's Polly. Is that you, Duncan? Is everything all right?'

'Not really. Can I speak to Dad, please? Is he there?'

'Yes, of course. I'll get him for you.' There was a pause and Duncan heard the receiver being handed over.

'Duncan?' Henry asked anxiously. 'What's happened? Are you and Sarah okay?'

'We've had …' His voice faltered. Sarah wept behind him. 'We've … er … we set light to the chip pan. 'But it's all right, it's out now.'

'What?' Henry bellowed.

Rosalie could hear the anger in his voice as it travelled down the phone line and across the kitchen.

'Sorry, Dad.' Duncan was really struggling to speak coherently.

Rosalie darted forward and snatched the telephone from him.

'Henry, it's me. There's been a bit of an accident. Nothing too serious.' She clamped her teeth and pressed her lips together as Henry started firing questions at her.

'No, they're okay – a bit sooty and upset but no injuries as far as I can tell.'

Rosalie did not see Duncan quickly hide his wrist. He knew he should run cold water onto the scald, but he didn't want to admit he was hurt.

Rosalie turned around and looked at them both as she continued her explanation.

'They were just trying to help me by making a start on the tea before I got home.' She listened again. 'Yes, the kitchen is in a bit of a mess,' she added. 'As soon as they've had a shower and changed their clothes, perhaps I could run them over to the pub and they can stay with you for a couple of days. Would that be okay?' After another pause, she said, 'Yes, I think it'll take a while. Yes. Okay, we'll see you as soon as we can then.'

Chapter 33

'Oh my God,' Henry exclaimed about an hour later when Rosalie herded the twins into the lounge-bar at The Fighting Cock. 'Sorry Quinny,' he said aside to the rector.

Quinny nodded absolution and turned around to see why his landlord had blasphemed.

The two children looked bewildered and agitated as Rosalie returned from her car carrying their bags. Sarah's eyes were pink and swollen. Duncan's face had turned white and he was holding the top of his right wrist with his left hand. The scald was hurting a lot now and the skin had blistered back to expose red, raw flesh. He was desperately trying to conceal the fact that he felt very sick and his legs were weak and about to collapse under him.

'What the hell has happened to you two?' Henry roared as he came from behind the bar. He opened his arms and bent towards them.

Sarah launched herself into his embrace, clung onto his neck and started to cry again. Despite her having showered and put on fresh clothes, Henry could smell burnt chip fat.

Rosalie watched, unable to prevent a spear of jealousy entering her soul.

'The smoke seems to have infiltrated everywhere, even upstairs,' she started to explain apologetically. 'It's got onto everything, even the clothes in the wardrobes and drawers.' She coughed quietly.

Shock at arriving home and finding all but a blazing fire in her kitchen was beginning to affect her too. Rosalie was imagining all the bad things that could have happened: the twins being burnt by the fat; the fire taking hold in the kitchen and spreading throughout the house; the smoke forcing its way into their lungs and rendering them unconscious to await their fate.

She knew she had been wrong to leave the twins on their own. But Henry had refused when she asked for help and she did not feel like assuaging his conscience in order to take all the blame.

'I had an appointment, if you remember?' she reminded him. 'I did ask you to look after them.'

'Why didn't you take them with you?' Henry demanded, oblivious that yet another of their private and personal disputes was being aired so publicly. 'They could've sat in the waiting room while you went in, couldn't they?'

'Well, I didn't, did I? Instead I foolishly thought you would do something to help me. But of course, you couldn't be bothered.' She looked wildly around the lounge-bar for hints of the leaving do Henry had used as an excuse. 'I see the party must've finished early!' It was a statement not a question, but Rosalie wanted Henry's answer anyway.

'As a matter of fact, it was cancelled at the last minute. Several people were called out to an emergency. It's being held next week, if you must know!'

Quinny and Max were sitting at the bar. The rector had his back to the couple, but he was aware of the children's discomfort and confusion behind him. He pinged his rubber band, turned around slowly and caught a glimpse of Duncan holding his wrist.

Quinny stood up and wiped his lips on the cuffs of his shirt sleeve. He glared first at Rosalie, then Henry and inhaled deeply before shouting above their bickering.

'Why don't you two put your children first for once? If you looked you would be able to see that Duncan has obviously hurt himself. And Sarah, poor love, is standing there shaking. They're probably both in shock, but neither of you are bothering with them. For goodness sake, pull yourselves together. Stop acting like kids and get on with being parents!'

Henry and Rosalie were stunned to silence. The room suddenly seemed to pulsate with potent electricity: when spoken out loud, the truth felt heavy and sickening. As they looked guiltily around; there were several customers sitting at various tables staring back at them, the argument being too public for anyone to even pretend not to have heard. Quinny pulled his jacket on and left the bar.

'The bugger didn't even pay for his pint,' Henry muttered.

'Serves you bloody well right,' said Max. He finished his own drink and set the glass noisily back onto the bar top. 'Better go see if he wants a lift anywhere.' He stood up and followed Quinny out.

Polly drew both Duncan and Sarah into the kitchen and retrieved the First Aid kit from its shelf by the door. Whilst she administered to Duncan's scald, she quietly questioned both to see if either was injured elsewhere.

Henry and Rosalie soon joined them, shame-faced and contrite. They forced themselves to remain calm as they discussed the damage to the Old Police House. When Polly had finished, the twins silently slipped upstairs.

Duncan's was the smaller of the two spare bedrooms; Sarah had claimed the larger to make up for the fact that her room at the Old Police House was smaller.

Originally, Nora and Woody had intended to use these as Bed and Breakfast accommodation, as there was a second bathroom in between them. However, soon after the pub opened, Nora acknowledged she wouldn't be able to manage an additional enterprise, especially with Woody's deterioration.

Duncan and Sarah had only a vague knowledge and understanding of their paternal grandfather's troubles. Their own problem now, as they sat side by side on Duncan's bed, was facing their culpabilities regarding the chip pan fire.

Sarah felt the weight of guilt because she had set the pan on the cooker ring, turned it on and then wandered off. When she returned, she forgot the basic rule of cooking, that you always, *always*, check the temperature - be it oven, ring or grill, or in this case a bright, albeit small red light - before you did anything.

Duncan, on the other hand, felt responsible because he was the elder of the twins - no matter what anybody thought of his assumptions. He also believed that Sarah was the scattier and he the more sensible. Although Sarah resented this, he realised it was one of the main contrasts between them. He thought it was the reason both their parents treated them so differently. But he could voice none of this.

After a while, they heard footsteps ascending the stairs. There was a quiet knock before their father opened the door.

'Your Mum's gone back home,' he informed them, still holding onto the door handle and not quite stepping into the room. 'She'll need to ring the insurance people for them to come out and have a look at the damage. Hopefully, they'll pay for any repairs and redecoration that needs doing.'

'What about the cooker?' Duncan asked, placing his arm around Sarah's shoulders as he sensed her tears were close to falling again.

'Well, yes, that'll need replacing. But don't you two worry about it. It wasn't your fault.'

'But it *was* my fault,' Sarah cried. 'I turned the ring on then …'

'No, it wasn't your fault,' Duncan interrupted. 'It wasn't anyone's fault. If it was, it was mine, I wanted the chips. I should've got up and cooked them myself, or at least helped you.'

'Neither of you are to blame,' Henry said quietly. 'It was my fault. I didn't help your mother when she asked.'

'She went to see the doctor,' Duncan said defensively.

'Yes, I know. But she said it wasn't important. She thought I was too busy to help her.' Henry pressed his lips together and felt very ashamed.

'Can we stay here, please, Dad?' Sarah suddenly begged. Her blue eyes were shining with tears and her face bright pink. Beside her, Duncan looked just as pale as he had when he first arrived.

'Yes, of course you can. But you'll have to bring your school stuff over, all your clothes and sports gear. At least its Saturday tomorrow, so that'll give us a couple of days to get things sorted out.'

'No, no. I can't wear my uniform. It'll stink of smoke,' Sarah sobbed.

'We can get everything washed before Monday,' Henry stated.

'What about my blazer? That'll have to be dry-cleaned. We'll never get it back in time.'

'I'm sorry, love, but you'll have to go to school without it for once.'

'Please, can I have a new one?' Sarah suddenly blurted. 'I'm too big for it now anyway. Please, Dad.'

'Well, we'll have to see what your mother says,' Henry placated. He felt very guilty because they were both so upset, but he didn't want to make any promises that would fuel the war between himself and Rosalie.

'But she'll just say it was my fault and that I'll have to put up with the smell.' Sarah's voice was hysterical.

'It is pretty bad, you know, Dad,' Duncan intervened. 'My stuff's ruined too. God knows what we'll do about our homework - our geography books were on the kitchen table.'

'Okay, okay. I'll see what I can do.'

And that was the day everything changed. Rosalie acknowledged Duncan had grown up. Duncan's account of what happened became the official version. Later, he told his mother that he and Sarah wanted to stay at The Fighting Cock for a while. Although it was a relatively small fire, the Old Police House needed completely re-decorating. The smoke had permeated all the rooms, upstairs as well as down. The beds, carpets, curtains and cushions, plus the upholstered furniture all had to be renewed. Even the clothes in their bedroom cupboards and drawers smelt of smoke from the burnt cooking fat. Luckily, Rosalie's house insurance covered most of the replacements.

'So I can buy all new outfits with my share?' Sarah asked her mother, looking down at the insurance cheque Rosalie was showing her.

'No, I'll draw out enough for what you need. And remember, you have to buy clothes for school as well as any fancy bits and pieces,' Rosalie explained.

Sarah was fast growing into a fashion-conscious young lady; she wanted to use her sudden losses to build up a complete new wardrobe: Duncan concluded that, at least, some good had come of the incident.

Sarah tried to thank her brother many times for taking the blame, but he shrugged it off, saying that it really wasn't her fault. The scar on Duncan's wrist caused by the burning fat itched as it healed. He smiled to himself sometimes because it reminded him of how happy Sarah had been with all her new clothes, shoes and bags, trinkets and make-up - everything a teenager needed to impress her school friends.

But even the seriousness of this incident could not stop their parents fighting. And Duncan, luckily, still liked chips.

Chapter 34

Henry looked over towards the window and the car park outside. The grey sky doming above the world continued to let the rain pound down and the puddles were quickly filling up. It was Tuesday, usually the quietest day of the week. There were just two customers, Quinny and Max.

'Don't you two ever do any work?' Henry asked as they waited for their pints.

Quinny studied the hunting scene on the pump handle next to the one Henry was using. It depicted horsemen in bright red riding habits transferred onto the white ceramic, representing a remnant of a far away age.

'It's good to see a proper fire,' Quinny commented, nodding his head towards the hearth in the corner of the lounge-bar. The fireplace had been removed from his own front room at the rectory when the central heating was installed and, although the whole house was warm now, he missed the homeliness of real flames.

'Cheers' he said as Henry handed his glass to him. He held it up to the light and peered at it. 'Bit cloudy, isn't it?'

Henry grunted and moved away. For want of anything better to do, he went through to the kitchen and made a mug of his tea/coffee concoction. He looked in the mirror as he waited for the kettle to boil.

At the age of thirty-five, Henry's dark hair was threaded with a few silver strands. But his beard, being reddish rather than brown, showed more grey. He was aware he had gained a little weight recently, mostly around his waist. He tried to stand upright as much as possible but, with his height and the fact that most of his work involved reaching forwards and bending, he was inevitably becoming a little hunched. In contrast, whenever he saw Rosalie, she seemed to pull back her shoulders and straighten herself in order to seem taller.

Henry's thoughts were with Rosalie most of the time. This probably explained why the attempts at flirting by forward and eligible ladies from the other side of the bar failed completely. Henry would only ever love one woman. Rosalie. He filled his time either working, and there was always plenty to do at the pub, or he looked after their children, who were now almost fourteen.

'So, Henry,' Max enquired when Henry returned to the bar with his drink. 'What've you got your kids for their birthday?' He had come into the pub this morning specifically to ask this question.

Goldwin's black Labrador gundog, Tess, had just had a litter of six puppies. There were three bitches, two yellow and one black, plus one yellow and two black dogs. Three pups had been pre-ordered, by their genders rather than colour, and two had had interest placed in them. But the last one had not yet incited any curiosity; he was only two-thirds the size of his litter-mates. In fact, potential buyers looked at the poor little runt and shook their heads.

On Monday morning, Fergus Goldwin told Max that there wasn't much work at the farm for the coming week.

'As your wages will be a bit short, you can sell the last pup and keep the money as compensation,' Goldwin said.

Max was aware that the Stickleback twins wanted a puppy. But he also knew that Rosalie had repeatedly refused. He thought, however, that maybe Henry might relent at some point.

'I've got no idea what to get them, although I expect

Sarah will have something in mind, for herself at least. Duncan is usually a bit less specific. Why?' Henry was suspicious of Max.

'Well, boss's got a spare pup from his bitch's last litter,' he stated, looking Henry in the eye with genuine hope.

'Going cheap, is it?' Henry asked.

'No, dogs bark. Sparrows go *cheep*,' Quinny reliably informed them, earning a look of disdain from Max and a grin from Henry. 'Goldwin usually charges a fortune for those gundogs of his. What's wrong with this one if you've got it to sell?'

'It's the runt, if you must know!' Max advised them sourly.

'And you're trying to foist it onto me,' Henry commented flippantly.

'I aren't *foisting*. You'll have to pay, you idiot,' Max snapped.

'Good job *you* don't call your potential customers *idiots*, isn't it, eh, Henry?' Quinny joked.

'He bloody well does. Idiots, and worse,' Max spat.

'So,' Henry interrupted. 'Tell me a bit about this pup then? Is it a boy or girl? What colour is it? Not that I've said yes. Rosalie would have my guts for garters if I bought it for the kids without asking her first.'

'That's the trouble with you, Henry. You're scared of yer missus.'

'Yeah, and so are most sensible husbands I know. Scared of their own missuses, that is. Just look at the Ervsgreaves! And Stan and Vera.'

'Well, at least those men actually live with their wives, which is more than can be said for you!'

'Now, now, you two,' Quinny intervened. 'I came in here

for a quiet pint, not to witness the start of World War Three, thank you.'

'Yeah, well.' Henry turned around as the main door was opened. Three men walked in and across to the bar, the shoulders of their jackets damp from the rain. 'I'll go and serve these customers. At least they might actually pay for their drinks.'

'You'd better hope the beer's cleared by now then,' Max said as Henry receded.

Quinny watched Henry greet his customers, the landlord clearly enjoying their conversation. Henry indicated over to the corner where the rector and Max were leaning on the bar and grinned. When the drinks were dispensed, money tendered and change given, Henry returned to them.

'So, Max. Tell me about this pup, then. Like, how old is it? And how much?'

'You're interested in it, then?'

'I didn't say that, did I?'

'You asked about it,' Quinny stated helpfully. 'That gave him hope.'

'I'm just curious.'

'Well,' Max said slowly. 'What time can you knock off? You can drive me up there today and have a look.'

'Bit soon, isn't it?'

'Gotta be quick, Henry. Or someone else'll snap it up.'

'Don't think so, otherwise he wouldn't be badgering you,' Quinny added.

'Badgers, sparrows, pups,' Henry commented. 'Good job I got rid of most of my cockerel bits.'

'Yeah, where did they all go?' Max asked.

'In the cellar. Why, d'you want some?'

'Not bloody likely. You ought to try and sell them back to

the stall-holders and junk shops you bought them off.'

'No, I'll keep them - might even bring some back out, now and again, like. To brighten the place up when you miserable so-and-sos start moaning.'

'There you go again, Henry. Insulting your customers. You'll never stay in business that way,' Quinny said, enjoying the banter.

'Well, I wouldn't stay in business from what I earn off you two anyway.'

At that moment, Polly bustled in through the door, her navy overcoat damp from the rain.

'Morning boys. Behaving yourselves, I hope,' she said as she removed her outer layer to reveal a mustard-coloured dress with a high hem-line. The frilled neck was low and the sleeve cuffs terminated just below her elbows. Her waist was nipped tight with a belt of the same shade and fastened by an enormous silver oval buckle.

Polly was conscious that she was being watched, especially by the three men who had taken the table closest to the fireplace in the corner. They stared as her long legs and black patent stilettos marched confidently across the carpet before reaching the tiled floor serving area where the bar suddenly hid her lower figure. They turned their attention to the cleavage on view above. She hung up her coat on the kitchen side of the adjoining door and then returned to start work.

'Anyone need serving?' she asked Quinny and Max, then looked over to the group of three and finally to various other customers. They all shook their heads and raised their glasses towards her. 'No, then I'll just ...'

Without actually saying what she was going to do, she walked towards the tables and started to collect the empty glasses.

'Right, now Polly's here, I'll go,' Henry stated.

'Just get me another pint, then - to fill in the time, like, 'til you're ready,' Max said.

'I'll have to speak with Rosalie before I make any decisions. I'm not going to see the pup unless she agrees the kids can have it.'

'Coward,' Max taunted. 'As I said, afraid of his own missus.'

'Yup, that's right. And if the truth be told, old boy, you're afraid of her too!' Henry stated as he left the bar. 'I'll see Rosalie tomorrow.'

Chapter 35

The next day, Rosalie was in the front garden at the Old Police House in Pepper Hill. Gardening did not interest her and she resented the time she was forced to spend keeping the area tidy. The sun was shining and the recent rain had softened the soil. She was attacking the weeds in the long flower bed by the hedge with disproportionate energy; they felt her disapproval as she strangled their stems and wrenched their roots from the ground. Wisps of her wiry blonde hair were escaping her ponytail, the ends catching in her eyes and making her temper scorch. Henry arrived just as she removed her gardening gloves to retie her hair.

He saw the scowl creeping across his estranged wife's face as she watched him park. His heart plummeted. He inhaled deeply whilst pulling on the handbrake and switching off the engine.

'Hello Rosalie,' he said cheerfully as he climbed out of his car. 'Have you got a few minutes? I want to talk to you.'

Rosalie looked around, heaved up her shoulders then let them fall again with a deep sigh. She had only just started weeding. The burgeoning snowdrops and the early show of crocus buds were being drowned by a carpet of illicit greenery. Also, the grass needed cutting, both here in the front and at the rear. To add to the house's general ramshackle appearance, the outsides of the windows were grimy – she'd had a disagreement with the cleaner after his last visit and would now have to either wash them herself or engage someone else.

'Oh, go on then, I could do with a break,' Rosalie relented.

Henry was surprised; she did not normally greet him with such civility.

'Come inside,' she continued. 'I'll make us a cup of tea - well, you'll want to do your own disgusting brew, no doubt. I'll just have an ordinary cup.'

Rosalie secured the fork she had been using into the ground, pushing the prongs down with her foot until the sole of her wellington boot rested on the soil. She threaded her gloves into the fork handle and marched around the side of the house to the back door. She removed her boots before entering and then led Henry into the kitchen. The room had been redecorated since the chip pan fire, and an updated cooker, fridge and washing machine were located in the same places as before.

'By the way, I keep meaning to ask, how's Nora?' Rosalie enquired as she took off her coat and hung it on the peg on the back of the door. 'I haven't heard anything from her for a long while.' She moved to the sink, turned on the tap, lathered her hands with soap and gave them a good wash.

'She's okay - I think,' Henry replied. 'I had a letter a couple of weeks ago which said she and Alice were taking a few days' break in Ireland. I really don't see why she wants to be away all the time, though.' Rosalie detected more than a slight hint of annoyance, maybe even envy, in his tone. 'I mean, I thought she would want to see more of her grandchildren, even if she isn't particularly keen to spend time with me.'

Rosalie waited until she had filled the kettle before speaking. 'Well, perhaps she's at a time in her life when she just wants some freedom from all the responsibility. You know, she wasn't able to take a holiday since moving into the pub with your Dad, so I guess she took the opportunity when it presented itself. And I presume she's doing an actual job of some kind - I mean, it isn't illegal, this *encouraging* people to gamble in the casinos, is it?'

'I don't really know. But it must be wonderful to be paid for permanently being on holiday.' There was heavy sarcasm in Henry's voice.

'We don't know if that is definitely the situation. Maybe her and Alice had a big win at the beginning and have invested a lump sum and are now living off the interest,' Rosalie suggested brightly.

Rosalie thought wistfully that she would like a holiday herself, but she did not want to be away from her children. The theme park about thirty miles away was offering cheap rate mini-breaks over the Easter holiday and she had been wondering whether or not to treat the twins. But she'd hesitated because Poskett told her that the offer probably only referred to the basic accommodation plus use of a couple of the facilities, with all other activities having to be paid for separately.

'Yeah, well. Pigs don't really fly either,' Henry replied quickly. The awkward silence was filled with the sounds of Rosalie setting out the cups, saucers and spoons, a coffee jar, tea caddy and sugar.

Henry glanced around the kitchen; it was untidy but looked lived in. He spotted the tall, ceramic cockerel-embellished mug on the kitchen windowsill. He reached forward and picked it up.

'Hey, I'd forgotten you had this. Do you use it?'

'Not to drink from, no. I just keep it there,' Rosalie answered. 'Occasionally I put spare spoons and things in it. Why, would you like to have it for your tea/coffee concoction, like the one at the pub?'

'Well, it would be the right size,' he said with a smile, holding it comfortably, his fist around the handle.

Rosalie took the mug from him and ran hot water into it. She then squirted a tiny amount of washing up liquid onto the squidgy and gave it a thorough clean.

'D'you remember the day we bought the two mugs?' Henry asked lightly, clearly reminiscing. 'You insisted they be washed up properly before anyone drank from them, and suggested putting them into the glass-washer?'

He smiled broadly. Rosalie turned towards him and she saw the young man she'd fallen in love with. Her heart jolted inside her chest and she immediately felt as if, for a long, long time, she had been cheated out of something precious.

'Yes, and you said something like *Can't do that 'cause it's for washing glasses!*' Rosalie mimicked Henry's way of speaking. 'Happy days,' she added quietly. 'Well, maybe not really so happy, were they? So soon after … everything.'

They both fell silent until the kettle boiled and switched itself off.

'Do you want to come and make this yourself?' she asked, indicating to the washed and dried cockerel mug plus the ingredients laid out on the work top. 'I'm not sure I remember how to do it now.'

'Of course.' And Henry stepped forward.

Henry was so close that she could feel the heat from his body and smell the shower gel he used. Their forearms touched as Rosalie nudged her own cup in his direction. The electricity between them caused the hair on her neck to crackle and, in response, the fibres of Henry's woollen jumper, the sleeves of which were pushed up to his elbows, extended invisibly towards her. They turned and looked into each other's eyes, Rosalie glancing upwards and Henry leaning down.

It was a moment. A moment when everything could have changed. Instead, it caused such confusion that Rosalie felt herself tremble.

'Do mine as well, would you, please?' she asked. 'I've just got to go and …' She walked quickly out of the kitchen, down the hall and up the stairs before her mind had thought of an excuse to leave the room.

In the bathroom, she rested her elbows on the sides of the wash basin. A wave of utter confusion swept over her. Why couldn't she relent and apologise? Then maybe they could start again. Or at least be friends.

But then she remembered the locket, still with the giant, ugly teddy bear in the wardrobe, and the pictures Henry had replaced with - of all things - a diamond. A second-hand diamond at that. And because her own engagement ring was tarnished by association, she could never wear that again either. She did, however, continue to wear her wedding ring, although she could not explain why.

'Tea's ready,' Henry shouted up the stairs a few minutes later.

'Okay, I'll be down in a minute,' she called back. She glanced at herself in the mirror. She looked like a vagabond. She untied her hair, brushed it and secured it once again in a ponytail, watching her reflection and noting that her almost permanent frown was deepening the lines around her mouth and between her eyebrows. She breathed deeply and forced herself to relax.

Rosalie was pleased that Henry was sitting down at the kitchen table when she returned. She took the opportunity to seat herself opposite him.

Henry smiled when he noticed she'd tidied her hair. He raised the cockerel mug to his lips and took a sip. Rosalie looked suspiciously at her own drink.

'Don't worry, I haven't poisoned it,' he joked.

'No, I didn't for one minute think you had.' She lifted the cup tentatively towards her. 'Did you put sugar in it?'

'No, I didn't think you took sugar. Do you want some?'

'No, no. It's fine.' She finally drank a sip. The tea was just how she liked it: Henry had remembered perfectly. She experienced a sharp sensation inside, bouncing somewhere between her heart and the base of her stomach.

But thinking about her heart reminded her again of the locket fiasco. She looked down at her hands, her eyes resting on her wedding ring. She and Henry were not divorced; they had never even discussed it. Rosalie did not want to leave Henry, but she did not wish to live with him either. Henry was a traitor to his promise and to her memories, and she couldn't understand why he still didn't see that his actions had hurt her so much.

Rosalie felt her mood darken. But, when she looked up into Henry's face, she suddenly realised she did not want to spoil such a rare moment of peace between them. She searched her mind for a neutral topic to discuss.

'It's the twins' birthdays soon,' she eventually said. 'And I wondered if you think they're now actually old enough to take responsibility for a pet. I mean, I know I would be the one looking after it - or at least supervising them. What d'you reckon?'

Chapter 36

'Max rang,' Polly informed Henry as he walked back into the lounge-bar at The Fighting Cock, his mind still confused from his chat with Rosalie.

'Did he say what time to meet him? I'm supposed to be driving out to the farm today to have a look at a puppy for the kids' birthdays,' he replied.

'Ah, well. That won't be necessary.' Polly paused. 'Now let me see if I can convey exactly what he said and how he said it. It went along the lines of "tell him not to bother to come because the little bugger has gone and died on us!"'

'Oh,' Henry said. He felt a mixture of dismay, disappointment and compassion, all in equal measures. Although he understood that the pup was still with the bitch, he wasn't sure if any animal in Max's care would receive the best treatment it should expect. Equally, he was glad the poor little chap had passed away whilst he still knew only the security of his mother's nurture, and before Henry had bought it. He did not wish to cause any more heartbreak and disappointment than he already had.

'Right. Well, I'd better go ring Rosalie and tell her. Typical, it would happen now, wouldn't it? Especially after she's finally agreed that the kids could have a dog.'

'She actually agreed, did she?' Polly asked incredulously. She had witnessed several of the discussions about a dog over the years since Sarah's appendectomy which, if she remembered correctly, was when the subject was first raised.

'Yes, she thinks they're now both old enough to look after it. And, I think secretly that she likes the thought of having something around the house with her all day – you know, as company.'

'You did warn her, didn't you, that she'd probably be the one who ended up taking it for walks, picking up its poo, feeding it, grooming it and vacuuming the hairs when it's moulting, which I think is most of the time? Not to mention the cost - food, vet's bills and all that.'

Henry frowned as he listened. It was unlike Polly to be so negative.

'I'll help with the money side of things,' he said quietly. 'I've told Rosalie not to worry about that.'

Henry scanned the customers in the pub, most of whom he knew well, with the exception of one group of four occupying the table nearest to the door. They looked like two retired couples and were nursing near-empty glasses. Polly followed his gaze.

'Right, I'll go and see if they want refills,' she said.

'And if you do hear talk of any litters of puppies, let me know, will you please?' Henry added. 'Meanwhile, like I said, I'd better go and ring Rosalie, although she'll probably be back outside in the garden again by now.' Polly raised her eyebrows in question. 'I interrupted her weeding when I arrived.'

'Right,' Polly said nodding knowingly. 'I wondered why she'd been so keen to have a chat with you.'

Chapter 37

Rosalie admitted she felt disappointed when this first puppy became unavailable.

'We'll have to find something else for the twins' birthdays,' Henry said.

'I'll sort out a couple of smaller gifts, but I think they'd probably appreciate money rather than us spending a fortune on something they don't want,' Rosalie responded.

'Teenagers, eh?' Henry stated with amusement. When he and Rosalie were that age, their worlds were as carefree as they hoped Duncan and Sarah's were. Although they were both thinking the same thing - that, at their age, their catastrophe had yet to happen - neither said anymore. They were both aware that memories of their lives would always be divided by that dreadful day: there was *before* their parents died - with its light, sunny and carefree days; and *after*, when the heavy darkness and guilt descended, taking away their younger selves and replacing them with a desperate searching question - why them?

Three weeks later, Duncan cornered his father.

'Why don't we get Mum a puppy for her birthday?' he asked.

'That might be a good idea, son,' Henry agreed with suspicion. 'Let me have a think about it.'

Henry chose a quiet moment and mentioned this to Rosalie again. He was pleased when she agreed.

A week before Rosalie's thirty-third birthday, Henry had been in Cliffend and, on the way home, he called into Bladestraw's, the vets' surgery.

'Do you happen to know of anyone with puppies for sale?' he enquired of the receptionist. She directed him to the general noticeboard in the waiting area. Dotted amongst information posters were several *Pets For Sale* cards. He noted the telephone number of a farmer called Loggen in Bexnith, a village about five miles north of Pepper Hill. Loggen was advertising 'Labrador pups for sale. Ready from the first week in April onwards'. Henry dialled as soon as he returned to The Fighting Cock.

'Come over and see me. I've only got three left now and two of those have been spoken for. I'll keep the last one in reserve for you - it's a chocolate, a dog, colour's a throw-back from its grandsire. The bitch is yellow, the sire black and all bar one pup came out black as well. Only the odd little chap left now. What did you say your name was? Stickleback?'

'Yes, Henry Stickleback.'

'Right. I'll just write that down with your phone number. What is it?'

Henry recited his number.

'Are you related to the chap who runs The Fighting Cock over in Ashfield?' the farmer asked.

'Yes. That's me.'

'Okay. Well, we had a do there a couple of months ago, meal for eight. Just after Valentine's, round about the time the pups were born, if I remember correctly. You set the tables up right near the fire - a real fire.' Henry remembered the party now. 'Food was excellent. Who was that lovely bar maid, by the way?'

'I think you probably mean Polly,' Henry replied. He wondered if he should explain that Polly was gay but none the less was attractive to men. But he thought this might cause embarrassment and he didn't want to discourage this gentleman from visiting the pub again.

'Good,' Loggen continued. 'Well, I can see the pup'll be going to a good home. And be fed well – you have to be careful with Labradors, though. I once heard a vet say you only know when a Lab is dead because it finally stops eating. Ha-ha.'

'Oh.' Henry was a little disturbed by this comment, especially after the demise of the pup Max had tried to sell him. He didn't quite know how to respond and wasn't sure if he could trust this man. But he said, 'I'll see you in a couple of days then.'

As arranged, Henry drove over to Loggen's farm at Bexnith.

'Here they are,' Loggen said with some pride as he led Henry to the barn.

Inside, Henry breathed in the dust from the straw, soil, sawdust and pasture detritus that outbuildings tended to accumulate. Penned off with rectangular bales in the corner, a yellow bitch lay on a deep bed of straw suckling three pups, two black and one brown.

'The pups have weaned but, like all young'uns, they'll take advantage of free milk if they can get it.' He seemed to laugh at his own joke, although Henry couldn't see what was funny; surely this was a fact of life. 'Four have already gone,' he continued. 'And these two here …' He pointed with his walking stick at the two black ones, '… as I said on the phone, are already spoken for. But that little chap …' The end of the stick moved towards the last one, a tiny, chocolate coloured dog-puppy; '… is available.'

'Let me have a proper look at him then. Will the mother mind?' Henry asked, thinking that Rosalie would probably have killed anyone she thought would take her babies away from her, including him, their father. In fact, especially him.

'No, no. Not so long as I'm here with you. Otherwise she might think you're about to steal one of her li'luns and take a chunk out of you.'

'Well, I suppose, from her point of view, that's exactly what I am going to do,' Henry stated. He carefully leaned over into the penned area and the bitch immediately became, although not agitated, certainly a little wary. She stood up and very definitely placed her own body between Henry and her pups.

'Let me,' the farmer said as he stepped over the bales. 'Come on, Lady. I'm sorry but you've got to let them go.' To Henry he explained, 'She was a bit miffed when the others went, so I think she's guarding these more carefully.' He looked back at the mother and added, 'bet you'll be glad to have a bit of peace and quiet again when they've all gone, though, won't you, old gal?'

He moved quietly and gently. Lady looked up hopefully at him and wagged her tail. She licked her lips as he bent towards the pups who were searching for the teats that had been abruptly pulled out of their mouths. He bent down, rubbed the top of Lady's head then picked up the designated puppy.

Holding the creature confidently with his palm under its stomach, his fingers on its chest and between its front legs, he held it up for Henry to take. The pup's limbs flailed in the air, his head bobbed uncomfortably and his skin wrinkled then unfolded as he turned as far as he could, constrained as he was in the farmer's hand.

A shaft of sun shone on the soft fur which Henry could see comprised colours from light ginger to almost mahogany brown, giving an overall effect of milk chocolate. As he took the pup, he felt a loose layer of fat beneath the coat protecting the solid little body of bone and quivering muscle. He could also feel a regular and rapid heartbeat from its chest. He studied him hard – not, Henry admitted to himself, that he could distinguish good canine features from bad.

The pup stared at Henry, but his blue eyes were not in focus. He sniffed the air in an attempt to identify who or what was holding him away from the safety of his mother. Henry saw the stubby legs and disproportionately large paws with their slender curved claws and sturdy pads supporting each individual toe. The tail, wide at the rump but tapering to a thin, whip-like end with a dainty curl upwards, was wagging furiously, but more to aid his balance than in delight.

The pup had a definite smell: milk, poo, straw and something else – something unique. Henry had never smelt it before, but it would remind him of this moment throughout the pup's life, in the same way that, whenever customers brought very young babies into the pub, or he saw them in the street on one of his rare trips out, he would instantly be transported back to the moments after the twins' births when he held them, first Sarah, then Duncan.

He continued to inspect the pup, whose brown nose was tinged pink on the inside of the continually tweaking nostrils. In fact wherever skin showed, it was flesh-coloured pink – the rims of his eyes, around his claws and pads and his belly. He yawned widely, displaying pink gums, white needle-like teeth and a thick, fleshy tongue. He closed his eyes and twitched his whiskers, then licked his lips and swallowed rapidly.

The pup then whimpered; the bitch's ears were instantly alert. She leapt easily over the straw bale and sniffed agitatedly at Henry's trousers, her claws clipping the concrete floor. She then stood on her hind legs, teats dangling underneath in a damp and undignified display of her maternal right to protect. She pawed at Henry's elbow.

'Get down, Lady,' Loggen ordered. 'He won't harm him.'

Lady flashed a glare of resentment at her master but promptly obeyed and planted both front paws on one of Henry's feet.

Suddenly, the pup's wrinkle-skinned, sturdy little legs began to flap again and he leant forward in an attempt to reach his mother. He whimpered and Lady responded by jumping up at Henry again.

'I'll have him,' Henry said decisively, suddenly feeling proprietorial. 'Yes. If Rosalie doesn't want him, I'll keep him at the pub.'

Chapter 38

Rosalie's thirty-third birthday was on 14th April. It was a Thursday, the day before the children returned to school after their Easter holiday. Henry thought it was crazy that they should start on a Friday, but Duncan explained the beginning of term was staggered for the different year groups; the younger ones returning on the Thursday, the twins' group on Friday and the students taking exams this year not until Monday. He was secretly pleased they would be at home for Rosalie's birthday, the puppy's first day with them.

'Dad's bringing your present over later,' Duncan informed his mother at breakfast time.

She could see that her son was excited. Sarah, also bursting with enthusiasm, seemed to have her hand clamped permanently over her mouth in an attempt not to let the secret escape. Rosalie smiled indulgently as she opened their card. *Happy Birthday to the best Mum in the world,* Sarah had written exuberantly with many kisses below. Duncan was a little more reserved - *Happy Birthday Mum, from Duncan.* With one X.

Henry had wisely told Rosalie he was collecting the puppy on the morning of her birthday. Duncan and Sarah, however, believed it would be a surprise.

Sarah had been shopping with her Dad during the previous week to purchase a basket for the pup, together with food, bowls, blankets, a collar and lead, plus toys, a soft brush, and chewing sticks to help with teething. These were all now in the boot of Henry's car as he drove to Bexnith. He had arranged to meet Loggen at ten o'clock and intended to drive straight to Pepper Hill afterwards.

Rosalie and Henry had not exchanged gifts since before their fateful wedding day, but he had bought a birthday present for his estranged wife this year, the puppy itself was from the Sarah and Duncan. And, although he knew this particular gift would not set a precedent, he hoped it would nevertheless be appreciated. It was a book entitled *How To Look After Your New Puppy*. He predicted that Rosalie would presume the printed word could not tell her anything she didn't already know or couldn't work out for herself, but he hoped the twins would both read it and put into practice some of the advice given.

The man at the pet shop in Cliffend recommended that, besides all the other paraphernalia, Henry should purchase a pet carrier - which Henry thought looked like a cage. It was enormous, but the shop owner had assured him it was the correct size for an adult Labrador. Henry'd had to fold down the back seats and manoeuvre it into the car through the boot hatch.

The puppy was placed in the carrier for the journey from Bexnith to Pepper Hill. He looked tiny and lost, even tucked into a blanket inside. He obviously missed his mother and siblings, and was unaccustomed to the motion of this strange and frightening experience. He cried continually.

Henry wished he'd thought to ask one of the twins to come and keep the pup company for its first journey. His lack of experience was already showing, because the puppy was very distressed and he wondered if he'd done the right thing in buying it. He couldn't reach to stroke him, all he could offer were soothing words, but these didn't seem to comfort him. The pitch and volume of his fear and misery rose, accompanied by the unmistakable smell of poo filling the air inside the car. In despair, Henry pressed the button to lower the driver's window, concluding he would have to return to The Fighting Cock to clean up. He wondered if he could persuade Polly to sit with him from Ashfield to Pepper Hill.

Unfortunately, Polly had not yet arrived at the pub. Mrs Mawberry refused to help, stating quite categorically that 'clearing up after a puking and pooping pup was definitely not in my job description!'

Henry removed the soiled blanket and wrapped an old towel around the pup. He cradled him, despite the drool cascading from both corners of his mouth. Wiping this away, Henry stroked him with strong but firm caresses. Eventually, the pup fell asleep and Henry carefully placed him back in the carrier.

He finally set off for the Old Police House, but was soon caught behind a tractor towing a very wide crop-spraying apparatus. During the crawl to Pepper Hill, he recalled Loggen's advice about making an appointment with a local vet (he had, of course, recommended Bladestraw's in Cliffend, where Henry found his advertisement) to start the pup's vaccination programme.

'And he will have to be microchipped - well, it isn't a legal requirement yet, but the farmer recommended it, especially if you're going to register his pedigree,' Henry told Rosalie as he handed over the pup. 'Mind you, I looked into all that - bloody expensive it is too. If you aren't going to use him to breed from, I wouldn't bother. But I did find out from the paperwork that his birthday is 16th February.'

Henry could see Rosalie wasn't listening. She was holding the puppy with the same maternal possessiveness as when the twins were born.

'Oh, let me have a hold,' Sarah stated a little too loudly. She reached forward and almost levered him from Rosalie. This made the pup tremble and whimper.

'You'll have to learn to be a bit quieter around him while he's still young,' Rosalie warned as she removed Sarah's hands whilst still cradling the puppy. 'And be gentle. He isn't one of your old toys that you and Duncan used to fight over, you know.'

Sarah's face switched from bright and hopeful to disappointed and hurt. Having not had any previous experience of puppies - or any young creature for that matter - she did not realise she was being noisy or inappropriate, or that she might upset him.

Duncan and Henry both observed this unfortunate exchange.

'Come on you kids,' Henry cajoled. 'Mum'll need a lot of help looking after him. Shall we have a look in the paper to see if there're any puppy training classes that he can go to in a few weeks' time? I'm sure you'll all be able to share him, but I think that today, as he is very frightened and missing his own mother, it might be a nice idea to let your Mum spend time with him.'

Henry looked at Sarah, whose blue eyes were shining. She had folded her arms across her front - not, as many teenage girls did, to hide their newly developing and unfamiliar figures, but as though in an effort to comfort herself.

Duncan watched silently. He had wanted a puppy for so long, but suddenly it seemed as if an intruder had gate-crashed their family. He felt confused.

A little while later, when everyone was more settled and Rosalie had finally relinquished her hold on the newly named Ben to the twins, they began to understand the demands of their new pet.

It was a sobering lesson for fourteen-year-olds. Inside the Old Police House in everyday life, Duncan had to take a lead role - not exactly be the man of the house, but sometimes both his Mum and sister needed advice and help from a different, a masculine, point of view.

And he was the tallest. Although he would never say this in front of them, he knew he was also the strongest. He now looked over to Henry, who had somehow been allowed to remain with them since Ben's arrival.

Henry smiled knowingly at his son: for him, the realisation that parents needed their children's help had come the day he discovered Woody's secret stash of whisky on the shelf under the bar near the cash till at The Fighting Cock. He had learnt that Nora, from then onwards, relied on him not to act like a child. To make mistakes as he grew, yes; but not to be unreasonably demanding for the sake of it.

When it was Duncan's turn to hold Ben, he relished the strange warmth and weight of the squirming, hairy little body on his lap. Then he discovered that the warmth was also wet.

'Arhhh! He's just piddled on me!' he exclaimed, holding Ben at arm's length away from him and back towards his sister.

Ben whimpered at having been disturbed. Sarah quickly retrieved him. She had been quietly reading *How To Look After Your New Puppy*. Even now, only a few pages into the book, she felt much more informed and superior to her brother.

'You have to take him out to the garden every hour, regardless of whether or not he asks to go,' Sarah said.

'Come on little fella, we'll go and let you explore …'

'You can't let him out without a lead,' Rosalie interjected. 'And he hasn't got used to his collar yet.'

The bright red collar was in stark contrast to his brown coat; Sarah touched it gently then checked he hadn't grown in the last few minutes and that she could still place three fingers between the pup's neck and the leather.

'Where's his lead?' Henry asked.

'It should be with the bed and bowls and his food. My goodness, when do we feed him? When did he last have something to eat?' Sarah asked urgently.

'Well, I expect he was fed at the farm before I collected him,' Henry said. 'But he was sick on the way here. Perhaps you could leave it a while longer and let his stomach settle a bit more then try him with just a little. I'll bring the basket and things in. He might need a drink, though.'

'Where shall I put all this?' Henry asked Rosalie a few minutes later as he carried in the new dog bed - a plastic basket-shaped shell with a soft padded cover inside - heaped up with everything Ben could ever need, including the lead.

'Here, let me give him some water,' Duncan offered, retrieving the bowl from the basket. He filled it and placed it on the kitchen floor. Sarah carried Ben through from the living room and put him in front of it. His head bobbed up and down as he sniffed the surface before he pounced forward and plunged his front feet in it. He pawed at it then started to scrab as if he was digging a hole. The water sprayed up over his plump, little chocolate body and he panted, showing his pink tongue and sharp, white teeth.

'No, stop it, Ben,' Rosalie said, attempting not to shout as she received a spray of water. But then she appreciated the comical side of the scene and laughed as much as the twins. A pool gathered around the bowl as Ben splashed wildly, whining and yapping as he did so. Sarah tried to mop up the spillage while Duncan encouraged the pup by saying,

'Go for it, mate!'

Henry stood slightly behind everyone else as they all watched Ben's antics.

'Thanks Dad,' Sarah said, looking up as she spoke. She gave Henry the smile that would always win him over no matter what happened - which, up until this moment had been no worse than setting fire to the chip pan in Rosalie's absence.

'Right, well I've got to get back to the pub.' Henry bent forward and stretched his hand over to coax the back of Ben's head, which was wet from the water digging.

'Yes, thanks Henry,' Rosalie added, looking up at him and treating him to the same smile as their daughter had just two minutes earlier.

Henry's heart thumped painfully as he quietly slipped away. Walking back to his car, he felt lost and excluded but, at the same time, he was pleased to be part of a plan that seemed to have brought so much fun into their lives.

Chapter 39

George's team at MaCold had completed their latest project ahead of schedule; despite this, he couldn't leave Aberdeen in time to be home for Rosalie's birthday on the Thursday. Instead, he spent the day finishing one or two personal tasks before setting off on the long drive after lunch the following day.

George's next planned assignment was not due to start for another six weeks. For a few months, he would be based at MaCold's Cliffend yard - formerly Tasker's where he had started work whilst still attending school.

He had decided to sell his flat in Aberdeen because, even if he did return to the Granite City at some time in the future, he thought it would be easier to rent somewhere to live. The property held no nostalgia for him. He had bought it as an investment, but it was unlikely to have gained any substantial value during his ownership. It was really just a base where he slept, sometimes relaxed and ate, but it was not a home. He was now happy to let the estate agents handle the sale.

George did not attempt the entire journey back to Pepper Hill in one day; he stopped overnight at the hotel he had used regularly over the years. He hadn't told Rosie the exact details of his schedule, just that he would arrive at the Old Police House late Saturday morning.

'Happy birthday for Thursday, Rosie,' he said when she opened the front door to him. He interpreted his sister's scowl as a question as to why he hadn't let himself in, rather than because he used her shortened name. 'Sorry, my key's buried somewhere in my luggage. And sorry I missed your actual birthday.' He realised he'd just apologised twice in the first three sentences he'd uttered. As he stepped into the hall, he held out his arms to give his big sister a hug.

'I'll put the kettle on,' she said when she stepped away and retreated to the kitchen.

George moved into the living room where Sarah was impatiently watching over Ben who, despite the noise of an arrival, was still asleep in his basket. Duncan stood anxiously behind them.

'Hello, mate,' George said to his nephew. He was about to stretch out his arms to him as well when he sensed a reluctance. He extended his hand instead and Duncan gratefully took it. Although it was a brief shake, George could feel Duncan's sapling frame was growing into adult strength.

In contrast, as soon as Sarah could wrench herself away from the puppy's basket, she flung herself at her uncle and held her arms around his neck while he lifted her feet off the ground in a genuinely happy greeting. Rosalie watched with impatience.

'My *favourite* uncle,' Sarah said when he set her back on the ground.

'I'm your *only* uncle,' George reminded her with a smile.

He glanced down at his niece. She was now about the same height as Rosie, and therefore considerably shorter than both him and her brother. She probably would not grow much taller. George chuckled when he compared the twins to himself and his sister. He clearly remembered how much bigger he was than Rosie when their parents died. Duncan would be about the same age now as he was then, although of course Rosie would've been two years older than Sarah.

'And you'll have to wait for your present, young lady. I couldn't find what I wanted to get you in Aberdeen, so I'll have to have a look next time I'm in town.' He turned and said, 'Rosie, yours is in the car, no doubt somewhere with my key.'

'I'm not just glad to see you because you might've brought me a present,' Sarah said with a tone of hurt sounding in her voice. 'I wanted to show you Ben.' She stooped down to the basket again. 'But he's asleep.'

George crouched next to Sarah and gently touched the soft, brown fur of the puppy's flank.

'How are you all getting on with your new family member?' he asked. 'You haven't allocated him my bedroom have you?'

'No.' Sarah was eager to explain. 'The first night, Mum slept downstairs in here on the sofa while he was in his basket - we thought he might be lonely after being used to sleeping with his Mum and all his brothers and sisters. Last night, I stayed with him.'

'Yes, but you didn't let him out in time when he woke up, and he weed on the floor,' Rosalie interjected.

Sarah winced and George could see her enthusiasm visibly deflate.

'At least he'd got as far as the kitchen, so it was easy to clean up off the floor - easier than the carpet, anyway.' Rosalie turned to her brother to explain, 'I want to get him into the habit of going outside as soon as he wakes up just in case he needs to go to the toilet.'

Sarah started to stroke Ben.

'Don't wake him up when he is asleep,' Rosalie snapped.

Sarah withdrew her hand and stood up again. She looked at her mother with a bewildered expression.

George was a little surprised at Rosie's sharpness. Duncan, however, was accustomed to his mother's outbursts, especially towards his sister. He often thought she singled Sarah out for criticism for no reason; sometimes she seemed to be as angry with Sarah as she was with Henry.

'We'll take Ben out as soon as he wakes up, Sarah. Want to come, Uncle George?' Duncan offered in an attempt to defuse the atmosphere.

'We'll see,' George said quietly, understanding that Duncan was trying to broker peace. 'Maybe you and Sarah could see to him while I get settled.' *And speak to your mother about her temper,* he added in his thoughts.

'Right then, who would like a cup of coffee?' Rosalie asked.

'Yes, please,' they all replied in chorus.

'You haven't tried your Dad's famous mixture of tea and coffee, have you?' George asked the twins.

'Not likely,' Sarah said emphatically. 'The smell is enough to put me off.'

'I had a little one day,' Duncan admitted. Rosalie tried not to show her surprise. 'But it was bloody awful! Shan't try it again!'

'Good,' Rosalie said. 'And mind your language, please. You're not at the pub now. Here,' and she handed around the mugs of coffee. 'We can see Ben from the kitchen table if we go and sit down,' she directed.

Ben continued to sleep, oblivious to those around him.

'How long are you staying?' Rosalie asked George when they had settled. 'Not that you have to say, it's your home as much as ours. I meant for me to know how much extra to buy when I'm shopping for food and things.'

'Well, I'm home for a break. We've just finished a big

project in Scotland and there's a new one starting in Cliffend in six weeks' time. I'm waiting to be told when to report at the office.'

'Ben's waking up,' Sarah said, indicating to the dog basket. 'I'll take him out. Come on, Duncan.' She stood up, retrieved Ben's lead and went through into the living room. She clipped it onto his collar before the puppy had time to finish yawning. She picked him up and scurried out into the garden, avoiding Rosalie's eyes as she did so. Duncan followed.

'Well, d'you want to put your things upstairs while I start cooking lunch?' Rosalie asked George as she finished her coffee and started to gather up the mugs.

'In a minute. First, I want to know why you're in such a bad mood.'

'I'm not in a *bad mood,* as you put it,' she retorted defensively.

'Then, why are you snapping at Sarah? She looked really upset at one point there.' George kept his voice even; he was quite dismayed at the obvious antagonism between his sister and her daughter.

'Oh, I don't know.' Rosalie sighed as she sat back down at the table. 'She never seems to do as I tell her to – look at the mess with Ben! And then she contradicts everything I say. She seems much worse after she's been to stay at the pub. And of course now the twins have the pup, I've told them they can't just go swanning off over there whenever they want and leave me here to look after him.'

George took a deep breath. Looking straight at his sister and in full knowledge that she would not like his next words, he ventured, 'Rosie, tell me if I'm wrong in this, but wasn't Ben your birthday present? Wasn't it you, in the end, who suggested the idea to Henry?'

'Yes, but that was only because the kids had been crazing me for ages to get a pet.'

'You told me, when we spoke on the telephone about it, that you knew you would end up looking after it, didn't you?'

'Yes, but I thought it would be more than two days before they got fed up!'

George could see that Rosalie was very angry now. They remained silent for a few minutes, staring at each other. George thought his sister seemed to grow older each time he returned home. But every time he left PepperAsh, he shut the door on the trials and dramas here, and concentrated on his life elsewhere. Rosie was only thirty-three, but she looked tired and careworn. And she needed to brush her hair.

In contrast, Rosalie saw her younger brother had gained a little weight; he had a healthy, outdoor complexion. He looked happy; after all, he was leading the life he wanted.

Rosalie relented. 'I'm just tired of always being the one who has to tell them what to do and then listening to the arguments when they don't want to.'

'Why, who has been doing – or not doing – what?'

'Sarah doesn't want to stay on at school for her A-levels. She's got some silly notion about becoming a travel agent or something. She wants to go and work abroad. She's been learning French at school, but the careers officer said she would need to study at least two languages, and spend a summer in one of the countries. She's only fourteen now, but expects to take a six-week holiday abroad the year after next. I've said no. I know she'll be sixteen then, and she's said that a couple of friends would go as well. But she won't be old enough. Besides which, I can't afford it ...'

'You can, you know. And I expect Sarah knows that too,' George interrupted.

'Yes, I know, we still have money from Mum and Dad, and no doubt Henry would contribute - not that he knows any of this. At least I don't think he does.'

'Why don't you talk to him?' George suggested, realising this would provoke an angry response. But Rosie surprised him.

'I can't see him being too pleased if his *favourite* twin disappeared.'

'That sounds as if you think he thinks more of Sarah than Duncan.'

'Well, it's obvious he does,' Rosie retorted furiously. 'And if you actually bothered to spend any time here with your family, you'd be able to see for yourself!'

George looked up sharply at Rosie's face, surprised at the venom in her voice. She began to blush and, to hide her embarrassment, she moved quickly across the kitchen to the sink. She lifted the vegetables out of their rack and started to prepare lunch. But George felt he could not ignore this comment.

'My job takes me away, you know that, Rosie. I get home when I can, but I work long hours and, if something needs to be done, I have to see it though!'

'You could have stayed at MaCold's place in Cliffend.'

'I would still be just an engineer in their fabrication yard - one of half a dozen. I wanted to get on, work my way up. And to do that, I had to go where the projects were.'

'And that just happened to be at the other end of the country. Meanwhile leaving me here to look after the house and the twins.'

'I'm sorry that you feel the house is a burden, Rosie. It's your home, and every house - home - needs a certain amount of looking after. Even if you were living at Tidal Reach you'd have to do maintenance. And as for you bringing up the twins on your own, you've brought that situation on yourself. You could be living with Henry - either at the pub or across the road from there.'

'You don't know anything about Henry and me!' she shouted. George hoped the twins hadn't heard. He stood up and looked out of the window down the garden towards where they were walking with Ben.

Sarah was training the puppy to heel. Although he had occasional distractions, he was responding well. When he lay down on the grass, either through tiredness or boredom - George was not an expert on puppies and didn't pretend to know which - she picked him up and held him. As Duncan stroked the little dog in his sister's arms, George could see they were smiling. George breathed in, not enjoying the situation with his sister, but understanding that he needed to intervene.

'What are they doing out there?' Rosalie asked.

'Just training the pup to walk on the lead.'

'Oh, I expect they'll spoil him and, when he won't do as they want, they'll just hand him back to me.'

'They look as if they're coping fine.' George was beginning to feel irritated. 'Look, Rosie ...'

'Don't call me Rosie!'

'I understand that you get a bit overwhelmed at times, but criticising the kids - particularly Sarah - won't put things right. Especially when the problem is with you and Henry.'

'It isn't all about us. Sarah just seems to ...' Rosalie did not finish her sentence. She suddenly remembered the argument she'd had with her own mother just before Annie and Derek left for their fateful holiday. George sensed this change.

'You'll drive her away, you know,' he ventured softly. 'It actually sounds as if you're jealous of her. And if you are, Rosie, you need to ask yourself why? Are you so dissatisfied with your own life that you have to take it out on your daughter?'

Rosalie remained silent. The potatoes were on the chopping board and she selected one to peel then picked up the knife.

George decided it was time to leave her and go outside to join the twins.

Chapter 40

After lunch, Sarah gathered Ben into her arms and carried him into the garden. In silence, George helped Rosalie with the washing and drying up, and then looked out of the kitchen window. The sun was shining, illuminating the newly green shoots on the trees. He could see that the grass would soon need cutting, and piles of last year's leaves should be tidied from the flower beds. A restlessness crept over him and he felt guilty for not helping Rosie as much as he felt he ought.

'I'll just go out and keep Sarah and the puppy company for a few minutes,' he told his sister.

Rosalie sniffed. 'Well, I have to slip over to Poskett's in a little while. Duncan's got football practice this afternoon, so that leaves Sarah looking after Ben.'

As George approached his niece, he could hear her encouraging Ben to '"Go toilet" and "Do wee-wee".'

'Does that work?' George asked. 'Telling him to "Go Toilet" like that, I mean?'

'It's what it says in the book to say,' Sarah replied, her smile broad with genuine pleasure that someone was taking an interest. But George looked confused. 'The *How To Look After Your New Puppy* book that Dad bought Mum,' she explained. 'I've read it – twice. It says you have to use distinct words or short phrases when teaching your new puppy, especially with toilet training.'

'Right.' George drew out the word, unable to keep the note of scepticism out of his voice. He looked downwards. Ben took two or three rather awkward steps forward, then hunched his back over his front paws, lifted his tail and strained.

'There's a good boy, Ben. Good boy! Isn't he a good boy, Uncle George?' Sarah enthused.

George had to look away. He did not know whether to laugh or be disgusted as Ben produced a sausage-like line of yellowy-brown poo which curled into a small circle on the ground. Steam rose from the heap and an unpleasant smell soon reached George nostrils.

As soon as Ben had finished, Sarah made an extravagant fuss of him before pulling out a black plastic bag from her pocket.

'Now you pick it up like this,' she began to explain. Again, George had to turn his head; he was suddenly reminded of the mess in the twins' nappies Rosie changed when they were babies. He shook away the images.

Ben, obviously confident that all was well with the world, began to play. His ears flapped as he moved; then he pulled them comically forward to attention whilst momentarily concentrating on a sound inaudible to human hearing. His mouth was open and he looked as though he was smiling; his little white teeth gleamed from under his pink tongue which bounced up and down in time with his excited breathing. He bounded away from them until he reached the end of his lead. He then turned to the side and started to run again, which resulted in him winding it around Sarah's leg. If he noticed the circle was decreasing, he showed no sign. His short legs were out of proportion with his body, and his feet were still enormous in comparison. But he looked as if he was having fun, which made George laugh.

Sarah placed the plastic dog poo bag over her hand like a mitten, she then bent down and picked up the still steaming pile. She folded the top of the bag over the offensive matter leaving it safely inside. She pulled the two top corners together into a knot to form a seal.

'See, it's easy. Just like when the butcher picks minced beef up from the tray on the counter. It can now go in the bin – best to double wrap it, though,' she explained as she tried to move but found she was tangled by Ben's lead.

Ben was now sitting down on his fat little bottom, wrinkles rolling from his shoulders downward in time with his frantic panting. He yawned widely, finishing with a high-pitched yelp of contentment before opening his mouth again.

'I'll leave the poo-picking to you, if you don't mind, Sarah,' George said, stooping forward and playing with the pup.

Ben rolled over onto his back. His legs paddled in the air as he squirmed from side to side while George rubbed his tummy.

'He likes that,' Sarah said as she freed herself.

George crouched down properly and continued. Suddenly, one of Ben's rear legs started to kick as if he were trying to scratch an invisible itch. They both laughed.

'He'll let you tickle him all day like that,' Sarah said.

'Yes, I expect he would,' George agreed. 'He seems to like attention.' He remembered the hours he had spent playing with the twins when they were younger.

George did not usually enjoy reminiscing: he preferred to deal with the problems of the moment and then move on, only referencing the past if it helped the present or prepared for the future. He could not understand Rosie's obsession with punishing Henry; in fact, George saw it as a very selfish way of depriving the twins of their father. He realised his brother-in-law had made a serious mistake in digging up the locket and replacing his and Rosalie's parents' photographs with the diamond from Nora's engagement ring. But, he thought impatiently, it was time they tried to forget the episode.

'It's just attention,' Sarah informed him, referring to Ben – and dogs in general. 'I read about it in the book.'

'Ah, yes. The book! I think I'd like to read this famous book as well, if that's okay.'

'Yes, of course,' Sarah enthused. 'It's got lots of helpful tips. For instance, dogs like company, and they form bonds with the people who look after them and spend time with them. Their human families imitate their packs in the wild. They have a hierarchy, with some being more dominant than others, but they all submit to one pack leader.'

'And who d'you think is the *pack leader* in his little family then?'

'Well, Mum thinks she is. And I suppose she is, because she's been there with him the most and, of course, she'll have to look after him when we're at school. But I think he prefers to be with me.'

George smiled to himself. 'Yes, I'm sure he does too.' He stood up. 'Well, as soon as your mother gets back from the shop, I've got to go into Cliffend.'

'Oh, can I come?' Sarah asked hopefully.

'You would be very welcome to, Sarah. But there's only one problem, isn't there?' Sarah did not comprehend, so George asked patiently, 'if you want to come with me and Duncan is playing football, who's going to watch Ben?' He raised his eyebrows towards his niece to emphasise the importance of the question.

Chapter 41

George stopped at The Fighting Cock late on the Saturday afternoon on his way home from Cliffend.

'Hello there,' Henry greeted as he walked in. 'How are you?' They extended hands, shook and grinned at each other.

'Fine, yeah, good, thank you,' George replied.

'Gosh, you're a sight for sore eyes, you know!' Henry realised that he hadn't seen George for almost a year: they had missed each other when he previously visited PepperAsh. He now noticed that George seemed to have gained a little weight and his hairline was beginning to recede. But he still looked the same - remarkably like Rosalie, but different in essence; he smiled more easily and seemed relaxed.

However, when George's eyes wandered around the lounge-bar of The Fighting Cock, the landlord felt uncomfortable.

George observed that the pub's interior was looking slightly dingy and dishevelled. The plush blue upholstery was turning threadbare and brown along the edges of the seats and on the arms where customers' elbows rested. The table surfaces were suffering the ravages of damp glass-bottoms and spillages, despite the number of beer mats available. The dark varnish was worn off in places, allowing the light wood underneath to show, and there were chips and scuffs along the edges. The carpet had several suspicious stains, plus a couple of scorch marks around the hearth area.

Henry followed George's gaze. 'Yeah, I know it could do

with decorating,' he said to pre-empt any comments. 'But they're talking about bringing a smoking ban into all public places soon, so I'll wait and have it done after that.'

'Good thinking,' George remarked.

'Anyway, what've you been up to recently?'

'Well, I'm home for a break. We've just finished a big project in Scotland and there's a new one starting in Cliffend soon. So I thought I'd come and show my face around here for a while, see what big sister is up to, you know? Good move with the puppy, by the way, they're all besotted - especially Sarah.'

'Let's hope the fascination lasts and it doesn't turn out to be a nine-day-wonder.'

'No, I think you're safe there. Rosie really is smitten. She looks like she did when the kids were little - all protective and bossy,' George said as he leant on the bar.

'She's always been like that, as you well know,' Henry joked. He held up a pint glass and indicated to George who nodded in reply. 'Well, bossy anyway.'

As they were speaking, a group of five younger people entered the bar, three women and two men. They were all wearing trainers, shorts and T-shirts. The bare skin on their arms and legs was red from exposure to the spring sunshine and their complexions pink; they looked as if they had been exerting a lot of energy. Cyclists, Henry deduced, but not the serious kind; it was lovely day for getting out in the fresh air. Not, he thought, that he would have a chance to.

Four broke off naturally into two couples, leaving one young woman on her own. George glanced at them as they chose their seats around a table. One of the men took their orders then walked up to the bar and stood next to him. They acknowledged each other with a nod.

Normally George wouldn't have taken much notice of other customers. But something made him recall the last leg of a long train journey back to PepperAsh when a young lady had sat down next to him. He turned around again and saw her talking to the others at the table. She looked up and across at him. She gave a shy smile.

The name Tina came into his mind.

Chapter 42

On Monday morning, the twins caught the bus to go to school, leaving Ben with Rosalie and George at the Old Police House. Rosalie had a list of jobs to do and hoped George would help.

'And I have to take the puppy to Bladestraw, the vet in Cliffend this evening for a check-up,' she told him at lunchtime. 'He's got to start his course of vaccinations. Luckily, they have a late surgery on Mondays. We've got an appointment at six-thirty. I'll take the twins with me so the vet can see us all together.'

They set off after school. Sarah sat in the back seat and held Ben on her lap. They had tried to place the pet carrier in Rosalie's car but it was too big. Sarah held Ben defensively, with a towel around him to mop up the dribble and drool. Rosalie wanted to comment that he wouldn't be able to sit like that when he was fully grown, but remained silent when she remembered George questioning her as to why she always seemed so critical of her daughter.

Duncan sat in the front passenger seat but constantly turned to see how Ben was coping with the journey. Rosalie gritted her teeth and ignored them. She was rewarded for her concentration when a lunatic vehicle suddenly appeared around one of the bends travelling very quickly towards them in the middle of the road. Both vehicles swerved to avoid a collision and Rosalie was quite shaken.

When they arrived safely in Bladestraw's car park, Sarah took Ben onto the grassed area surrounding the gravel so he could make himself comfortable. He walked nicely on his lead but liked to sniff everything possible, which slowed the pace of any exercise. On this occasion, however, they did not have to wait long before Ben obliged - despite having *gone* before they climbed into the car. He pooed first.

'You can pick that up!' Duncan told Sarah.

'Don't worry, I'm going to,' Sarah retorted. Whilst she bent over to practise how to safely, discreetly and hygienically pick up dog poo, as demonstrated in the book, Ben took two paces forward and squatted for a very long wee. The twins both laughed at this.

Sarah carried Ben into the surgery, talking quietly to soothe him in this new and strange environment with all its frightening sights and smells and noises. They reported to the receptionist who placed a tick beside their name in the appointment book.

'Take a seat, please. Mr Bladestraw is running on time.'

They sat down on the plastic chairs and Sarah held on to Ben. He yawned and looked around, sniffed, then turned in a circle on Sarah's lap and settled down to sleep.

'Puppies spend up to eighty-five percent of their time asleep,' Sarah advised her mother and brother, imparting more knowledge from the book. She stroked and coaxed Ben, rearranged the buckle on his collar and thumbed the shiny new name tag that George presented to them upon his return from Cliffend on Saturday.

'Just a little souvenir to celebrate Ben's arrival,' he had told them.

After a few minutes Mr Bladestraw opened the door from the consulting room.

'Ben Stickleback?' he called.

Rosalie was surprised that Ben now shared their surname but, on reflection, she supposed it made sense, as there could have been two pets called Ben in the waiting room.

Mr Bladestraw was a tall, thin man with stooped shoulders. His shirt sleeves were rolled up beyond his elbows and exposed the most prominent veins on the underside of his forearms, wrists and hands that Sarah had ever seen.

'Well, he's a fine little chap,' he stated as he felt along Ben's spine, around his hips and down his rear legs, lifting each before straightening and then bending them. He checked his feet, separating each toe with his fingertips. He then examined Ben's shoulders, front feet, and around his neck. He peered into each ear, looked at his eyes, and gently prised open the puppy's mouth to inspect his teeth. Ben seemed bemused at all the attention as he stood on the black-topped examination table in the centre of the consulting room. 'And he's here today for the first of his vaccinations, is he?'

'Yes, that's right,' Rosalie replied.

'Have you owned a dog before, Mrs Stickleback?' he asked when he finished listening to Ben's heart through his stethoscope.

'No. It's my first time - for the children as well. My husband got the name of the farmer who sold him to us off your notice board. Mr Loggen, he lives at Bexnith.'

'Oh yes. I remember. Bitch's name is Lady.'

'Right, well. Yes,' Rosalie murmured. 'I, er, don't know about that. *Bitch,* oh yes, you mean Ben's mother.'

Sarah's face turned scarlet with embarrassment at her mother's misunderstanding.

'A female dog, Mum, is called a *bitch,*' Duncan smirked as he explained.

'I know that!' Rosalie hissed abruptly.

'The sire - father - was a champion gun dog,' the vet

continued. 'But you weren't after a working dog, were you? You just want a pet.'

'Yes.'

'Well, Labradors make very loyal and loving companions. Be firm with him during training, though. And don't feed him too much. He'll always tell you he's hungry.' The latter instructions were given as Mr Bladestraw gathered the loose skin around the back of Ben's neck to inject him. Ben started with surprise but relaxed again when the temporary soreness was dissipated by a firm rub.

Rosalie felt quite proud when Mr Bladestraw complimented their preparations for Ben and his care so far. He said he was confident that Ben would have a good and loving home.

'Right, you two,' Rosalie addressed Sarah and Duncan as they travelled back to Pepper Hill. Duncan was holding Ben this time. But, whilst the puppy adored his young master, he had been more peaceful curled up on Sarah's lap on the way to the vet's. 'We need to sort out a rota for walking Ben. You heard what Mr Bladestraw said, after his second injection in two weeks' time he can start to socialise.'

'I can take him out after school,' Sarah volunteered, claiming the easier of the options. She always left her final preparations until the last minute. Duncan often had to ask the bus driver to wait until his sister appeared through the front door. 'And there's always such a rush before school. Duncan, you could walk him then.'

'Yeah, alright,' Duncan said. He recognised his sister's ruse, but he allowed himself to be manipulated. Life for Sarah was not as simple as it seemed to be for him: complications came in the form of homework, acne and fashion. And finally, maths!

Chapter 43

George left MaCold's at lunchtime and walked into Cliffend town centre. He needed to send a parcel to an ex-colleague from a former project in Aberdeen and thought he would take the opportunity to use the main post office rather than hope to catch Poskett at the end of the day. He had asked Rosie to do this for him, but she insisted that she needed to know exactly what was in the parcel, in case she had to fill out an official form.

'It's just a book about engineering on a nineteenth-century project,' he said, not wishing to explain the technical nature of the content.

'Sounds mysterious,' she had commented, obviously not satisfied and inviting her brother to explain further.

'It's for that chap I told you about ages ago. He used to work at MaCold's. He was offshore when he had appendicitis. He's a librarian now and has started to collect books on engineering.'

'You're sending a book to a librarian? Hasn't he got enough to look after already?' she enquired pointedly. George shook his head and decided to deal with the parcel himself.

When he arrived at the post office in Cliffend, there were three people in front of him, but only one young lady serving at the counter. He waited for his turn and, as no one came in behind him, he chatted to her during his transaction. He leant forward to read the name on her official badge. Miss B Guthrie. She looked familiar.

'I guessed you lived somewhere in PepperAsh,' she commented as she copied the sender's address – the Old

Police House, Pepper Hill - onto the form in her register.

'Yes, well I work away from home most of the time, but I've been back for a few weeks now.'

'D'you work for MaCold then?' she enquired, indicating towards the company's logo on his jacket.

'Yes, good detection. It's Tina, isn't it?' George said with a moment of enlightenment, but was then bewildered by the first name initial on her badge.

'That's right.' She looked up at him. The toughened glass screen with just the slot open at the bottom formed a barrier. It didn't just protect employees from threats or harm from the other side of the counter, but also maintained a professional distance and prevented too much familiarity. Even through this, though, Tina felt an attraction.

George was tanned and muscular, and had blond hair that was beginning to recede. He looked tall, but Tina was sitting down, which made most customers look tall. She noticed his hands were slightly calloused and his clothes were grimy from work. She assumed he was a few years older than her; his manner made her relax.

For his part, George thought Tina was polite and helpful. She tended to frown as she concentrated but her face became round and pretty when she smiled.

'Didn't I see you at the pub the other week?' she asked.

George suddenly remembered.

'Yes, the one in Ashfield, The Fighting Cock?' He felt a slight embarrassment at saying the name out loud. 'It's my brother-in-law's pub. That's my sister's husband.' Brother-in-law could mean that he himself was married and he felt keen to clarify this point. 'It's a long story. The pub name, that is.'

'Yes, I remember the landlord. Big chap, dark hair, ginger

beard - well a muted red, really. Hasn't he got twins? I went there once before and two youngsters were running amok around the bar - not little kids, nearly teenagers, I think. I wouldn't really like to guess their ages.'

'Yes, that's Henry. And his children, Sarah and Duncan,' George confirmed.

'Oh, right. And the landlord's got a strange name, hasn't he? Something fishy?'

'Stickleback. Henry. Like I said, he's married to my sister Rosie - Rosalie. She hates being called Rosie. They don't live together - God, it's complicated.' He paused. 'Anyway, that's my family history. How about you?'

'Well, you were right, I'm Tina, although my full name is Bettina. I don't use it very often, though. But the "B" has to be on my badge.' She looked down at her lapel.

'I like the name Tina,' George said, then cursed himself. Even to his own ears he sounded patronising. 'I, er ...' He cleared his throat and looked directly at her. 'Would you like to go for a drink? We could meet at the pub in Ashfield, or I'll come into town and pick you up.'

Tina blushed a violent red.

'We're not allowed to, er, as our area manager would say *fraternise* with customers, especially while we're at work. Sorry. Anyway, you don't know I haven't got a boyfriend.'

George looked away; it was his turn to be embarrassed.

Eventually, Tina quoted the price for the transaction and he handed her a five pound note. She delivered the change with a fixed smile.

'There you are Mr Tillinger.'

'George,' he confirmed.

'Mr Tillinger' she said with emphasis. 'Your receipt.'

Tina always felt a little annoyed at the men who tried to

flirt with her. 'All part of the job,' her area manager, Arthur Dentforth, had once said during a training session. Tina was not brought up in the conventional family unit. She could never fully trust anyone, especially men, which made her seem either suspicious or naïve. She'd had boyfriends, but relationships never lasted long: she was almost grateful when they finished.

'My name's George,' he repeated. He frowned as he looked at her. 'And I think we met before that time in the pub,' he said. 'On a train from Mattingburgh to here, Cliffend.'

A slow smile crept onto Tina's face. There were still no other customers waiting. She was bored. Life at home was tedious. She had been contemplating whether or not to rent a flat and live by herself, but she did not yet have enough savings. Every time she mentioned this, her grandmother became petulant and irritable.

The post office door opened and another customer entered. George swung around then turned back.

'Right well, thank you, Miss Guthrie, you've been most helpful. Bye.'

The sun was shining outside and George was relieved that he didn't have to return to work that afternoon. On the other hand, he did not want to go back to Pepper Hill just yet either. Whilst working away from PepperAsh and Cliffend, he spent most of his precious free time on his own. Living at the Old Police House, he sometimes found the constant company a little stifling.

He walked across the road to the café opposite the post office, vaguely recalling that the last time he had been in there was many years ago when he'd met Nora during his lunch break from Tasker's. On that occasion, she had intended to buy his new uniform for his return to school. He smiled at the changes in his life since then.

George found the seat by the window was free. From here he could watch the entrance to the post office. But he saw nothing more of Tina.

George returned to the post office the following lunchtime on the pretext of purchasing stamps.

'You could've bought these yesterday,' Miss Guthrie informed him.

He asked her out again. She refused again, but this time with a bemused smile.

George missed a couple of days but found an excuse again on Friday. It was the beginning of the second bank holiday weekend in late May. The weather was sunny and warm again; the town centre was busy. George now had more stamps than he thought he would ever use, but still the young lady behind the counter refused to accept his invitation.

The following day was Saturday and Tina was not working, but such was her curiosity as to whether or not George would visit her again that she drove into town and sat in the café opposite at the table by the window.

Around mid-morning, she saw George enter the post office. He reappeared a few minutes later and strode directly across the street towards her. She could not escape.

'So this is where you're hiding?' he asked accusingly as he approached her table. He now looked even taller than he had on the other side of her counter.

'How did you know?' Tina asked, feeling rather foolish.

'Your colleague with the moustache told me,' he informed her. 'He saw you in here.' George smiled. She smiled back. He sat down.

Chapter 44

Rosalie did not see her brother for the rest of the Bank Holiday weekend. George telephoned Saturday evening to say he was staying in Cliffend and would let her know when he would be home, but he did not give any details.

At lunchtime on Monday in the Old Police House, Sarah asked, 'Where's Uncle George?'

'He's met someone in town,' Rosalie replied. Although she hoped her daughter would not ask too many questions, she couldn't resist infusing a little mystery into her voice.

'But I haven't seen him since Saturday breakfast and I wanted to show him what we've taught Ben to do.'

Rosalie swallowed. She didn't think George would welcome any interruptions at the moment.

The telephone rang. By coincidence, it was George.

'You'll see your uncle later this afternoon,' Rosalie told her daughter when the call ended. 'He's bringing his new girlfriend to the pub for us all to meet each other.'

'What, you and Dad together? Gosh, I hope she knows what she's letting herself in for!'

Before Rosalie could scold her impertinence, Sarah went outside to find Duncan, who was patiently walking Ben round the garden.

The Bank Holiday Monday was extremely busy in The Fighting Cock public house. The weather had been quite hot all weekend, giving the traditional early tourist season in Cliffend and the surrounding area a good start. Henry had asked both Polly and Craig to work. Craig finished his shift an hour or so ago, but Polly was there until closing time.

At around four o'clock, George arrived. He walked in and saw his sister sitting at the table by the empty fireplace whilst Polly served behind the bar. Henry sauntered out from the kitchen, across the room and over to them. Tina was surprised by how tall he was; George towered above her, but Henry was a couple of inches taller than him.

'Henry, Rosie, this is Tina,' George said as an introduction. He then turned to Tina. 'Don't call her *Rosie* by the way, or she'll really flip. It's Rosalie.'

Rosalie blushed as she stood up and wiped her hand down her hip before holding it out to shake. Sometimes, she thought, if he wasn't so much bigger than her, she would flatten her brother - that would show him what it was like for her to *flip*. Then she remembered with shame the only occasion had she had really lost her temper - with Henry, the morning after their wedding.

'Hello,' she said as she silently appraised her future sister-in-law.

Tina's dark hair was loosely tied back, the ends were lighter than nearer the crown, but sun-bleached rather than due to having highlights tinted in. Rosalie estimated Tina was several years younger than George; she was maybe around twenty or twenty-one years old. She did not feel that this was a good thing. But to cover her initial misgivings, she knew she had to be friendly.

'Yes, it's Rosalie - George's older and much wiser sister.' She thought she was being friendly, but her words seemed to cause an instant shadow across Tina's eyes.

As the two women's palms touched, Tina could feel Rosalie's uncertainties in a slight trembling. Yet Rosalie felt only warmth from the younger woman. They relaxed and smiled at each other.

'Pleased to meet you,' said Tina.

'It's nice to meet you too, Tina,' Rosalie said warmly. Tina smiled again before looking back at George. Rosalie could see she was obviously smitten with him.

Rosalie felt somewhat side-lined. Although she had not thought of George's feelings when she initially fell in love with Henry, now she understood that he might have felt a little left out. But he hadn't said anything to her at the time.

'And this is Henry,' George did not describe Henry in terms of relationship; he had already explained the Sticklebacks' circumstances. They too shook hands and Henry asked the new arrivals what they would like to drink. He then walked back to the bar area to fulfil their order.

'So how did you two meet?' Rosalie asked. 'I know it sounds a clichéd question, but it's what everyone wants to know.'

'Well, he's a very persistent chap, that brother of yours, you know. He just kept on coming into the post office,' Tina stated with a grin.

'Yes, it took me a week of asking - and buying stamps I didn't need - before she agreed to come out with me.'

'That was Saturday morning, I believe. I haven't seen much of you since,' Rosalie added pointedly. She watched as George held Tina's hand and they exchanged an intimate look.

This time Rosalie experienced a definite twinge of jealousy. She had never met any of George's girlfriends before; although she knew he must have had relationships, he always kept that part of his life private, even from her.

'No, well. I didn't think you would like it, but we hired a boat from Perrona Dawn. We've been sailing it to Mattingburgh and back all weekend, and have only just returned it.' George knew this information would incite Rosalie. He could hear her voice ranting at him in his head - how dare he give business to the company who had killed their parents? How could he go on the same river in the same sort of boat, sailing along the same stretch of water and, knowing George's audacity, mooring at the same staithe? But George held Rosalie's glare, silently challenging her to say anything.

'Oh, that's a nice way to spend the weekend,' she eventually whispered. 'You had lovely weather.'

'Yes, we did,' Tina said boldly, aware of the tensions between brother and sister although she did not understand the cause.

'Where are the twins?' George asked Henry, who carried the tray of drinks over to their table.

'They're outside with Ben, training the poor little chap. They'll all be in soon.'

'Who's Ben?' Tina asked having thanked Henry for her glass of white wine. She took a thirsty gulp.

Henry watched warily.

'Our dog - well puppy really,' Rosalie answered. 'He's about three months old, a chocolate Labrador. The twins gave him to me for my birthday last month, but I think Henry really bought him for them.' She saw a flicker of confusion cross Tina's face. 'It's a long story.' Rosalie looked away then back again. 'Anyway, tell us more about yourself. George here hasn't really said much - man of few words, is my little brother.'

'Oh well, what would you like to know?' Tina asked with a smile.

'Do you live locally? How long have you worked for the post office? Do you know our Mr Poskett? He runs the post office and shop in Pepper Hill.'

'Well, I've been working there since I left school. I'm afraid I didn't do very well academically – I only managed to pass a couple of exams. I'm a complete disappointment to my grandmother.'

'Your grandmother?' Rosalie asked, chinking the ice cubes against the side of the glass of bitter lemon before taking a sip. 'Why not your parents?'

George raised his eyes to the ceiling, before saying to Tina, 'I did warn you you'd get the third degree from *big sister*, didn't I?'

Henry grinned at George in a conspiratorial manner.

'I don't mind. There's nothing much to tell. My mother, Maris, left me at the maternity unit in Mattingburgh hospital after giving birth. Grandma brought me up, we live in Fenstone. Grandad died – he was a fireman for most of his working life, he retired then had a heart attack a couple of months later. So it's just poor Grandma and me now.'

Tina lifted her glass again and nearly drained her wine.

Henry frowned and looked down at the floor.

Rosalie caught his dismay. Despite their constant antagonism, she was attuned to his moods. Tina's mannerisms reminded them both of something; it was not a pleasant memory. A spark ignited in Rosalie's mind and she felt the need to cause a distraction.

'What about your Dad?' she asked, then cried 'Ouch!'

George had jabbed his foot into her ankle in response to her lack of sensitivity.

'George, stop kicking me.'

'Sorry, Rosie' he said, without remorse. 'It's just a reflex action to your lack of tact.'

'Why, what have I done?' Rosalie whined.

'No, no, don't worry,' Tina said soothingly to George, before turning to Rosalie to explain. 'I don't know who my father is. My mother never told Grandma.'

'Oh, I am sorry. I didn't realise,' Rosalie said, glaring at George for not warning her.

'No, there's no reason why you should know. If the subject comes up in conversation, I tell people; if it doesn't, I don't. It isn't something I brag about, as you can well imagine.'

Rosalie nodded in agreement. She saw a glimpse of defensiveness which gave Tina's voice a hardened edge. And it made Rosalie feel protective towards her brother. She looked at him. His lips were smiling, but his eyes were cautious. Something was not quite right.

George had been a little anxious about introducing Tina to Rosie and Henry. But he had secured word from them both that they wouldn't squabble with each other while Tina was there. He could not have predicted, however, that Rosie's nosiness would cause such embarrassment.

The arrival of the twins and the puppy changed the group's dynamics as more introductions were made and Ben's antics admired.

George drove Tina back to Cliffend later.

'At least my sister and Henry were on good terms today,' he said.

'Why, what do they normally get up to?' Tina asked. She could not decide if she actually liked the pair and definitely would not be seeking their company in the near future if she had an alternative. George and Rosalie were very similar in looks - but, unlike Rosalie, George was calm and measured, polite and thoughtful. She could see the Tillinger family resemblance in the twins, but they also had a look of Henry.

Tina would have drunk a third glass of wine, if one had been offered. As it was, it took a long time before the second had been suggested. Yes, she decided, the Sticklebacks definitely needed alcohol to make them palatable.

Chapter 45

Tina's grandmother, Hilda Guthrie, did not like George.

'He's too old for you,' she informed Tina, in front of him during their initial meeting.

'There's only eleven years between us,' Tina responded indignantly. George wisely remained silent.

Three weeks later, Tina signed the lease on a flat in Cliffend and moved out of her childhood home. George all but joined her. Over the summer Rosalie and the twins saw less and less of him as his and Tina's relationship developed.

George could only ever concentrate on the matter before him but, up until now, this did not seem to cause too many problems with those close to him. However, Tina resented his ability to forget about her if he wasn't with her, whereas she thought about him nearly all the time. If any decisions had to be made, she would consult him. The fact that he did not reciprocate this was apparent when he was offered a management position with MaCold in Treemore.

George's single-mindedness did not stop at ignoring Tina; he seemed to almost forget about his sister, niece and nephew as soon as he moved to Cliffend.

But Tina remembered them, when it suited her.

'You could go and visit Rosalie and the twins while I'm away,' she told him, having just reminded him she was attending a course over the weekend. It was being held at the Perrona Dawn complex in Fenstone where they had conference facilities.

George telephoned Rosalie.

'Tina's deserted you, has she? And you thought you

could spare a few minutes to see if your sister and her kids were still in the land of the living, did you?' Rosalie's tone was sarcastic in the extreme. 'Well, if you're that bothered, come over for lunch and we'll take Ben out for a walk. I don't expect he'll remember you, though, it's been such a long time since you've been near him!'

There was a definite autumnal chill was in the air when George arrived at the Old Police House. And it wasn't just the weather outside.

Rosalie was a little curt at the beginning of the meal but she slowly thawed after realising how glad she was to see her brother happy. Duncan joined them for lunch. However, because he'd had little notice of the family gathering, he'd already made other plans for the afternoon.

'He's off with - what's her name? Lily,' Sarah advised her mother and uncle when Duncan excused himself from the table. 'I can't remember her surname. Her Dad bought the old airfield just up the road. Hammond? His first name's Vince ... something. Hallett, that's it. Dad knows him. He goes into the pub quite a bit. She - Lily, that is - is a couple of years younger than us. Delicate, petite - you know the type, can eat anything and stays as thin as a stick. She never smiles - always looks hungry.'

Sarah tried not to let her envy show. She was not thin, neither was she fat. But she was definitely now an inch or so larger around the waist than her mother. She didn't waste time with diets, she needed energy. Anyway, thin people always seemed to be miserable, in her experience which, even she admitted, was limited. Besides, Eammon Tanworth, who was in her class at school, liked her; he was always trying to look down her cleavage. And he was the best looking boy in her year.

By the time they finished their full roast lunch - despite it being Saturday - and let it settle then washed up and tidied away, Ben was bouncing around the kitchen, reminding them it was time for his exercise.

'We just need him to practice walking to heel on the lead and get him used to traffic,' Sarah said. 'We don't have to go far, just along the road to where the footpath leads off The Tunnel through the woods.'

The Tunnel was a length of road just beyond Pepper Hill on the way to Ashfield. The trees had been planted so close on either side that, for most months of the year, their branches reached across overhead and the density of the leaves almost eliminated daylight, making it feel cool and dark and mysterious.

'Well, I think it's a daft idea,' Rosalie observed bluntly. 'There's no pavement so we'll have to walk on the actual carriageway heading into the traffic until we reach there.'

'There shouldn't be too many vehicles about, it's Saturday,' George reasoned.

'Yes, well there may not be as many lorries and vans, but there'll be more ordinary cars and motorbikes, won't there? People will be going into town to do their shopping and things,' replied Rosalie.

'I'll wait in the hall until you're ready,' Sarah said. She was annoyed that her mother seemed to be dominating everything - as usual. She hooked Ben's lead onto his collar and was trying to keep him calm. He was excited at the thought of a walk and wanted to be on his way. 'I've got bags and treats and everything for him,' she confirmed, patting the appropriate pockets. 'Shall I start walking up the road and you two catch me up?'

'No,' Rosalie commanded. 'You can both learn to be

patient. Tell him to sit and keep him quiet.'

But Ben would not wait, even in the hall; he wanted to go outside.

'Mum, I'm just going into the front garden for a moment,' she called through to the kitchen where Rosalie and George were still not ready. 'I think Ben wants to go – you know, *go*.' She knew even Rosalie couldn't argue with the possibility that the pup might need the toilet.

However, Sarah opened the front door before the back one was closed. The hall door slammed violently.

'What d'you think you're doing?' she heard her mother shout.

'She said she was taking Ben out,' George placated.

'I've told them so many times before to make sure the back door is closed before opening the front one. They know it causes a draught and the other door slams. What if I'd been standing in the way?'

'Well, you weren't. Now please just get ready. And don't keep having a go at Sarah!'

'You always take everyone's side against me,' Rosalie complained.

'Now you're being ridiculous,' George said irritably. 'Come on, just put your coat on and we'll catch Sarah and Ben up.' George looked around. 'We'd better just let Duncan know we're off.'

'Duncan?' Rosalie called, her face scowling with annoyance. 'DUNCAN?'

'What?' he said as he opened the hall door and leaned in. 'What's going on?'

George quietly shut the back door and turned the key. 'Nothing, Duncan. We're just about ready. Sarah's gone out the front, Ben needed the garden. What time are you meeting Lily?'

Duncan glanced at his uncle and shrugged his shoulders, then explained in an embarrassed voice that he was catching the two-forty bus into Cliffend.

'Okay, well, enjoy yourselves, won't you?' George said. He waited until Rosalie had turned away before discreetly passing a bank note to his nephew. Lowering his voice he said, 'treat yourselves.'

Duncan placed the money in his jeans' pocket and blushed. 'Thanks,' he muttered.

Sarah was waiting with Ben by the front gate. She was using the time to maintain his training, telling him to sit and then lie down. Ben was mostly obedient and Sarah delighted in his responses.

The group started to walk with Sarah in front trying to discipline Ben, who wanted to sniff everything he could find. Whenever Sarah slackened the lead, his long, gangly legs became tangled. George let the distance between him and his niece and puppy lengthen in order to allow him to talk with his sister. Rosalie sensed George's ploy.

'Okay, little brother, what's on your mind?' she asked in a forthright tone.

'Huh, I might've guessed you'd sniff out trouble.'

'Trouble? What's gone wrong now?' Rosalie remembered just in time not to raise her voice.

'Shush,' George warned. 'MaCold's have asked me to consider managing a project. But it's in Treemore and Tina did not take the news very well.

Chapter 46

Easter was quite late in 2006, and the first meeting of PepperAsh's committee to organise the St Jude's Festival had been arranged to take place on the Tuesday afterwards, the 18th April. The church always had a choice of two dates on which to hold their patronal celebration - either 19th June, which was for Jude alone, or 28th October, when he shared his festival with St Simon. PepperAsh chose the nearest weekend if the dates fell during the week.

'It's like the Queen having two birthdays,' Max commented on the evening of Easter Monday in The Fighting Cock. He was now back working full time for Goldwin, who obligingly supplied him with endless reasons to moan.

Quinny, claiming rest and restoration after the rigours of Holy Week and the Easter celebrations, seemed to Henry to have spent most of the Bank Holiday in the pub.

'Well, we have to have an alternative, in case the June date coincides with Father's Day, don't we?' the rector commented sagely. 'But by the time we reach October, we're into the harvest festival season. And then, of course there's Hallowe'en at the end of the month.'

'Why don't you have this autumn fayre you're always talking about on the Saturday, then have harvest festival on the Sunday, call it something to do with lost causes - that's what old Jude's all about, isn't it? You can have done with the whole shebang in one go!'

'No, it's too far ahead to think about.' Quinny said before draining his glass. 'Hopefully, we'll stick to the June date.'

'It's some kind of democracy, isn't it, if you've already

decided on the outcome!' Max stated sarcastically.
An article appeared in the May edition of the PepperAsh parish magazine advertising the St Jude's Festival, which was to be celebrated over the weekend 17th and 18th June, just prior to the saint's day. There would be a flower festival in the church on both days, a fête at Pepper Hill's village hall and grounds on the Saturday, and a grand Songs Of Praise on the Sunday anticipatory for St Jude's day on the Monday. Mrs Ervsgreaves rubbed her hands together in glee as she mentally began to choose the hymns and organise the service.

The weather had been relatively warm during May and the first half of June, which encouraged almost everyone to begin preparations. Quinny watched with interest from a safe distance, either in the rectory or sitting at the bar of The Fighting Cock.

The request in the magazine asked for second hand items to be donated to the fête that could be sold on the bric-a-brac stall, new items as prizes for the raffle and tombola, and cakes, sweets, jams or pickles for the Home-Made stand.

Rosalie had half-heartedly started to sort through the remainder of her parents' possessions on several occasions, even once with George's help. So far, however, she had not managed to finish. But now she had a good reason to begin again.

The day was hot and Rosalie opened some of the Old Police House's windows to let in the fresh air. Ben was happy in the back garden, playing with one of his toys, which involved trying to entice treats out of a toughened hollow, ribbed rubber cylinder.

Rosalie gathered the empty cardboard boxes she had collected from Poskett's shop and took a roll of black bin liners from the cupboard under the sink. She carried these all up the stairs and along the landing to the room that had been her parents' room.

Luckily the Old Police House had five bedrooms, enough for her to leave this one intact, although it had been redecorated and the bed and curtains replaced after the chip pan fire.

Rosalie remained in the bedroom she occupied as a child but, when the twins needed rooms of their own, she'd moved George into what had originally been the spare room and Duncan into his: George spent little time at home by that point and, when Duncan received a train set for Christmas one year, he needed enough space to lay out his rail track.

Finally, Sarah's room was the smallest; she hadn't seemed to mind this, until one day during an argument about something completely different, she complained that at least her bedroom at The Fighting Cock was bigger than Duncan's.

Annie and Derek's personal belongings, at least those unaffected by the smoke from the fire, were still packed into their wardrobe. It was one of the old-fashioned, brown wooden kind; double-doored, tall, with room for a shelf inside above the hanger rail at the top, and a drawer at the bottom.

Her parents' shoes, Annie's handbags and such like were crammed into the drawer. Rosalie's heart dropped when she pulled everything out. There were three bags in all. Annie's best handbag, which was used for special occasions, weddings and such like, was stored in a protective calico drawstring sack. It was beige and gold, and matched her special shoes, still in their original box. Rosalie unpacked them all and set them on the floor, the handbag between the two shoes. A wave of despondency swept through her.

They - her Mum and Dad, George and Rosalie - had attended a relative's wedding during the summer holiday before Rosalie started at Cliffend High School. Although she couldn't remember the bride at all, or anyone else who had attended, she could clearly visualise her mother in the outfit bought especially for the day. The matching dress and coat had quickly faded out of fashion and Rosalie could not recall them being worn again. She had discarded them, together with most of their other clothes in the wardrobe, after the chip pan fire. But she found she was still not ready to relinquish the shoes and bag; they reminded her too much of the best of her mother.

With an overwhelming feeling of longing, Rosalie picked up one of the shoes and impulsively tried it on. It was at least one size too big for her. She stared at it, knowing that she wouldn't have worn them even if they had fitted; the pain of just seeing them was too bitter.

With a sigh, she laid the shoes aside to return to the drawer later. Next she found Annie's two everyday handbags. One was black - the organiser kind with multiple compartments and zips and hidden pockets. Rosalie searched through these, patting the insides, opening everything up and shaking the bag upside down to make sure nothing was hidden. A hairgrip, an old fifty-pence piece and a shopping list fell to the floor.

Rosalie picked up the list and felt tears flood to her eyes as she read the familiar handwriting: butter, cornflakes, marmalade, cheese, pork chops and blackcurrant juice. She couldn't remember when her mother had written this; it had probably just been a normal day when they did not realise how swiftly it could all end. She flattened out the creases, re-read the words then folded the slip of paper and slid it into her jeans pocket.

The other handbag was brown with a plain clip at the top, she rummaged through this, but it yielded nothing. She hugged it closely to her for a few moments, holding her breath against her loss.

Only Derek's best lace-up shoes, also still in their box, barely worn and probably bought for the same wedding, were suitable to be sent to the second hand stall. Rosalie bundled the remaining items that were of no use and which she did not wish to keep, into one of the black plastic sacks to be placed in the rubbish bin.

She then opened the doors to the main part of the wardrobe. Despair mingled with her despondency, but she forced herself to stretch up to the top shelf and retrieve Annie's wooden jewellery box. It was next to the strong box in which Derek had kept all his important papers.

She sat back down on the floor and lifted the jewellery box lid. It contained a mixture of loose trinkets and packaged items. She began to look through all the trays and boxes, and tears fell again as she held and caressed various pieces.

However, even through her grief, Rosalie recognised that, although memories of Annie wearing some of these - especially her watch - were painful, they were now not quite as sharp as they had once been.

After a few minutes, she decided she would leave the jewellery. She returned the box to the top shelf next to the strong box, thinking she would wait until George was here to help with these.

Next, she began to remove the packages, plastic carrier bags and objects wrapped in brown paper or bubble-wrap from the wardrobe. And, as she worked her way through, sorting things for the sale and others to be thrown away, she eventually found the big brown teddy bear that Henry had given to her. It was safely ensconced at the bottom, still within its large cellophane bag that had protected it from absorbing smoke from the chip pan fire. As she pulled it out of the wardrobe she could see the golden locket, containing the treacherous diamond, remained around its neck.

She was in a dilemma as to whether she should send the bear to the sale and risk Henry seeing it, or push it back into the wardrobe and leave the decision for another day. She started to open the cellophane bag to take out the locket, resolving to keep that regardless of the bear's fate.

Kneeling on the floor, she eased the bear out of the bag and felt a wave of sympathy. In any other circumstance, she would probably have treasured it - for itself because it was soft, comforting and cuddly, and because it was a gift from Henry. There was a rip in one of the shoulders which Rosalie thought she had noticed before, but wasn't quite sure.

Then the golden locket stole all her attention. She held its heart shape in her fingers; it felt substantial, as if it understood its own importance. For several minutes, she studied the decorations etched onto the front.

As she slid her thumb nail into the edge at the side of the locket, she warned herself that it no longer contained the photographs of her parents. She was still overcome with an incredible disappointment when she flicked it open and the diamond glared defiantly back at her.

Rosalie's body was blocking the light from the window

but, even in shadow, the gem glistened and gleamed, as if making the statement that not even hiding it in darkness could dull its lustre.

She was already feeling maudlin; now tears threatened to cascade over her cheeks as she stared at it. She was truly saddened that this brilliant stone had resulted in years of heartache for her and Henry - and, she was aware, for the people closest to them.

Then, like a rock-fall in her stomach, she realised that it was not the diamond causing the rift, but herself.

The two tiny heart-shaped photos of Annie and Derek were safely ensconced into a small ring box that was returned from the Thrimbale Hotel in Cliffend the morning after her and Henry's wedding day. She had not looked at them for many years. The box also contained her engagement ring, which she regarded as part of the treachery against her.

She wondered if Nora had known about the replacement diamond; she hoped not because that would mean she had condoned it being placed in the locket and not used for Rosalie's ring. She did not know who was aware of the truth, the real reason why she had left Henry. Possibly only Nora and George, and she didn't think either was likely to have shared the story.

With these uncomfortable thoughts disturbing her, Rosalie carefully placed the bear on the floor, stood up and walked to her own bedroom.

The box with the photos and the redundant engagement ring was in an ottoman she'd bought to replace a blanket chest ruined by the smoke from the chip pan fire. She was in the habit of piling discarded clothes on the padded top, today these had been joined by two coat hangers.

She moved the garments and hangers onto the floor, crouched down and lifted the lid. A mass of debris met her eyes - she tended to dump things in here that she didn't know what else to do with. However, she knew approximately where the box would be. She lifted out a photo album and her two framed vocational certificates - one for eighty words per minute in shorthand, the other for forty in typewriting - the highest of her achievements from her sojourn at Clifftech.

And there underneath was the ring box. Carefully retrieving it, Rosalie felt her heart beat quicken. She opened the lid.

Inside was the ring. The gold shone. The stone was set low so as not to catch on anything as she wore it.

The diamond glittered.

Substitute diamond.

Traitor diamond.

Rosalie had worn this ring for nearly two years before she and Henry married. She'd thought it was beautiful, exquisite (seeing the certificate a few moments before prompted shorthand outlines to squiggle into her brain again). She removed her wedding ring, which she continued to wear despite her and Henry not living together as husband and wife: she was, after all, still Mrs Henry Stickleback.

She carefully drew on the engagement ring.

It still fitted.

She wriggled her fingers to admire it, turning her hand towards the window in order to catch the sunshine onto the gem. It flickered and tiny specks of colour shone out. A shaft of bright red dominated, then ruby, scarlet and crimson; the colours of passion. In a slight movement they were gone, quickly replaced by yellow and orange, green then blue, all shining from different planes on the stone's surface.

Rosalie slowly stood up, still angling the ring towards the window. Leaving the ottoman open, she walked out of her bedroom and along the landing to her parent's. The big brown teddy bear remained on the floor in front of the wardrobe. The locket was still open, exposing the diamond inside.

Rosalie tried to remember if she had been wearing the engagement ring that morning when Henry had given her the locket with the bear. She couldn't recall - it was such a long time ago. She draped the locket over her finger until it was next to her ring, thinking this was the first time she had compared the two diamonds.

They were a similar size, but even Rosalie's untrained eye could see that they were not the same cut.

But they both were incredibly beautiful - clear yet full of colours.

Suddenly, at last, Rosalie felt the continuity, from her parents through Nora to her and Henry, which he had sought to create. Tears prickled her eyes again and blocked the back of her throat.

She tried not to cry. She was so used to disguising her upset in case the twins saw; she had to be strong for them at all times. She needed all her energy and courage to fight Henry. But what else could she do? She felt as if she had unexpectedly reached a junction in her journey. To continue straight ahead would lead to more loneliness ending with a bitter old age. Or to take a chance and turn into an unknown road which would be exciting, dangerous …

She looked around the room. It felt extremely empty and cold, nothing like Annie and Derek's domain any more.

If George were here she would ask for his advice. But she

could hardly expect her younger brother to give guidance on her relationship with Henry. Her children were too young, Nora was miles away, and Quinny wouldn't understand. Her friends from school and college had their own lives, complete with different worries and problems. She always felt as if they thought she was just a *silly drama queen* (she'd been in a cubicle in the Ladies' at Clifftech one day and heard one of them call her that). Polly would listen to Rosalie, she was sure; Polly was always good to the twins – dispensing good, godmotherly advice. But Rosalie felt Polly blamed her for the rift between her and Henry.

The two diamonds, side by side, continued to glitter and tantalise her. She was mesmerised by their lustre. She remained on the floor for a long time trying to find the solution: to unlock her heart to Henry, or continue on her own?

She suddenly decided that she could not change, not if Henry stayed the same. And she could not make herself vulnerable to his love again by forgiving him.

Then, very hastily and motivated by her decision, she pulled off the engagement ring and strode back to her own bedroom. She replaced the ring in the box and, remembering the shopping list she'd found in one of Annie's handbags, she retrieved it from her pocket, carefully folded it and slipped it in as well. She then hid the box underneath the framed certificates and photo album in the ottoman, closed the lid and replaced the clothes and coat hangers on top.

In her parents' room once again, she recommenced sorting the things from the wardrobe into boxes for the fête; the items to be thrown out were jammed into the black bin liners.

When she was satisfied with her choices, she sought a

needle and a length of brown cotton. She returned to the bedroom and picked up the big brown teddy bear, unfortunately causing the split in his shoulder to lengthen. Some of the stuffing fell out. Rosalie gathered it up off the floor and pushed it back inside before sewing the seam together. Once this was completed, she returned it to its cellophane bag, which she then left amid the boxes and bags in front of the wardrobe.

Chapter 47

On the Friday morning before the fête, Rosalie deposited the second cardboard box of items into the boot of her car. It was another bright, sunny summer's day. Rosalie had shut the door from the kitchen to the hall to keep Ben safe while the front door was open. Earlier, she had taken him for a long walk; now he was happily chewing a piece of cow hide in the shape of a bone.

There was one more box to fit into the car before she finished, along with two bags of rubbish destined for the bin. The only thing left upstairs in her parents' room that she was undecided about was the teddy bear.

Rosalie carried the last box downstairs and set it on the concrete behind her car. Distractedly, she noticed there were rather a lot of black ants scurrying around on the ground. The hot weather was drawing them out and they seemed very busy in their own little world. They were pushing cones of earth up through the cracks as they emerged, which reminded Rosalie of mini volcanoes. They then marched across the concrete and disappeared beneath the surface again, whilst more and more followed behind.

She sat on the lip of the car boot, basking in the sunshine, her mind drifting for a few moments. She suddenly felt movement on her leg and, as she absent-mindedly swiped off an ant, she thought she would have to walk across to Poskett's shop later to see if he stocked any powder to get rid of them.

Her reverie was interrupted by the telephone ringing indoors. She stood up and walked slowly inside to answer it. It was Henry.

'Quinny's been on at me to donate all the cockerel bits and pieces that we collected years ago to his fête thing.' He cringed at this reference to their shared history. 'And I've decided to just keep old Morris and Mortimer - d'you remember them? The two bookends that used to sit one either side of the mantelpiece.' He did not wait for Rosalie to reply. 'And my mug, of course. And the plate you bought me for my birthday. I wouldn't get rid of them! Or the doorstop - that's still useful, so I'll hang on to that as well. Anyway, I'm taking it all up to the village hall this afternoon, and I wondered if you'd like me to stop off and collect your stuff.'

Rosalie sighed. She had been thinking about Henry quite a lot since undertaking the clearing out session. She smiled now at the sound of his voice.

'That would be brilliant, thank you Henry. But I've just brought most of it downstairs and put in my car. Tell you what, though, I'll meet you up at the village hall in about half an hour and you can help me unload. How about that?' Rosalie smiled to herself, thinking this could be destiny intervening, despite her previous decision.

With the car fully loaded, Rosalie went back upstairs to finish tidying her parents' room. She pushed the remaining items into the black bin liners; she did not want to look too carefully at them in case she decided to keep anything. She carried the bags downstairs, set one of them on the ground and opened the lid of the wheelie bin.

There was not much room inside and, as she pushed the first bag down to make room for the others, she heard Ben bark. As she looked around, she could see flying ants beginning to pour out of one of the volcano mounds in the concrete near the rear of her car. She quickly flicked the bin lid shut and picked up the other bag to remove it from the ants' path. She slammed her boot closed but was then distracted by Ben barking again.

'What's wrong, little chap?' she asked as she went round to the back garden. He was still a slim dog, quite gangly, in fact - not quite a puppy now, but not an adult either. He was standing near the gate and wagged his tail furiously at her as she approached.

She spent a while coaxing and soothing him, his gorgeous chocolate fur shining in the sun and his eyes searching for reassurance. She fed him his midday food: Mr Bladestraw had recommended that his daily ration be divided up into three meals whilst he was young, thus giving him small but frequent portions when they ate as a family.

Afterwards, Rosalie took Ben for a quick walk around the back garden, played *ball* with him until he was tired then settled him into his basket in the kitchen. Suspecting Rosalie was about to go out and leave him, Ben whimpered but finally snuggled down and hid his head under his blanket. She switched the radio on as company for him, closed all but the small top window in the kitchen, locked the doors and left.

It was only a short distance up to the village hall but, as soon as Rosalie pulled out of her gateway, a taxi drove up quickly behind her. The driver began to hoot furiously and gestured for her to go faster. She ignored him and he finally overtook just as she indicated to turn right into the hall car park. Still annoyed with the impatient and ill-mannered driver, she parked near the rear door where Henry'd had his barbecue set out for the Bonfire Night celebrations many years before.

Chapter 48

Henry arrived a few minutes later.

'Hello there, Rosalie,' he greeted her. 'It's good to see you.' He climbed out of his car and opened his boot lid.

Henry's donations filled two grocery boxes and a couple of sturdy bags. He took three journeys to convey them into the hall where the good ladies were organising the donated items for the various stalls. Rosalie was about to carry in her second load when he walked over to her.

'Can I help you with your last bits?' he enquired.

'Yes, please. There's just these to go,' and she pointed into her boot. Henry leant in and lifted the remaining box and black bag with ease.

As she drove away, Rosalie realised that she had enjoyed the brief time spent in Henry's company. Again, thoughts of their possible life together entered her mind.

'I must be mellowing in my old age,' she chuckled to herself. She indicated to turn left, exited the village hall car park and set off on the very short drive back down the hill to the Old Police House. The sun was still shining, the day was pleasantly warm and she was feeling the glow of early summer.

Still grinning, Rosalie caught sight of something black on her arm. She felt the same tickling sensation on her skin as earlier. She glanced down then jumped in alarm at three ants marching with purpose towards her wrist. Instinctively, her feet clamped down onto the clutch and brake pedals and she veered the car to a standstill beside the lay-by outside Poskett's shop and post office.

There was an impatient hoot, similar - but louder - to that delivered by the taxi on her previous journey. A lorry came to an abrupt halt only a few feet behind her. The angry driver hung out of his open window and bellowed abuse.

Rosalie ignored him as, looking down, she saw a platoon of ants scurrying with purpose across her lap. She unbuckled her seatbelt and opened her door in one movement. She tumbled out of her car and into the road, heedless of oncoming or passing traffic.

The lorry driver swore at her again as she frantically swiped and brushed at her arms and legs, her hair and face, screaming and squawking as she did so. She could feel a thousand tiny feet crawling over her and her attempts to flick them away became more and more manic.

The driver sounded his horn with a couple of short blasts before holding his hand down. The noise was deafening and eventually brought Poskett out of his shop.

Henry had just left the village hall when he saw the lorry's brake lights flare red, accompanied by a squeal as the vehicle lumbered to a stop. The horn by now was sounding incessantly with Rosalie in the middle of the road hysterically waving her arms.

To Henry's horror, she started to unbutton her blouse. He managed to squeeze his car past the lorry on the nearside, half creeping along the pavement, and parked in the lay-by. He ran the short distance towards Rosalie. At the same time, the lorry driver removed his hand from the horn and climbed out of his cab.

'Stay there, mate,' Henry shouted as he dashed past. 'What's wrong?' he then asked Rosalie urgently as he attempted to shield her from the other man's sight. She had removed her blouse, flung it on the ground and was still hitting at her skin. Another car approached from the other direction. To Henry's relief he saw it was a woman driving, although the distinction hardly seemed relevant: his wife was still undressing in the middle of the road.

'ANTS!' Rosalie screamed as she scratched through her hair, wearing nothing on top except her bra. 'Get them off me!'

Henry stepped forward, uncertain as to what to do.

'No, don't touch me!' she yelled as she backed away. Her hands then started to ease the waistband of her skirt away from her skin.

Henry feared she would undo this next. True to his prediction, she thrust the skirt downward and stepped out of it before screaming again. Henry could see a cluster of tiny black bodies on her leg.

'*Ouch, ow, ow,*' she cried. 'They're biting me. Help!'

'Here, mate, tip that over her,' the lorry driver said. He opened a litre lemonade bottle and handed it to Henry, who eyed the bubbling liquid dubiously. 'It's only fizzy water. And if you don't do it, I will – with pleasure!'

'Okay. Rosalie, I'll just …'

Henry aimed at the biggest group of ants on her legs. Although only throwing a fraction of the liquid, it swept the insects away. But Rosalie did not seem to appreciate his intervention.

'*Ahhhhh*!' she screamed. 'You bastard! I bet you enjoyed that!'

'Oh, give it 'ere, mate,' the lorry driver said with exasperation as he snatched the bottle which, to Henry's horror, was now bubbling wildly. He tipped the remaining contents over Rosalie's head and doused the rest of her underwear-only clad body, aiming the last cascade at a persistent individual running in circles around her shoulder. The final dribble splashed onto her face. Her eyes widened, she took in an enormous breath and was about to screech when a bright blue, white and yellow police car arrived.

PC Owen Yates parked alongside the lorry, facing the other vehicle and effectively blocking the road. The lady driver looked up when he stopped but then turned to continue her hunt of the back seat of her car. She eventually stepped out holding a large moss-green beach towel which she offered to Rosalie who allowed it to be draped around her shoulders as she stood shaking, dripping with liquid and glaring from the lorry driver to Henry.

Eventually, she smiled weakly at the woman and mouthed, 'Thank you.'

PC Yates pulled on his hat, took a deep breath and walked forward.

'What's going on here?' he bellowed officiously. He was in a bad mood. 'Oh, no. Not you two again,' he cursed as he recognised the Sticklebacks.

'These idiots have just thrown lemonade over me!' Rosalie screamed. 'I was already covered in ants and now they've made it worse!'

'It was supposed to be water - fizzy water,' Henry said to the police officer.

'IT'S LEMONADE!' Rosalie screamed.

The woman beside her echoed 'lemonade' softly as she nodded her head in agreement.

'Oh Christ,' the lorry driver cursed. 'I gave you the wrong bottle. Sorry mate.'

Rosalie screamed again as she slapped more ants off her.

'They're in your hair as well, love,' the woman driver said which made Rosalie scratch savagely at her scalp.

'Right,' PC Yates commanded as he held up his hand with the palm towards the group. 'What exactly happened here?'

'I was driving down the hill and caught up with this woman,' the lorry driver volunteered with disdain as he pointed at Rosalie. 'She suddenly rams on her brakes, jumps out of the car and waves her arms about! And then she starts taking her clothes off.'

Rosalie hugged the towel tightly around her. She felt sticky from the lemonade and writhed as she imagined ants creeping all over her skin.

'I handed what I thought was a bottle of water to this chap here,' and the lorry driver indicated towards Henry.

'I'm her husband,' Henry stated.

'I know,' PC Yates confirmed.

'Estranged,' Rosalie added with venom.

'I KNOW!' The ferocity of PC Yates's voice made the air around them tremble.

The lorry driver looked at each of them in turn and shrugged his shoulders.

'And he just daubed a bit over her,' he continued. 'But I knew that wouldn't get rid of the little buggers so I sluiced her down.' Satisfaction sounded in his voice. Then his face dropped its smile. 'Didn't know it was the new lemonade bottle, though,' he confessed sheepishly. 'I thought it was the other bottle - just ordinary water. Come to think of it, it did fizz a bit when I handed it to him.'

Rosalie cried out suddenly as tiny mouths began to bite into her again. She ran frantically across to the Old Police House, pulled her spare key from behind the hanging plant container – the other being on the ring with her car ignition key, unlocked the front door and ran inside. Henry made to follow.

'Oi, wait there,' PC Yates shouted.

Henry stopped, not really knowing what to do. Rosalie's car was still in the middle of the road, the woman driver glanced around and then stepped back to her own car. The lorry driver looked at his watch and grumbled that he would be late getting back to Cliffend. Poskett, realising the group was blocking access to his shop, mentioned this to the police officer.

'Right!' PC Yates yelled, interrupting any further complaints. 'You,' and he pointed to the lorry driver. 'Get back in your vehicle.' The man shook his head, but turned and did as he was told. Next PC Yates ordered the woman to reverse her car and leave sufficient room to allow the lorry to pull out around Rosalie's. He then told the lorry driver to wait until he had drawn back so he could reverse far enough to clear the stationary car.

The lorry driver gave the horn a loud blast as he left the scene and, ignoring the thirty miles per hour speed limit, accelerated noisily towards Ashfield. The woman in the car also drove away, shouting that she knew where Rosalie lived and would call in for her towel tomorrow.

PC Yates then turned to Henry and lectured him as if the entire debacle was his fault. Eventually he departed. Henry scanned the interior of Rosalie's car to check if there were any ants visible. Unable to see any, he climbed in and adjusted the driver's seat. He drove into the entrance to the Old Police House and parked in the driveway. He walked back to his car outside Poskett's shop and sighed as he started his engine. Despite their earlier conversations being friendly and hopeful, he decided to wait a couple of hours before ringing Rosalie to see if she had recovered.

Chapter 49

A year later, in the spring of 2007, Rosalie could see a parallel developing between herself at sixteen and her daughter now. The twins' GCSE exams would start immediately after the Whitsun half-term holiday and Sarah was beginning to panic.

'But you've covered all the topics in each of the subjects' syllabuses,' Rosalie tried to reason one evening during the Easter holidays. 'You have a revision timetable written out and, if you stick to it, you should have plenty of time to go over everything you'll need.' In her heart, however, she could feel the same uncontrollable fear that had overwhelmed her nineteen years previously.

'Yes, well, if it was so easy, Mum, how many GCSEs did you get?' Sarah quickly responded. Rosalie realised she'd fallen into the trap her daughter had baited.

'They had only just been introduced when I was your age. I was in their first year,' she replied with a calmness her racing heartbeat belied. She could have added that her parents had only just died, but she thought that would be too cruel.

'Exactly, Mum. They were a lot easier when they first came in. You don't know how hard they are now.'

'I'm sure the ones you'll sit are no more difficult than those I took,' Rosalie snapped. She closed her eyes and rubbed her forehead.

Upon reflection, she couldn't remember if she had ever told her children that her last half-term at Cliffend High School was a disaster. She wasn't sure how Sarah would react if she knew her mother had experienced a devastating panic attack immediately before the first exam started which caused her to be taken out of the hall and, because of her circumstances, she was not allowed to sit the remaining papers.

The following year at Clifftech, she only took three subjects, other than her shorthand and typing qualifications. By the end of her college course, her mind had flitted too much between grief and her infatuation with Henry for her to fully concentrate on her studies.

'Well, I don't care!' Sarah almost screamed. Her cheeks were red but Rosalie could see it was with fear not anger. Then Sarah hung her head which allowed her hair to fall and hide her face. 'It's maths that I'm really worried about,' she confessed quietly.

'Yes, I know, sweetheart,' Rosalie said with a sigh. 'But, if you take your time and read the question thoroughly before you start. Go through it several times and say the numbers in front of you to make sure you have them the right way round...'

'I CAN'T SAY THEM OUT LOUD, MUM. I'LL BE IN AN EXAM!' Sarah shouted.

'What's going on in here?' Duncan asked. The noise of another argument brought him down from his bedroom.

'It's the exams,' Sarah said. Her face was scarlet by now and the corners of her mouth curved downwards.

'Look, I've told you,' Duncan said slowly with exasperation sounding in his voice. 'Just take your time. It doesn't matter what grade you get, just do your best.' He stepped into the living room towards his sister, but she backed away. He respected her reticence, but finished by saying, 'and show your workings out, that's what they always say, isn't it, Mum?'

'I don't know why I bother telling you two anything,' Sarah yelled. 'You never listen, either of you. I said I can't do them, but no one takes any notice.' She then stormed out of the room. Rosalie expected her to slam the door, but she left it defiantly open.

'I don't understand why she's so worried. She got a C for maths in her mocks. She's much better at English and history than me, so she'll do okay there,' Duncan explained needlessly.

'Well, whether she passes or not, I just don't want her to be upset. Anyway, has she said anymore about what she wants to do after the exams?' Rosalie asked.

During her last year at school, Sarah's ambitions had swung from becoming a teacher, hairdresser, waitress, nurse (a reflection upon her time spent in hospital with appendicitis), a mechanic (which Henry thought might be very handy) or an engineer (like her Uncle George, but she could not specify an area). Sarah had also thought about childminding but, having volunteered to help with a children's party at the village hall one Saturday afternoon which had been extremely chaotic and messy, she'd decided she didn't particularly like young children after all. Finally, following a presentation at school, she sent away for information about joining the RAF.

'I don't really know what she wants to do this week, but she's already asked Dad if she can earn a few pounds during the summer by collecting glasses at the pub.'

'Oh, has she?' Sarcasm tinged Rosalie's reply. Duncan was already helping his father, when he wasn't with Lily. Their teenage romance had survived to its first year's anniversary. 'And what did your Dad say?'

'The same as he always does, Mum,' Duncan stated

wearily.

'And what was that?' she enquired as she placed her hands on her hips; she already knew the answer.

'That Sarah would have to ask you first. But, if it's okay with you, then it's okay with him.'

'Coward,' Rosalie scorned. 'He never wants to take responsibility and say something definite.'

'Yeah, but if he did, you would tell him he was wrong, so he can't do anything right anyway.' Duncan rarely intervened in his parents' feuding, but sometimes matters erupted and everyone became involved. He started to leave the kitchen but then turned back to her.

'You haven't forgotten you're driving me over to the pub later, have you?' he asked.

Chapter 50

Rosalie drove into The Fighting Cock car park and Duncan noticed the pub sign squeaked as it blew back and forth in the strong breeze. He wondered if he ought to offer to repair and repaint it. Henry had been talking about redecorating and refurbishing the inside of the pub after implementation of the smoking ban, but Duncan saw that the outside could also benefit from a tidy-up. These were jobs he could undertake during slack times. He had also been helping Shaun at Tidal Reach with this septic tank emptying business and was already adept at driving and manoeuvring the tractors and trailers around the small holding.

Duncan didn't want to return to school in September but understood that he would need solid plans for his future to present to his parents for not studying for his A-levels. He knew his future included Lily, and he wanted to start earning and saving towards that.

Duncan had endured a good deal of teasing from his mates about his relationship with Lily, especially as she was two years younger than him. Her father, Vince Hallett, told him that he did not mind their being friends and going out together, as long as that was all. Vince was not stupid, he knew how teenage boys' minds worked, but he didn't wish to think about his daughter in that way, nor did he want anyone else to.

He left his wife, Irene, with the task of dealing with Lily and, so far, he'd had no reason to suspect anything had happened. But he knew the youngsters would find a way to misbehave, if they wanted to, regardless of any warnings of dire consequences from either set of parents. Both Henry and Rosalie were aware of the similarity between these two and themselves as youngsters.

Vince had spoken to Henry about the teenagers' relationship and had been assured that Duncan was well aware of his responsibilities as the older of the two, especially as he was now sixteen and Lily was still two years away. The parents watched and saw a firm and solid friendship building, regardless of anything else that might be happening.

Henry had just returned to the bar from changing barrels in the cellar when Duncan and Rosalie walked in. Whilst wiping his hands on an old towel, a wide smile brightened his face when he saw them.

'Hello, you two. It's good to see you.'

Rosalie wondered if he really meant it or if it was just the usual greeting for everyone who came into the pub.

After a few minutes talking, Duncan's face reddened. He cleared his voice.

'While you two are both here, I want to have a word about Lily,' he ventured.

'Oh, right,' Rosalie said, allowing a smile to creep into her voice. 'How is she? I haven't seen her for a few days.'

'She's fine, thanks, Mum.' Duncan hesitated and looked down at the floor. He then lifted his gaze and held his mother's eyes with his. 'Actually, I've got something to ask you.'

'Permission to marry her?' Henry joked as he walked forward. 'You'll have to ask Vince about that, not us. And, you're too young - well, you're just about old enough, but Lily's definitely too young!'

Duncan blushed again and Rosalie guessed Henry might have been quite close to the truth.

'Don't tease him, Henry,' Rosalie intervened. 'This sounds serious.'

'Yes, it is, actually.' Duncan shuffled. 'Yeah, Lily and me are thinking of getting married …'

'Congratulations. But, as your father just said, you're a bit young – not that we can talk!' Rosalie stated brightly.

Henry reluctantly nodded his agreement.

'Well, hang on a minute and let me finish. I don't mean right away. We know we'll have to wait several years. It's just that, I don't want to go back to school, regardless of my exam results. I want to get on and start earning a living. I know Tidal Reach is empty at the moment, from when I've been working over there. And I, well …' His cheeks were furiously red as he tried to explain, thinking how fanciful he must sound. 'I know I'm still only sixteen and can't take the tenancy on myself until I'm eighteen. But I wondered if you two would hold all the legal side of it until then, and I could do the work. Shaun wants to get rid of the business and I've learnt a lot from him. He's willing to carry on 'til I get my full driving licence next March.' Duncan paused for breath, before adding, 'I think I could make a go of it, especially if I was living on site, so to speak.'

'You want to move into the cottage?' Rosalie interrupted. She was flabbergasted at this revelation; Duncan had not said anything to her about it before.

'Yes, if that's all right.' He looked from one to the other. 'You see, Shaun can't get the timings right for draining out the effluent. Because he isn't there all the time, he has to leave one tank emptying overnight and start the second one in the morning. If I was there, I could do them both, one straight after the other.'

'I don't understand why they can't both be done at the

same time,' Rosalie stated.

'Because of the drainage capacity. Even though the same amount of fluid eventually filters down through the ground, it takes a certain amount of time to cleanse the ...' Duncan faltered in his explanation.

'And when would you start this venture?' Henry asked in order to save his son's embarrassment. Unlike Rosalie, he was not surprised at the proposal; he knew Duncan wanted to start working properly and could see the logic in his ideas.

'As soon as possible. Shaun says he's had enough, but he'll carry on until I've passed my driving test, and got the paperwork sorted out and the proper insurances and license in place. I know this will all be expensive so, if it's okay with you, Dad, can I carry on working at the pub until then - and afterwards, probably, when I'm not busy with the other.'

'What does Lily say? Have you asked her? What about her parents?' fired Rosalie.

'I expect, given time, Duncan will tell us everything,' Henry interrupted Rosalie's barrage of questions.

'Yeah. Lily's happy with the idea, she says,' Duncan replied. 'As long as it doesn't smell.'

This statement caused laughter, which relaxed the trio; they could all appreciate the irony and Lily's innocence. But Henry and Rosalie saw Duncan's determination and knew the young couple would need a great deal of support.

'I think what we need to do,' Henry said cautiously, 'is invite Vince and his wife over to have a proper discussion.'

Chapter 51

The marks for the GCSE examinations came out on the third Thursday in August, the A-level results having preceded them the previous week.

When Sarah received hers, she was bewildered. She had gained an A grade in maths, but only B's and C's in other subjects where she thought she would've scored higher. Interviews with the Cliffend High School's careers officer had been arranged for pupils who, at the end of August, were still undecided as to what they wanted to do.

In Duncan's case, Henry had willingly agreed that he could divide his time between working with him at The Fighting Cock and helping Shaun at Tidal Reach.

Sarah, however, suddenly seemed secretive, still claiming that she didn't know what she wanted to do. When she asked for a lift to school to attend her interview, Rosalie was enthusiastic.

'We can ask about the courses at Clifftech as well as see if any companies have offered anything to the school,' Rosalie said.

'No, no, I don't want you to come into the interview with me,' Sarah stated, suddenly horrified.

'That's ridiculous,' Rosalie snapped. 'Why ever not?'

'Because you'll only tell them what *you* think I should do,' she stated defiantly. 'And you won't listen to what I say.'

'But we want what's best for you,' Henry said. He thought that if she had to choose one parent to accompany her, she would have chosen him. It was a shock to learn that she didn't want either of them.

Sarah now regarded him, her blue eyes were narrowed and her jaw firm. He could see she was scheming something.

'Well, if that really is true …' she began.

'Of course it's true,' her mother interrupted.

Sarah turned to face Rosalie.

Henry could see two very stubborn and obstinate people preparing to commence battle.

'You promise you'll agree to whatever I decide - and not interrupt when I'm explaining?'

Henry misinterpreted this as a signal that one of them could go with her.

'Of course we will, sweetheart,' he said quickly. Sarah looked back at him. He thought she was mellowing. 'We'll abide by your wishes, whatever they are.' His voice was placatory, but Sarah did not look convinced.

Duncan, who was listening by the door as usual, spoke up.

'Be careful, Dad. She's probably got something planned and is lulling you both into a false sense of security.'

'Shut up, Duncan!' Sarah seemed to bite the words. 'It's okay for you with all your brilliant results.' Duncan had gained mostly A grades, with the exception of art and geography.

'Well, it isn't as if I'll ever want to draw atlases or maps,' Duncan had shrugged when he read his results.

'That's cartography, you idiot,' Sarah had stated. 'You won't need to do much of that when you're emptying slurry tanks and pulling pints!' Her words had been harsh but her voice was soft and teasing.

Now, with only half an hour before her allotted appointment at Cliffend High School, they were all in silent deadlock in the kitchen at The Fighting Cock in Ashfield, twenty minutes' away.

'Dad, will you drive me there, then? Mum, you can come in the car as well, but neither of you can come into the interview!' Sarah finally dictated.

'Don't be ridiculous, young lady,' Rosalie repeated, offence stinging her tone. 'Anyway, you can't tell us what to do, we're your parents.'

'I'm sixteen, I can do what I like!' Sarah retorted.

'Within reason, you can,' Henry soothed. 'But in this case you might want our help – especially if money is involved.'

'I'll speak to Uncle George, he'll help.'

'Don't you dare involve your Uncle George! He's got enough to worry about with his own work,' Rosalie scolded. George and Tina had moved to Treemore and, in truth, Rosalie knew very little of his life there.

'Oh for God's sake, you lot,' Duncan suddenly exploded. 'Get in the car and I'll go into the interview with her – stop her selling her body to the highest bidder, or joining the army or whatever other crazy schemes she's got up her sleeve!'

'They won't let *you* go in with her,' Rosalie stated, her frown deepening the lines on her forehead.

'They will if I tell them that you two've been rowing again and can't make up your minds what to do. Anyway, you haven't got long now before her appointment. So, let's all be on our way and, if we can't come up with anything better by the time we reach school, as I said, I'll go in with her.'

They travelled in Henry's car to Cliffend High; Rosalie sat angrily silent in the front seat whilst the twins sank down in the back. When they were about half way there, the engine reached a certain level of drone that seemed to envelop all passengers within themselves. Sarah hoped this was the point at which their parents would not be able to hear her talk to her brother. She leant over.

'Thanks for volunteering,' she whispered.

'Well, it's what you wanted, wasn't it?' Duncan hissed back. 'That's why you left it so late and made such a fuss.' When Sarah didn't reply, Duncan guessed her silence confirmed his suspicions. 'Anyway, what *do* you want to do?'

'There's a training scheme at Perrona Dawn, the course is called Leisure Management. It lasts five years and I'll be paid while I'm learning - not that much though, but something. But if I start at sixteen, I'll need Mum and Dad's permission because I'll have to live in at the complex - it's in Fenstone, not the one here in Cliffend.' She paused. 'I can't really see Mum agreeing to that, though, can you? Especially with the connection to Granny and Grandad Tilly's deaths.'

Chapter 52

'The answer is no!' Rosalie stated firmly with barely contained anger. 'No! I will not sign the forms. You are not going to work for that … *that* company.'

Mother and daughter were standing in the kitchen at the Old Police House with the forms awaiting signatures on the table. Duncan had wisely taken Ben out into the garden. Although brave in most situations, even fool-hardy and fearless at times, the two year old chocolate Labrador did not like raised voices, especially if one of them was Rosalie's: there seemed to have been a lot of arguments recently.

Sarah never shouted at Ben. Her scolding consisted of old-fashioned nagging and finger pointing which usually culminated in Sarah laughing at the confused pup's expression and then playing with him. But Sarah was not laughing now, she was furious.

'I can do what I want when I'm eighteen,' she responded to her mother defiantly. 'You won't be able to stop me then!'

'I can stop you coming back here to live when it all goes wrong, young lady,' Rosalie retorted. 'But then I expect you'll just run to your *Daddy*, like you always do.'

'I really don't know why you're so against me doing this course,' Sarah continued, ignoring the jibe about Henry. 'Most parents would be pleased that their kids had thought about what they wanted to do with their lives. It isn't like you've ever had a career, is it?'

'No, I've been too busy bringing you two up. And mostly on my own,' Rosalie spat in return.

'Dad has helped. And he's always wanted to do more, but you won't let him.'

'He's done enough as it is. Anyway, he hasn't exactly given himself a career, has he? He just fell into looking after the pub when his mother disappeared. And now it seems that Duncan is following suit – when he isn't talking about taking over from Shaun, that is.'

'Well, Uncle George has a career!' Sarah's pretty face contorted as she struggled with this battle. And although she didn't want to hurt her mother, her immaturity and lack of restraint would not prevent her using every fact available as ammunition. 'And he started his training when he was younger than me. Why was it okay for him, but you don't think it's right for me?'

'Your Uncle George's circumstances were much different. He had – we both had – just lost our parents …'

'You always give that as a reason for everything you two did when you were young that you don't want Duncan and me to do!'

'Well, it made a big difference to our lives.'

'Don't you think the fact that you and Dad live apart and are always arguing makes a difference to us?'

'At least we're both still here!' Rosalie could feel herself growing dangerously upset. The resentment from years of being alone and coping with this kind of drama was bubbling near the surface of her reason. She felt overwhelmed with fighting against something she knew to be fundamentally wrong: her daughter was too young to leave home. Sarah still needed her Mum and Dad. Nearly two decades may have passed since Rosalie's parents had died, but the pain of their loss was still as raw. She didn't want to lose her daughter as well, however selfish that might seem.

'But George still went off and did what he wanted to do,'

Sarah added vindictively. 'He was living in Aberdeen when he was sixteen, wasn't he?'

'Yes, but he acted a lot more grown up than you do!' Rosalie was suddenly surprised at the amount of bitterness in her words. She had known for a while that there was a new Leisure Management course at Clifftech. With tourism being one of the main local employers, it was always highly probable that one of the twins would eventually choose to work in the industry. She was aware that students could be sponsored by a holiday firm which would mean living on the job. If it had been any of the other companies, she would probably have agreed. But it was Perrona Dawn who, in Rosalie's eyes, was responsible for her parents' deaths.

Sarah was reeling from having been made aware of yet another of her shortcomings.

'You've always been jealous of Dad and me!' she suddenly blurted out.

She too was feeling the effect of years of pent up frustration: in her opinion, her parents' constant niggling was instigated almost entirely by her mother. At times, both Sarah and Duncan almost dreaded speaking of one to the other or, more truthfully, saying anything about their father to their mother.

From time to time, Rosalie and Henry seemed to call a truce, such as when he helped Sarah and Duncan buy the puppy for their Mum's birthday. But harmony on that occasion had ended abruptly when Rosalie was left with Ben for a week whilst the twins went to Derbyshire on a science field trip with the school. Henry refused to have Ben at the pub, saying he couldn't watch him all the time when he was working. And, of course, Mrs Mawberry was allergic to dogs. Or at least she claimed to be. Ben was moulting at the time so there would have been a lot of hairs to vacuum up.

Secretly, Rosalie had enjoyed being in sole charge of Ben. He was a contented little dog, and Sarah and Duncan, to their credit, had accomplished the pup's toilet training quite quickly. Rosalie had frantically but quietly dashed around doing her housework while Ben napped during the day. It reminded her of when the twins were small: they had to be constantly watched from the time they started to walk until the day they began pre-school.

But this argument between mother and daughter had been brewing for some time. Rosalie was now silent for a few moments, leaving the harshness of Sarah's statement to echo around the kitchen. The fridge hummed into life and Sarah mistakenly thought the lull meant she had gained an advantage. She was childish enough to believe that, by continuing this futile shouting match, she could win without Rosalie being seen to have been defeated. She was also as stubborn and determined as her mother; nothing was going to make her give up her ambitions, even if she had to wait another two years before she could embark upon the training. But by then she would be eighteen; others her age would have a two year advantage. This latter realisation spurred her on to attack again.

'Yes, well, if it was a lack of parents that made Uncle George grow up, then perhaps it's because I've had parents who argue all the time that has held me back and not allowed me to do the same.'

Rage caught Rosalie. At the very second Duncan entered the back door with Ben following on his lead, she impulsively sprang forward and slapped Sarah's face.

The smacking sound reverberated around the kitchen, shocking Sarah into holding her breath as she immediately clutched her hands to her cheek.

'Mum!' Duncan shouted, his voice suddenly squeaking with horror at the incident he had just witnessed. 'Mum, what are you doing? Leave her alone!' He turned to his sister but, although she was trembling all over, she swung away from him.

Duncan wanted to reach the telephone and call Henry, but he dared not move from between his sister and mother, his slim body acting as a barrier against any further violence.

Of the two parents, he was aware that his mother had the more volatile temper and a tendency to shout if things went against her. But neither had ever hit them, even at the height of previous troubles.

The silence was broken when Ben whined. He sensed conflict and was not happy. Rosalie saw her chance to retreat but still retain a little dignity. She stepped forward, bent down to scoop him up. She held him comfortingly to her, stroked his head and whispered softly, close to his ear.

Duncan relinquished his end of the lead.

'I'll just take him outside,' Rosalie said. 'He might want to do a wee-wee.' And she led Ben away.

Duncan did not like to say that they had just been for a walk and all such functions had already been performed.

Chapter 53

Rosalie closed the back door behind her. As soon as she had gone, Sarah clutched at her brother and wept on his shoulder. By then Duncan too was shaking.

'Can you ring Dad, please?' Sarah sobbed. 'And ask if I can stay with him until I start my course? He'll sign the form for me, I know he will.' She was still determined to enrol, despite her mother's objections.

'Yeah, of course.' Duncan's voice sounded as if it were breaking for a second time. 'But I'll have to tell him about this,' and he indicated to the closed back door.

'No, don't. He'll just say it was all my fault for provoking her,' she protested.

'No, he won't,' Duncan stated adamantly. He was sure Henry would support Sarah even if he hadn't witnessed the argument leading up to the slap.

Five minutes later, when Duncan had settled Sarah enough to dial his father's number, he heard the engaged tone. 'I'll try again in a while,' he said, noticing Sarah was still holding her inflamed cheek. 'Meanwhile, we'd better go put some things together. We can come back again later and get some more. But I think we'd better stay out of Mum's way for the rest of today.'

Sarah removed her hand from her cheek and Duncan could see a bright red mark. In contrast, the rest of her face was ghostly white and her blue eyes shone with tears.

Duncan was very angry with his mother for slapping Sarah: he did not believe that whatever she said warranted physical attack. He knew Sarah was going to ask to go on the course; he was also aware that this would cause an argument. He suggested they try to arrange for their parents to be together when she asked, but Sarah was adamant that it would be impossible to get them in the same room and be civil to each other for long enough to allow her to explain, quoting their lack of support when she attended her careers interview. But Duncan now wished he had tried harder to persuade her; after all, they listened to him when he told them about Lily and Tidal Reach.

But a frightening truth was beginning to dawn. Duncan realised that, although he was sixteen years of age and much taller and stronger than his mother, at this moment he was a little afraid of her: not, he reasoned with his own bravado, in case she tried to hit him, but of what he would do if she struck Sarah again.

Rosalie was very angry with Sarah for her defiance and insolence, but she was also shocked at her own actions. She knew she needed Henry's help, however much it riled her to admit it. She patted her pocket for her mobile phone but realised she had left it behind.

She talked calmly to Ben as they walked across the road to the telephone kiosk outside Poskett's shop and post office. She had a little money in her pocket and pushed a couple of coins into the slot as soon as the phone at the pub was answered.

'Henry, it's me, Rosalie,' she announced, her voice sounding strange even to her own ears.

'Oh hello.' Henry could not prevent the concern sounding. 'Is everything all right?' Rosalie very rarely rang him, and never just for a chat.

'No. I, er, was wondering if you could come over straight away.' She remembered a similar feeling of humiliation when Duncan telephoned his father after the chip pan fire.

'Why, what's happened?'

'I'll explain when you get here. Or at least, I'm sure the twins will.'

Henry thought the second sentence had sounded a little defiant, more like Rosalie's usual feisty self.

'Right, well. I'll have to ask Craig to cover. Polly isn't due in yet, but I'm sure he'll manage not to bankrupt me while I'm gone.'

'Well, if it's too much trouble ...' Rosalie snorted, returning to normal. But then she remembered why she was calling. 'Whatever you feel is necessary,' she finished in a quieter tone.

'Mrs Mawberry's still here, I'll ask her to keep an eye on things as well.'

Mrs Mawberry had answered the telephone when Duncan rang again.

'He's on his way to yours now,' she advised him.

'Oh, right. Okay. Thank you.' He then replaced the receiver. 'He's coming over,' he told Sarah. 'Mum must've phoned him.'

Sarah was sitting down at the kitchen table now; she still hadn't packed. She wouldn't leave her brother's side until she thought she would be safe to go upstairs. She didn't want her Mum to return until her Dad was here too. Then she thought of Ben and wondered if he was likely to come to any harm being with her mother.

Sarah had never before been this afraid. She did not know exactly what she was frightened of, but she felt it was her fault. She asked herself, if she hadn't argued with Rosalie, would this have happened? If she didn't want to get away from the constant bickering between her Mum and Dad, would she still wish to leave home? If they were just normal parents - like her school friends' mums and dads - could they have all lived happily at the pub?

Sarah did not know the real reason why her parents had only spent that first night of their marriage together. But she knew it had something to do with the stupid teddy bear which she thought was upstairs in the back of Granny and Grandad Tilly's wardrobe.

She hung her head and moved her hand away from her cheek. She wanted to look in the mirror but somehow couldn't summon the energy to move. She felt worthless, reduced to nothing. If this was how conflict with her own mother ended, she wondered if she would ever cope with members of the public in a crisis. She thought her career in leisure would be tainted, having had this kind of beginning.

Henry suddenly entered the kitchen. Sarah looked up at her father and started to sob again. He crouched down and gathered her in his arms, wanting to comfort her and make her world safe and secure again.

But she was not a child anymore, he realised, and there had to be a reason why she was so upset. It was Duncan who explained that he had slipped outside with Ben to give Sarah a chance to ask Rosalie in private if she could attend the leisure course, which meant she would have to live at Perrona Dawn in Fenstone. He said he purposely hadn't gone far from the kitchen and returned when the shouting started. He then relayed the scene he actually witnessed.

'Where's your mother now?' Henry asked when he'd finished.

'Still out with Ben, I think,' Duncan replied.

'Right, I want you two to come over to Ashfield with me.

We'll get you settled then I'll speak with your Mum.'

'But I need you both to sign these forms for me to start the training course in September - the date's only three weeks away now,' Sarah wailed, picking up the two offending sheets of paper from the table. 'She won't let me go. It's not fair.'

'Like I said,' Henry stated quietly, calming the turbulence gathering inside him. 'I will speak to your mother later.' After a few moments, he asked, 'Does she know that I've said I would sign if it's okay with her?'

'No, I didn't get that far. Mum just flew into a rage as soon as I asked.' Sarah did not want Rosalie to know that she had already spoken to Henry, who had agreed in principle but, as usual, would support Rosalie's decision either way.

Henry and Rosalie had agreed when the twins were born that they would not be manipulated by them when they grew old enough to be aware of the situation (rather sooner than either had anticipated, as it happened) or by other people.

Henry now looked at his daughter, the doubt clear in his eyes. He could see the contrast between Sarah's reddened cheek and the paleness of the rest of her face. Although he would not condone the fact that Rosalie slapped Sarah, he did not fully believe Sarah had been calm and reasonable in her approach to the subject.

He had never raised a hand to either Duncan or Sarah and was not aware that Rosalie had before today. He himself had not been struck as a child by his mother or his father, but he knew his mate Sid's father was violent towards him, his brother and sister and his mother. He often wondered if that was why Sid drifted into crime, because he could see by the example his father set that brute force achieved what he wanted - and, as a consequence, why he had served a prison sentence for grievous bodily harm.

'Right, just go and get a few things together and I'll drive you both back to the pub,' Henry instructed quietly. 'I'll leave a note to say I'll ring your mother tomorrow. It'll give everyone a chance to calm down and think this through a little more clearly.'

'But, Dad …' Sarah started to object.

'No, we'll do this my way. No more arguments, please. If your Mum still says no tomorrow, you'll have to wait a couple of years before starting at Perrona Dawn. You might have changed your mind about working there by then, anyway. Until then, stay at school for your sixth form and take your A-levels. But if your Mum says yes, you can start the course in September. I can't go against her in this, Sarah. You do see that, don't you?' Henry said.

'But she hit me! I don't want to live with her if she thinks she can hit me.'

'You can both come back to the pub with me – for tonight, anyway. And we'll deal with the rest tomorrow,' Henry assured his daughter. 'Meanwhile, just go and put some things together, please.'

Sarah stood sullenly, picked up the forms off the table and slouched through to the hall door. She paused for a moment, then turned and shut it quietly behind her.

Half an hour later, Henry and Duncan realised they had not heard a sound from Sarah for quite some time.

'I'll go up and see how she's getting on,' Duncan volunteered.

Less than a minute later, Henry heard Duncan call Sarah's name. Then he yelled, 'Dad, she's gone!'

Dear Reader

If you have enjoyed reading my book then please tell your friends and relatives and leave a review on Amazon.
Thank you.
Franky

More **PepperAsh** stories coming soon.

Have you read the first one in the series,
The PepperAsh Clinch?

Acknowledgements

I have scribbled stories for years, but it was not until I joined the Waveney Author Group that I achieved my ambition to be published. I would like to say an enormous thank you to Suzan Collins for all her kindness, support, and practical help. Thank you, also to the other members of WAG. I would also like to thank Pat for proof-reading my novel, and Alex for her encouragement.

And finally, the biggest thanks of all goes to my dear husband, John, for all his hard work and support, especially on the technical side.

Cover: John Sayer

Editor: Alex Matthews
www.bookeditingservices.co.uk

Reader: Pat Vellacott

The places featured in the PepperAsh stories are all fictional, although there may be a passing resemblance to towns and villages around the coastal area of the Suffolk/Norfolk border. The characters, personalities and their predicaments are also completely fictional.

About the Author

Born in Felixstowe, Franky moved to North Suffolk as a small child. She still lives close to the Norfolk/Suffolk border, with her husband, John, and their yellow Labrador, Boris.
Franky trained as a shorthand/typist/secretary and worked as such in a variety of industries, including a rock and sweet making factory, an offshore oil and gas platform construction company, and as a local government officer. Other employments include music engraving, and over two decades as a parish council clerk.
Her hobbies include music - she plays tenor recorder, guitar, piano and church organ, and the last of these led to her becoming the chapel organist for twenty years in a local prison.

Her other interests are dressmaking, walking her dog in the countryside and reading.

This is Franky's second novel, and also the second in The PepperAsh series, The PepperAsh Clinch being the first.

If you would like to know more about Franky and to follow her on Facebook please go to Franky Sayer Author.